the BLUE
AMULET

MARK OF THE FAERIE SERIES

THE BLUE AMULET

Book II of *Mark of the Faerie*

Patricia Rae

RaeDiance Productions

Books may be ordered through booksellers or from the publisher's website:
www.MarkoftheFaerie.com

Hard Cover ISBN: 978-1-7345528-4-3
Paperback ISBN: 978-1-7345528-3-6
E-book ISBN: 978-1-7345528-5-0
Library of Congress Control Number: 2020914454

Cover and book design by Longfeather Book Design

I dedicate this book to M. Kay Howell
—a fellow author, mentor, and an angel on Earth.
Thanks, Kay, for taking me under your wing.

chapters

☙

MAIN CHARACTERS FROM BOOK ONE
"CURSE OF THE CHOSEN ONE"

Isaboe McKinnon: The beautiful young wife and mother who lost twenty years of her life after she unwittingly passed through a portal into the realm of the Fey.

Connor Grant / Braden MacPherson: A Scottish warrior who also spent twenty years in the realm of the Fey, and is now destined to be Isaboe's protector.

Margaret McDougal: A rough pub owner, and Isaboe's best friend and savior.

Lorien Rankish: The control-hungry, manipulative, and deceptive Fey Queen from the land of Euphoria in the realm of the Underlings. Her goal: To take possession of Isaboe's half-fey child so she can rule both worlds.

Demetrick: The powerful and genius wizard whose plot to stop Lorien's twisted plan included saving Braden MacPherson from a British prison.

Teina and Finn: The pixies who communicate with mortals through the Blue Amulet.

Rosalyn: A powerful sorceress.

Lieutenant Colonel Jonathan Blackwood: The demented British officer who abducted Isaboe, dragging her through the streets in Inverness.

Marta and Henry Cameron: Isaboe's adopted parents.

Saschel and Cecelia: Isaboe's adoptive sisters.

Deidra and Tomas MacFarland: Isaboe's other adoptive sister and her husband.

Nathan McKinnon: Isaboe's deceased husband.

Benjamin and Anna: Isaboe's two grown children who believe she died twenty years ago.

Turock the Dwarf, and Leo the Giant: Rosalyn's companions and two misunderstood souls, sharing her canyon ridge top sanctuary. Combining their efforts, the three of them have carved a home out of a cave, offering safety from a cruel and unjust world.

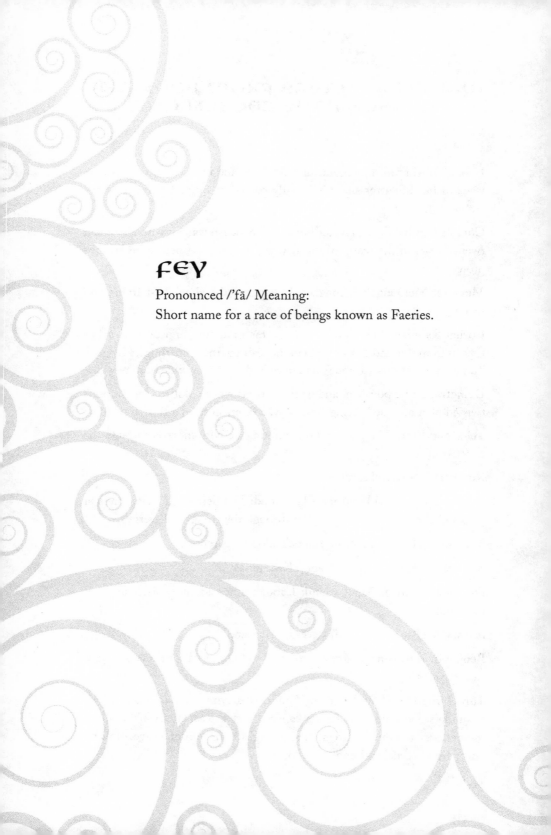

ƒEY

Pronounced /ˈfā/ Meaning:
Short name for a race of beings known as Faeries.

CHAPTER 1

LILABETH

Connor Grant's ride back down Lochmund Hills went much faster than it had on the way up. Desperate to be back in Edinburgh with his beloved Isaboe by nightfall, he had ridden hard all day, but knew that both horse and rider were in need of a break.

The sound of tumbling waters drew him to a small mountain creek that was obscured by dense underbrush. Fed by the autumn rains, the creek was high and lapped at the greenery beyond its banks. After dismounting, Connor led his horse down to the water's edge so both could quench their thirst before heading out on the last leg of his journey into the city.

For most of his life he had never been far from Scotland's nature, but today everything looked different, as if he were seeing the world through new eyes. Standing along the creek bank, Connor quietly observed the nature around him. The idea that a race of beings—Underlings, as Rosalyn and Demetrick had called them—could live unnoticed among mortals was disturbing. That their presence could be hidden completely unless they chose to show themselves was unsettling. He found himself looking at every tree, every rock, even the life-giving water with suspicious scrutiny.

After man and horse had quenched their thirst and eaten enough to keep them going, Connor led his mount back toward the road, but stopped when a small noise caught his attention. Not entirely sure what it was, he paused to listen. When it came again, he thought it sounded like the whimper of a child.

The pathetic sound came from downstream, behind a thick patch of brush that grew out over the bank. Connor stood silently for a few moments, and when he heard it again, turned back to investigate. Leaving his horse, he quietly made his way up the bank, following the sound of the muted cry. Suddenly the crying ceased and Connor froze. All his senses went on alert.

"Hello," he called, but there was no reply. "I heard ye crying. Are ye hurt? Hello?" Moving back toward the creek, he made his steps quiet and deliberate, looking for something small and injured. As he stepped out of the brush, a rock suddenly flew past his face, missing his head only by inches. Instantly drawing his sword, Connor spun in the direction of the assault and found himself face-to-face with a young girl holding another good-sized rock ready to be launched.

"Take another step and I'll knock your head off! And this time I won't miss!" The intense look on the young girl's face left little doubt she had every intention of carrying out her threat.

"Whoa, lass, I mean ye no harm," he said as he slowly returned his sword back into its scabbard. "I heard crying and only came to investigate, to see if I could help. Ye can put the stone down. I'm no threat."

"How do I know he didn't send you?" With the rock still in her hand, the young girl held her ground and seemed determined to defend herself. But her wide, brown eyes were filled with fear and desperation.

"No one sent me. I was just passing through, watering my horse when I heard ye whimpering." It was then that Connor noticed a red stream running from where the girl stood in the shallow creek bed as the water washed over her feet. "Ye're hurt. Yer foot, it's bleeding."

The girl's long, dark hair tumbled down around her pale, tear-stained face. The thin dress she wore clung to her young frame. Soaked and shoeless, she stood shivering in the freezing mountain water.

Connor fancied himself wise enough to take a step back and reassess the situation. Shooting a quick glance around, but seeing no one, he took a steadying breath. "Are ye out here alone, all by yerself? Are ye lost?" The girl didn't answer as her quivering lips began to turn purple. "I have some supplies in my saddlebag. I can help with that cut on yer foot. Just put the stone down. It's gonna be alright. I won't hurt ye, I promise."

Apparently, there was something in the way he looked or spoke that was convincing. Slowly the girl lowered the rock and dropped it into the creek with a plunk. "My foot, it really hurts," she whimpered as she found a seat on a large boulder, its surface a safe distance above the water. When she picked her foot up, blood dripped steadily into the creek.

"Stay here. I'll be right back." After hurrying back to his horse, Connor pulled a handful of cloth strips and a blanket from his saddlebags. He walked back to the creek where the girl sat waiting, and as he approached, she turned her large, tearful eyes to look up at him.

Easily lifting the girl from the boulder, Connor sat her down on the grassy bank and wrapped the blanket around her shoulders. He knelt down beside her and carefully began to wrap the wound on her small foot. All the while, she cried softly, sniffling back tears.

"Why are ye out here all by yerself?" he asked.

"I'm running away."

"Oh, ye're a runaway, aye? Things not so good at home? Mum and Dad treat ye badly?"

"My momma's dead, and it ain't my father I'm running from."

"No? Then what are ye running from?"

"Why do you care?"

"Well, ye hardly seem old enough to be running around by yerself with nothing on but a slip of a dress, catching yer death of cold and bleeding in the creek. There must be someone who will be missing ye."

"I won't go back there! Do you hear me? I won't!" the young girl snapped defiantly.

"Alright, alright, no need to work yerself into a fit. What's yer name, lass?"

"Lilabeth."

"That's a pretty name. Who are ye running from, Lilabeth?"

"Sir Brentworth MacKennsie." No child should ever know the kind of loathing that Lilabeth spat into the name.

"Sounds like ye dinnae care much for this MacKennsie fellow."

"I hate the maggot." Lilabeth's eyes darkened as her mouth drew into a thin, tight line.

"Those are pretty strong words."

"He's a disgusting bastard!"

"Hmm. So, this disgusting bastard, MacKennsie, who is he to ye?"

"He was my master. I was his servant."

"Not much of a servant if ye're running away from him, are ye?"

"He's worse than the slime of a sea slug! I'll never go back. Do you hear me? *Never!*"

"Aye, I hear ye," Connor said as he finished wrapping her foot. "There, that ought to stop the bleeding. So why do ye hate him so much?"

"Because he's a foul-smelling buzzard and a blood-sucking leach," Lilabeth snarled as Connor tried not to chuckle at her language. "My father owed him a lot of money with no way to repay it. So instead of payment he sent me to work off his debt. I was told I would be a house servant, but I ended up a *bed* servant." There was shame and defiance in her eyes as she silently dared him to judge her, to laugh at her misfortune, and it gave Connor a swell of respect for this speck of a girl. "I will never let that filthy maggot touch me again, ever!"

Connor now understood Lilabeth's loathing, and her fear, but she also wasn't his problem. He silently regarded her for a moment. "How old are ye Lilabeth?"

"Fourteen," she said, sniffling back tears.

"So, what's yer plan? Where are ye going?"

"I'm going to my auntie's home in Lollyhock, my Mum's sister. She'll keep me safe. MacKennsie will never find me."

"What about yer father's debt? Won't MacKennsie go after him now that ye've run off?"

"My father can go to hell!" she spat. "What money we had left after Momma died he spent on liquor and gambling. That's how he became so indebted to MacKennsie. He don't care 'bout me, or what happens to me, so why should I care 'bout what happens to him?"

"So ye're gonna take off by yerself on this lame foot all alone to Lollyhock?"

"Aye."

"Even if ye had two good feet to walk on, it'll take ye at least a week to get there. Ye'll probably freeze to death before then, unless someone less friendly finds ye first. Did ye not think this out before ye took off?"

"I ran when I had the chance!" Lilabeth shouted. "I didn't get many opportunities." Taking a shaky breath, she tried to calm down before continuing. "MacKennsie sent me on an errand to gather supplies with the ol' cook, Bree. She's old and can't run a lick, so when she wasn't looking, I slipped away. I didn't have time to think. I just ran!"

Still kneeling next to her, Connor looked at the girl wondering what, if anything, he should do for her.

"I'm not asking for your help." she said, as if she knew what he was thinking. "I'll make it on my own." She stood and began limping up the side of the bank.

"Wait," he said as he stood. Letting out a sigh of frustration, Connor knew he couldn't just ride off and feel justified about leaving her. "Let me take ye into Edinburgh. I'll put ye on a coach that will take ye to Lollyhock."

Lilabeth turned around, glaring at him. "Why? What do *you* want from me?" she asked suspiciously.

Connor chuckled and shook his head at her unspoken accusation. "Look, I'm only offering to help ye. That's all. Ye'll never make it on foot. Ye'll most likely die before ever reaching Lollyhock."

"I'd rather be dead than have that slimy bastard ever lay a hand on me again!"

The sound of horses galloping along the road made them both suddenly freeze and Connor could see the fear on Lilabeth's face. He looked up the creek bank and waited until the horses had passed. When he turned back to where the girl *had* been standing, she was gone. She'd slipped off into the underbrush, into the shadows of the fading light and disappeared.

"Lilabeth? Lilabeth!" he called out, but there was no answer. "Ah bugger!" he mumbled as he ran his hand through his hair. Standing on the edge of the creek bed, Connor glanced around, wondering what to do next. He had to get back to Edinburgh, and back to Isaboe. She was his main concern. Nothing else should be, or could be more important right now. Deciding that Lilabeth had set off on her own determined path, he tossed aside any concern he might've had for the child, and made his way back to where his horse waited patiently. But when he came around the bank, he found Lilabeth holding the reins, looking at him with big, sorrowful brown eyes.

"Oh, now ye've changed ye mind, aye?"

"I can't go back there, and I don't want to die out here. Please, help me." Having apparently found a sympathetic soul, it appeared that Lilabeth had decided to take her chances with him.

"I'm not takin' ye to Lollyhock."

After a few uncomfortable moments of silence, the young girl finally nodded her head. "Fine. Then I'll go back to Edinburgh with you. And you will pay for my coach fare to Lollyhock?" Maybe she was over-playing the victimized role, looking at Connor with her large, doe-like eyes, but it was working.

He let out an exasperated sigh. "Ye dinnae even ken who I am. What makes ye think *I* can be trusted?"

"If you were a bad man, you wouldn't have bandaged my foot, or given me this blanket. You're my only hope, so I have to trust you," she said between renewed tears.

"How did I become the bloody savior of damsels in distress?" he growled. Lilabeth was not his problem. Even if she had no chance of making it to Lollyhock, this girl was of no importance to him. But something deep inside told him otherwise. He knew that leaving her to survive on her own would very likely be a death sentence.

Connor heaved another sigh, this time in resignation. He knew what he had to do. "Goddamn bloody hell," he grumbled under his breath. "I wanted to be in Edinburgh by dark, but now, I don't think I'll make it." Connor glanced to the sky before looking back at Lilabeth with a stern glare. "We ride fast. Hopefully we'll at least be riding into the city by nightfall."

Lilabeth limped over the few steps to hug Connor around his waist, catching him off guard. "Thank you. I promise I'll be no problem."

"That's yet to be seen," he grumbled, pushing her away. "Now, do ye need help, or can ye climb up into the saddle yerself?" He was frustrated, but more with himself than her. Being burdened with the responsibility of a runaway servant-girl was hardly something he had counted on when he left the Lochmund Hills that morning. Watching the young girl trying to mount his horse unsuccessfully only added to his irritation. In one swift movement, he picked her up and dropped her into the saddle, a little harder than necessary.

"So, what's your name?" she asked as he mounted up in front of her.

"Connor."

"Connor what?"

"We won't be together long enough for formal introductions. Connor is all ye need to ken." He knew his reply was rude, but he couldn't keep his irritation from bleeding through. Jerking on the reins, he spurred his horse into action, quickly bolting them up the side of the bank and back on the road to Edinburgh.

CHAPTER 2

AN ILLUSION AT TWILIGHT

Connor pushed his mount hard until darkness swallowed the land. After stopping for a short rest, they continued at a slow trot as the road wound through a forest of thin aspens. But eventually, he pulled his horse abruptly to a halt. Turning to look back over his shoulder, a puzzled expression crossed his face.

"What's wrong?" Lilabeth asked.

"I dinnae recall passing through this forest on the way out of Edinburgh, and we should be close enough to see the lights from the city by now." Connor had tracked men and horses during his years as a soldier, and could find his way back to almost anywhere, as long as he had been there once before. "Even in the dark, something should look familiar. I must've taken a wrong turn somewhere," he mumbled before dismounting. "Looks like we'll be makin' camp here tonight. I'll be able to find my bearings better in the morning," he said, lifting Lilabeth down from the saddle.

Though he made the statement casually, he couldn't deny his disappointment at not making it back to Edinburgh by day's end. He knew Isaboe was in danger, and he needed to be with her as soon as possible. But Connor was also smart enough to realize that he had somehow gotten lost and had no idea which direction led back to the city. As much as he didn't want to stop, there was no other option but to wait till daylight.

The sky held the promise of a clear night, but even without rain, it would still be a cold one. In the ebbing evening light, Connor managed to coax a small fire to life as Lilabeth sat and watched him.

"I'll go gather some more wood." Lilabeth stood, and limped a few steps only to pause when Connor spoke up.

"Stay here, near the fire," he grumbled. "Ye dinnae ken what's out there, not to mention ye can barely walk."

She seemed tempted to argue, but a swift, frigid glare from Connor ended the discussion faster than it began. She floundered in silence for a few moments before taking her seat. "Uh, I never asked why you're going to Edinburgh."

"And I'll thank ye to keep it that way." It had been a trying few days, and he was in no mood to share. After a simple meal of dried beef strips and stale bread, Connor offered Lilabeth a cup of hot coffee. He had put a kettle on the fire earlier, and the water was finally hot.

"No, I don't drink coffee, but thanks anyway," she replied.

"Well, ye might want to on a cold night like this. It'll warm ye up on the inside."

"So would some tea. I noticed some wild yarrow mint over there that would make some very nice tea." Lilabeth pointed to a bushy area growing low under a tall tree, where the herb was barely visible in the dark. After taking another sip of his coffee, Connor briefly glanced in the appointed direction, but offered nothing else.

When she realized that he had no intention of assisting her, Lilabeth slowly limped her way over to the herb patch. There was just enough light from the small fire for her to tear off a handful of leaves. As she limped her way back, she ground the leaves and stems fiercely in her palms. After pouring a mug of hot water, Connor placed it on a small rock, close to the fire.

"There's enough here for two, if you'd like some," she said, dropping the leaves into the cup. "It's especially sweet this time of the year. I remember when my mum used to brew it. The whole house smelt like heaven with its sweet aroma, and we would sip on it for days. Would you like to try a cup?"

Connor only shook his head.

"Oh, come on, Connor. I know that a cup of tea ain't much, but it's all I have to offer. I know you don't really want me along, and there ain't no way for me to repay your kindness. Please, it's not much, but it's all

I got," Lilabeth pleaded as she held out the cup, her wide, dark eyes reflecting the flames of the fire, as well as the innocence of her offer.

Connor considered himself a bit stoic, but even he couldn't deny the girl's honest exposure, or her sincerity and he let down his guard. "The coffee tastes bitter tonight anyway," he lied as he dumped what was left in his mug onto the ground.

When her benefactor took the offered cup of tea, it brought a smile to the young girl's face. Her smile radiated through the darkness, changing the tension between two strangers into something more relaxed—a sense of ease.

Reaching into his bag, Connor pulled out the flute and began playing a lighthearted tune, soothing the mood even more. When the song came to an end, Lilabeth applauded enthusiastically. "That was very good. Have you been playing long?"

"Aye, since I was a child. My grandpa taught me."

"Would you mind if I played you a song?" she asked.

"Ye ken the flute, aye?"

"Yes, I learned from my mum. She was very good on the flute. She was very good at a lot of things. I miss her so much," the young girl whispered as a look of sadness fell across her face.

"Then by all means, play me a tune." Connor handed Lilabeth the flute, which she took eagerly.

"And you drink your tea while it's still hot," she ordered as she prepared to show off her own talents.

Lilabeth was indeed quite skilled, and the melody that drifted from the instrument was a haunting ballad, almost a spiritual tune.

Scooping out the leaves from his cup and tossing them into the fire, Connor made himself comfortable while sipping the yarrow mint tea. The sonata enveloped him with its intoxicating rhythm, and he felt the melody as much as he heard it. Closing his eyes, he laid his head back against the saddle and felt his soul gently sway, as if he were dancing on air, swept up in the hypnotic serenade.

Waking with a start, Connor instinctively grabbed the dirk he kept at his side. Lilabeth jumped back from the tip of the blade that was only inches from her face. It was still dark, and the fire had long since gone out, but the night sky was full of stars, and a partial moon cast a nocturnal glow. At first, he could only make out her silhouette as she squatted down next to him. But then, her large, dark eyes reflected what little light was available, and he could finally see her face. "What do ye want?" he asked, annoyed and unnerved.

"Connor, I want to show you something. Come with me," she said, almost in a whisper.

"What? Go back to sleep," he growled.

"There's something you have to see. Come on. Get up." But Connor waved her off before turning his back to her. "Please Connor. Just come with me before it's over. You have to see this."

"I havta see what? What are ye talking about?"

"I can't explain it. You'll have to see for yourself. Come on, hurry!" Lilabeth grabbed his hand, pulling him to his feet.

"This better be important!" he grumbled. Allowing her to lead him through a small grove of trees, they followed a path that was strangely illuminated by a mist swirling across the forest floor. "Lilabeth, where are ye taking me?" he hissed. As he followed the girl, Connor also thought it odd that her limp seemed to be gone, as if her foot was no longer injured.

"We're almost there, *shhh*," she whispered, holding a finger up to her pursed lips. They continued through the trees until reaching a clearing, and in the center a small pond was glistening eerily. The still water reflected the night sky, full of starlight that twinkled on the mirrored, black surface. Moonlight cast strange shadows around the edge of the clearing, and they stood silently, as if they had invaded a sacred place and were waiting to be invited.

"What are we doin' here?" Connor whispered.

"Just watch." Lilabeth's answer was barely audible as she stared wide-eyed into the center of the pond.

Connor was nearly ready to turn and leave when the reflected lights of the night sky began to slowly move across the surface of the water. But there was no wind, and the water itself was unmoving. When he glanced at the stars above, they remained stationary in the sky, though when he again looked out across the pond, the lights were swirling in circles, as if dancing to an unheard song.

"What the hell?" Unable to believe his eyes, Connor stood in bewildered amazement at what he saw unfolding before them. Suddenly the lights lifted from the water's surface. Continuing their dance in the air, they gracefully ascended, one by one, until the night sky was full of small, shimmering, translucent lights, circling upward in iridescent columns. A soft, nocturnal melody floated eerily on the night breeze, whistling through the trees. It started out muted, but the sound escalated as the glimmering lights rose off the surface of the pond.

Soaring out in all directions, the lights dipped and dove through the trees, aviating around rocks, and gliding across the water, but never breaking the surface. More than once, Connor and Lilabeth had to duck as the strange lights streaked by just above their heads. The song of this surreal dance now filled the air, and the haunting sound was intoxicating. The night sky was alive with energy, accompanied by the sensual and haunting song of the twilight. Connor felt himself being swept up in the seduction of its aura.

"Aren't they beautiful?" Lilabeth asked in a breathy whisper as she gently slipped her hand into his.

"Aye, but...what are they?" Connor was trapped by the magical display, and he barely noticed when Lilabeth hugged his arm before dropping her head against his shoulder.

"They are the children of the Goddess Aphrodite," she whispered. "They have come out to bless the night and play in the light of the moon and stars. Very few have ever seen them, so we are fortunate this night. Their colors represent all the beauty of love, the love of Aphrodite. They're amazing, aren't they?"

Lilabeth's voice sounded different; warm and seductive, and when Connor finally tore his gaze from the dancing lights to look down at her, his jaw dropped.

"Isaboe?" Placing his hands on the girl's shoulders, he held her at arm's-length, closely examining her as disbelief registered across his face.

"Yes, Connor, I'm here for you. We are here in this beautiful place tonight, together, just as it should be." Wrapping her arms around his waist, Isaboe leaned into him.

Connor instinctively returned the embrace with matched intensity, but as confusion clouded his mind, he pushed her back. "But…how? How is it that ye are here? I dinnae understand?"

"Does it matter?" she whispered, as she wrapped herself against Connor and turned her face up to his. "All that's important is we're together. I never want to be out of your arms again. Kiss me."

He hesitated at first, trying to find the logic, but Isaboe was here with him, just as he wanted her to be. *Maybe it's a dream*, he thought. *Maybe Aphrodite's magic brought her here.* Having Isaboe in his arms was so enticing it proved to be more powerful than Connor's attempt at rationality. Giving in, he eagerly obliged, pressing his mouth against hers. All the desire he had for her came flooding out in a passionate, intense moment. He held her tight, afraid if he let go, she might somehow slip away.

"I love you so much, Connor. Please, make love to me. I need to feel your body next to mine," Isaboe whispered as she slowly pulled out of his arms, and lowered herself to the ground.

"Here? Now?" he asked, looking down at her reclining on the mossy ground in front of him. The magical lights continued dancing around them, casting a surreal light that glowed off Isaboe's delicate features. Tossing her hair off her shoulder, she ran a hand down the side of her neck and across her bosom, caressing her exposed white skin. As she slowly swept her tongue across her lower lip, he felt his heart stutter and quicken.

"Yes, now. You want me. I know you do." She reached up and pulled Connor down to lie next to her. Again, she kissed him deeply, her tongue eagerly searching for his as she caressed the back of his neck. As she pressed her warm body up against his, he felt the blood rushing to his loins. She felt perfect in his embrace, arousing and overwhelmingly tempting. God, how he wanted her!

Pulling away, she rolled onto her back and began unlacing the ties of her bodice, revealing the roundness of her breasts and the warm, pale skin that had tempted him for weeks. She reached for him, running her fingers over his chest and stomach before grabbing his hips and pulling

him over on top of her. Shuddering with desire, he ground down against
her, kissing her hard. The seductive night song and the illumination of
the lights intensified with the heat of their passion.

"I've waited long enough, my love. Take me now!" she demanded,
pulling at his pants.

Pushing up to his knees, Connor began fumbling with the buckle of
his pants, when suddenly, even in the fog of his desire, he knew something
was amiss.

Leaning over her, he looked closely into her brown eyes. *Brown eyes?*
Isaboe's eyes are green. Is it a trick of the light, or—no! Something's very wrong
here. The thought flashed like a bolt of lightning through Connor's mind,
pulling him abruptly from the grasp of sensual indulgence.

"Ye're not Isaboe!" he growled as he drew away from her. "What kind
of twisted magic is this? Who are ye? *What* are ye?"

It started out low, a methodical, evil kind of laugh. Lying beneath him,
the not-Isaboe was laughing in such a malicious way that it sent terror
down his spine. All the beautiful colored lights immediately disappeared,
and the night air became quiet and still, plunging them back into darkness. Connor now looked down into the face of Lilabeth, lying on the
ground in front of him, laughing.

"What kind of evil thing are ye? Ye've placed a damn spell on me,
ye *galla salach!*" Connor shouted as he backed away slowly, recoiling at
something so frightening, so wicked and immoral that he couldn't take
his eyes from it. Paying no attention to his footing, he tripped on a tree
root and tumbled over backwards, falling hard onto the ground.

In the moment it took Connor to stand back up, it was no longer
night. Brightness surrounded him as if a curtain had instantly been pulled
back, revealing the light of day. There was no transition between twilight
and dawn, and Connor found himself standing next to the cold remains
of the fire he had built. He was trying to make sense of what had just
happened, wondering how it could've happened, when that awful laughter
caught his attention.

Lilabeth sat upon a large bolder gazing down at him. Confused and
disoriented, Connor stared back at the woman who no longer looked like
a scared, young run-away. The innocence she had used to trap him no

longer existed. Her long dark hair hung loosely over her bare shoulders, and her dark eyes looked cold and menacing. The stark, blood-red of her lips stood out dramatically against her porcelain, white skin, and the simple smock she had been wearing earlier was now replaced by a clinging, black gown, slinky and seductive that hugged her curves like some perverse drawing. The loosely-laced bodice of her dress barely covered her rounded breasts, and the slit that ran up both sides of her garment, from her feet to her waist, promiscuously displayed Lilabeth's long, sleek legs as she glanced down at Connor, scoffing.

"*Please, please help me! I'd rather die than go back there!* You mortal men are so predictable!" Lilabeth said mockingly, taunting him with the words that had trapped him like a dumb animal into a snare baited with fresh meat. "Though it took a little longer to get you to come around, I think it was; *I have nothing to offer you but this cup of tea,* that finally did it. I have to admit, I'm rather proud of that one," she boasted.

Furious, Connor rushed toward Lilabeth in a blinding rage, only for her to vanish before his very eyes.

"Tsk, tsk, Connor. It will do you no good to be so angry." She now taunted him from the branch of a tree where she sat casually, dangling her alluring legs. "You can't help that you're just a pathetic man, driven by such weakness as lust. Oh yes, I know that you *lusted* for me. You would have taken me, but there was just that *one* split second of sense, wasn't there? Could you do it again? Should we *try* again?"

"*Ye filthy bitch!*" Connor ran up to the base of the tree, but the branch that Lilabeth sat upon was well above his head. His hands balled into fists, he glared up at her. "What evil thing puked ye up from the depths of hell?"

"That's both rude and insulting." Lilabeth leaned back against the tree, letting one leg hang freely while resting the opposite foot on the branch. The fabric of her dress hung down and wrapped around her leg in ribbons. "I'm a muse and a shape-shifter. I can take on the appearance of anyone or any living thing." She paused, and looked down at Connor. "Even a wolf," she said with a wicked smile.

The wolf; the black monster that had viciously attacked Margaret, inexplicably invading the Scottish Highlands where no wolves should be. "That was you?" Connor exclaimed, stunned at her confession. The attack may have been short-lived, but the damage was severe. He left Edinburgh not knowing if Margaret's arm could be saved, not to mention her life. "But why? Why attack her?"

"Margaret was too close. She needed to be removed. You, on the other hand, would not be as easy. I knew I would need a different angle with you. I had to find your weakness. Since you're mortal man, it wasn't difficult to identify," Lilabeth jeered. "Mortal men are so easy to deceive. All I needed to do was show a little flesh, add some big sorrowful eyes, and you were mush in my hands." She let loose an evil chuckle. "You saw what I wanted you to see; the blood on my foot, the innocence of my pillaged youth, and yes, your precious Isaboe. Lorien told me all about her."

"*Lorien!*" Connor growled through gritted teeth as the last of the fog from the fairie glamour cleared from his mind, and what had happened suddenly became crystal clear.

"Yes, she told me all about your noble sense of honor. That's how I knew you would fall for the poor little servant-girl." The elusive fey again swung her legs down and crossed her ankles, letting her feet swing under the branch. Realizing what he had allowed to happen, Connor felt fear and anger ramming into the center of his gut. Rosalyn's last words of warning before he left Lochmund Hills now came back to haunt him.

"Lorien needed me to intercept you, delay your travels back to the city. Had I not had the opportunity to distract you and provided the road you mistakenly took, well, you would have arrived at your destination too soon."

"Too soon for what?" Connor's rage was quickly replaced with panic. Isaboe's life was at stake.

"It was my job to detain you. She needed more time alone with your beloved Isaboe. More time that would be unencumbered by...you." Leaning slightly forward, she smiled down at Connor. "Did I also mention that I'm an entertainer? So, tell me, Connor; were you entertained?" she snickered with a wicked laugh.

"*Lorien!*" Connor spat the name with vile disgust. "I should have known. Rosalyn tried to warn me, but I...I had no idea how manipulative, how evil, how..." Connor mumbled to himself as he began to understand it all. He feared that his ignorance had already cost Isaboe more than they could handle.

Throwing himself into action, Connor pulled his gear together and saddled his horse, ignoring Lilabeth. His only thought was to get to Isaboe as soon as possible.

"You're wasting your time, lover boy. You are no match for Lorien. She will get what she wants. We did have fun though, didn't we?" As Connor kicked his horse into a rapid gallop, back in the direction of Edinburgh, Lilabeth's wicked laugh carried on the wind behind him.

chapter 3

the bitter taste of self disdain

By the time Connor rode into Edinburgh, the city was almost dark. Stopping only once to water his horse, he had ridden hard all day, berating himself the whole time for having been so easily fooled. Having no idea how much time he'd lost while caught in Lilabeth's trap, he prayed that it was just hours, and not days.

Rosalyn and Demetrick had both mentioned that time in the realm of the fey did not equate with time in this world, and he knew all too well the differences from firsthand experience. But had he actually left this world? Had Lilabeth actually taken him on an astral journey, or had it simply been an illusion brought on by intoxicating tea and faerie glamour? The lure of desire made him feel weak and pathetic, led only by instinct. Yes, Lilabeth had toyed with him and clouded his mind with fey magic, preventing logical reasoning, but he had taken the bait.

How could I have been such a damn fool? I didna heed Rosalyn's warning and fell into Lilabeth's trap like a stupid animal. How could I have not seen it? Please God, dinnae let me be too late. Connor mentally tortured himself for being so easily lured, but he had never suspected that Lorien would lay a trap for *him*.

Upon finally reaching the inn, Connor prayed desperately that his ignorance hadn't served Lorien's plan. Making his way quickly up the steps and down the long hallway, he reached the room where he had last held Isaboe. He rapped lightly on the door before hearing a voice inviting him to enter.

As Connor walked into the room, Margaret was sitting up in bed, leaning back against the headboard with her eyes closed. He walked over and gently touched her shoulder. She opened her eyes slightly, but when she saw him standing at her side, her eyes flew open wide. "Connor!" she exclaimed as she raised her bandaged arms to embrace him, cringing slightly from the pain.

He returned her embrace cautiously before sitting down in the chair next to her bed. "How are ye?" he asked as he examined the bandages on her forearms.

"I'm doing alright, considering."

"Where's Isaboe?"

"She's gone," Margaret said, her words heavy.

Connor's wide blue eyes flashed between concern and fury. "Isaboe's gone? When? Where'd she go?"

"She left yesterday. I don't know to where." With a couple of fingers that were exposed and un-bandaged, Margaret held up the letter that had been lying on her bed. "Why would she leave us? It doesn't make sense."

Tentatively, Connor opened the letter and read Isaboe's words.

Dearest Margaret,

I don't know the right words, or if there are any to tell you what I have to say. The doctor told me you are showing improvement. I pray that you'll be alright and make a full recovery. I can't tell you what your friendship has meant to me, nor can I tell you why I have to leave you. I will never forget what you have done. You have saved my life, though I'm not sure it was worth saving.

I'm going to find Anna and Benjamin on my own. I'm taking some of the money that Connor left, so I should be fine. Please don't try to follow me.

I'm sorry I cannot explain myself further, but please trust that I am doing the right thing, for all of us. Thank you for everything, I will never forget you.

Please tell Connor I'm sorry.

Isaboe

Connor held the letter in his hands and felt the weight of the words punch him like a ramrod into his core. He felt himself swirling down, like the sinking of a ship into turbulent black waters. The rage of anger and self-reproach was almost overwhelming as he sat and stared at the letter. "I'm too late," he mumbled, feeling the fear of what he now knew, what he had hoped wouldn't be the case. "I'm too late!" he exclaimed, shooting up out of his chair and crushing the letter in his fist.

"Too late for what? What are you talking about?" Margaret asked with a tinge of panic in her voice.

"I'm too *fucking* late!" he shouted as he kicked the chair hard across the floor. Throwing the crinkled letter down, he ran back out of the room, leaving the door open behind him.

"Connor, where are you going?" Margaret shouted after him. "What do you mean, too late? Too late for what? *Connor!*" But he didn't turn back. He left Margaret sitting on the bed, watching him leave just as quickly as he had appeared.

His horse had but a short rest when Connor was back in the saddle and again kicking hard into its flanks. Inquiries he had made of both the hotel clerk and of the stable keep had come up empty. Neither of them had any information on where Isaboe had set off for. He had no idea where to start looking and no plan of action. Reacting only from a place of fear and urgency, he bolted his horse into a gallop out of the city, into the dark perimeter beyond the street lanterns. But it didn't take long before logic took over, and he pulled back hard on the reins, bringing his horse to a halt in a flurry of flying dirt and rock. Feeling his chest heaving from the ride and from his burst of panic, he struggled to focus on what his next move should be, but he couldn't put his thoughts in order.

Isaboe was gone.

It was his own damn fault he had lost her, and somehow he had to find her again. The how, he didn't know. All he knew was that Isaboe had left on horseback, but not alone. Lorien was with her, and that only intensified the anxiety that twisted his guts into knots.

Connor hadn't eaten all day. His body was exhausted from the hard ride, but his mind was alive, darting in a million different directions all at once. Thick clouds filled the night sky, blocking any trace of moonlight as he gazed out into the darkness. Jumping down from his horse, he looked back at the dim glow that hovered over Edinburgh as his breath burned across his parched lips. He didn't know what to do, where to go, or how to move forward from this point. And in not knowing, he felt like a complete failure.

This was new and unsettling territory for him. Connor's training as a soldier had not prepared him to fight this type of enemy. He was up against not only a sinister and manipulative being, but one whose abilities were strange and unexplainable. From first-hand experience he had endured the magic of faerie glamour, been enveloped into its mind-altering effects. He could only imagine what Isaboe was going through at the hands of the Fey Queen.

The thought of Lorien and her wicked tricks made him angry, at himself for falling for them, and at Isaboe for leaving the city with her. Regardless of what Lorien may have said or done, it was stupid and childish for her to run off without him. But her naïve innocence was just one of the things he had grown to love about her, and another reason he had to protect her.

Connor's dull nails were biting half-circles into his palms, and he let himself feel it. Maybe he deserved some pain for his stupidity. But in that moment of realization, knowing what had already come to pass, he also knew he had to make it right.

As he mounted his horse with a heavy weight in his chest, Connor let out a deep sigh. Looking out over the dark horizon, he whispered her name into the night, "Isaboe." As the rain began to fall, he dropped his chin to his chest and felt the drain of exhaustion, but his heart wasn't ready to give up, and he raised his head. "Isaboe, if it takes my last breath, I swear I'll find you!" he announced his commitment to the foreboding night sky. He would find her, and protect her—from Lilabeth, or Lorien, or anyone else who ever tried to hurt Isaboe again.

Drops of cool water splashed against his face, but Connor was completely oblivious to the rain now falling steadily around him. He pulled on the reins and slowly made his way back into a city full of people that offered him nothing but emptiness.

Water dripped off his coat as he sat silently staring at the floor next to Margaret's bed. He felt the heavy weight of anguish hanging on him like invisible chains.

"Connor, talk to me. What is it? What did you mean when you said you were too late? Too late for what?" Margaret asked, after his long silence drove her to speak.

With a heavy heart he raised his head and looked at Margaret. "I ken what happened to her: the years she lost, her husband, her children, being taken to the world of the fey, all of it," he confessed.

Margaret's jaw dropped. "You know about that? Did Isaboe tell you?" He only shook his head. "Then how? How could you possibly know?"

Connor let out a heavy sigh before answering. "Do ye remember when I told ye I had to find a woman who lives in the Lochmund Hills? Her name is Rosalyn, and she's a… a sorceress, or something like that. She told me about Isaboe and what happened to her. She also told me I was chosen to be her… protector," Connor murmured the last word as he dropped his gaze, afraid that Margaret would see what a failure he was and hate him for it. When he looked back up at her, his eyes begged for understanding. "I thought she'd still be here when I got back, but…" Connor couldn't finish his sentence.

"What does she need protection from? Do you know why Isaboe would run off by herself?" Margaret asked. Her eyes grew wide as Connor shared with her what he felt he could.

"She's not alone. Lorien, the very one she needs protection from is who Isaboe left town with."

"Lorien! I've heard that name before," Margaret said, and Connor heard the fear bleeding into her words. "Who is this…Lorien anyway?"

"From what I was told, she is a very powerful Fey Queen who wants to take Isaboe back to her world, to the realm of the Underlings."

"But why? She just came back from there."

"Because of the child."

"You know 'bout that, too?"

"Aye."

"I don't understand. If this Fey Queen, Lorien, wants Isaboe's baby, why did she ever let her come back to us in the first place? Do you think that Isaboe's already gone? I mean, back to the realm of the fey?"

"No. It is only the child she wants and it has to come to full-term first. Isaboe is just…*God damnit!*" Connor shouted as he stood up and began pacing the floor while running his hands through his hair. "If only I'd been here. She was alone and vulnerable with that evil witch twisting her mind. I should've been here."

"Isaboe is just what?" Margaret asked.

Connor sat back down before looking at Margaret, his eyes pleading for answers. "Did Isaboe tell ye anything about where she might've gone, which direction, who she might've talked to, *anything*?"

"Connor, I've been out of it. I don't remember much. Today is really the first day I feel awake and alert, like I'm not swimming in some kind of a fog. I don't recall speaking to Isaboe before the other night, and she didn't say anything about leaving."

"Did she tell ye what she would be doing when ye arrived here in Edinburgh? She's looking for information on the whereabouts of her children, aye?"

"Aye, but if she found anything, she didn't say. Isaboe is just *what?* You didn't answer my question."

"Lorien only wants the child. Isaboe is just the woman carrying it. These… these fey creatures care nothin' about her."

"Why do they want her child?"

"I dinnae ken, other than there's somethin' special about Isaboe's baby."

"But why you, Connor? Why were you chosen to protector her?"

Margaret scrutinized him, and Connor stared back, not sure how much he wanted to reveal. "Why Isaboe?" he replied.

Margaret finally nodded, but gave no response. It was just one more of the unanswered questions that surrounded the mysterious Isaboe.

"She did mention that she planned to start at the church her mother attended. I believe she said it was the Greyfriars Kirk."

"What was Isaboe's mother's name?"

"Marta Cameron."

"I'll go there first thing on the morrow and see if she's been there."

"You can't just walk in and ask if Isaboe McKinnon has been there. Isaboe supposedly *died* twenty years ago. If she went to the church lookin' for information, she wouldn't have used her own name."

"What name would she have used?"

"I don't know, Connor. We never discussed that. I only know that she was going to start at the church. I still don't understand why Isaboe would leave us with no explanation."

"Rosalyn told me that Lorien is telling her lies. I dinnae ken what, but Isaboe obviously believed her. She must have felt that she had no choice but to leave with her." Connor hesitated before continuing. "If only I'd made it back sooner," he muttered. Running his hands through his hair in frustration, he stood and again paced the floor.

"Why did you leave her alone in the first place?" Connor heard the accusation in Margaret's voice, knowing she was right, but he couldn't face her. And he certainly wasn't about to share what Lilabeth had done to delay his return. Sure, he had been duped, lulled into Lorien's trap, but he should have known better, should have seen it coming. The only way to make it right again would be to find Isaboe before it was too late. There were no other options.

He finally turned back to Margaret "As soon as I can find out where she went, I'm leaving."

"Not without me," she replied assertively.

"Ye're in no condition to ride, and I dinnae wanna be hindered by…" Connor caught himself before finishing a statement he might regret, remembering that Margaret had set her own life aside to make this journey with Isaboe. "I'm sorry Margaret, I mean no disrespect, but I cannae wait."

"Connor, you can't leave me behind. Isaboe means as much to me as she does to you, maybe more. We are all in this together, so don't you dare leave without me."

"Margaret, these fey are very powerful, and they can mess with yer mind. We dinnae ken what we may be up against." Though visibly shaken by the intensity of Connor's statement, Margaret was adamant, and by the look on her face, Connor knew it was useless to try and reason with her.

After locking stares for a few uncomfortable moments, he finally conceded. "When will ye be ready to ride?"

"When you tell me it's time to go."

He managed to give her a weak smile before walking back to her bedside. "Ye're a good friend, Margaret. Get some rest, and I'll see ye in the morrow." Connor kissed her lightly on top of her head before turning to leave for the night.

CHAPTER 4

A PLACE TO START FROM

The following morning when Connor arrived at the kirk, he had no idea what he would ask. He just knew he had to come. This was his only lead. Attempting to keep his steps light and quiet, he made his way toward the altar when he saw a clergy woman walking toward him.

"Hello," she said with a pleasant greeting. "I'm Sister Jean. My I help you?"

"Good morning. Aye, I was wondering if a young woman has been here in the last few days asking for information on a former member of your congregation, a woman named Marta Cameron?"

"And, what is your name, sir?"

"Connor Grant."

"Yes, there was a woman named Kaitlyn Grant here a couple of days ago asking about Marta Cameron and her family. She spoke with Sister Miriam. Are you related to her?"

Hearing the name, he knew it had to be Isaboe, and was surprised that she had used his surname, wondering what was behind that, but now was not the time, and Connor decided to go along with the fabricated story. "Aye, I'm her husband. Any chance I may also speak with Sister Miriam?"

Holding his gaze, Sister Jean appeared to be considering his request when a number of other women clergy began strolling into the sanctuary, and she glanced in their direction before finally answering. "This must be your lucky day, Sir," Sister Jean said lively. "Please come with me and I'll introduce you to Sister Miriam."

Standing in front of the stoic, elderly woman, Connor was sure she could see right through his lie when he asked about the information she had given Kaitlyn Grant.

"Why don't you ask her yourself?" Sister Miriam regarded him with cautious reserve. Connor knew she wouldn't be easily coerced into providing the missing information.

"I would, if I knew where she was. That's why I am here, looking for information on where she's gone."

"So, you do not *know* where your wife is? A good husband would have his house in order, and his wife would not have run off." The stern look on the elder sister's face told Connor this was not going to be easy.

"Aye, a good husband would, and I'll be the first to admit that I've failed her. I left town a few days ago on business. I made sure she was well lodged and comfortable before taking my leave, and at the time, I felt confident that she would still be here when I returned. There are no words to express my distress when I found that she...she had left. Left with no word or indication as to where she might've gone. I understand that ye may question my ability to care for her, or her reason for leaving without me, but I can assure you my one and only concern is for her welfare. So please, if ye have any information about where she might've gone, I must ken." Connor's plea rang sincere. He hoped that the sister felt the truth in it, though she was still glaring at him judgingly.

"Why would she not wait for your return? Is there some reason that she felt compelled to leave without you? Maybe your concern and conviction for her welfare is not as honorable as you would have us believe."

Though Connor understood the sister's line of questioning, he was growing impatient with her scrutiny. Every moment he spent explaining himself, Isaboe was moving farther and farther away. He also knew that this woman might be his only source of information, and though his first instinct was to demand answers, he did his best to keep himself in check. "I understand yer concerns. Ye feel the need to protect her, and for that, I'm grateful. But she has not been well in the head lately, and though I knew that, I didna realize just how serious it was until I returned to find her gone. The longer she is out there alone, the more I fear for her safety. Please, do ye ken where she might have gone? I believe that she came here looking for information on her family, a brother and sister. Do ye know if she found anything regarding their whereabouts?" Connor's gaze was pleading as he looked into the sister's eyes.

A subtle shift crossed the woman's face, and Connor felt cautiously hopeful as he watched her features soften. "Yes, Kaitlyn was here inquiring about her family—Isaboe's children to be specific, though I had very little to offer her," the old woman finally conceded. "All I could tell her was the last known location of Isaboe's sisters, though I have no idea if she intended to seek them out."

"Where's the location?"

"Somewhere on Orkney Island, a small fishing port was all I could recall."

"And the name of Isaboe's sisters?"

"Their names were Saschel and Deidra. Deidra and her husband ran a small fishing business, but if I did know his name, I no longer recall it."

"Anything else?" he asked, clinging to the hope that Isaboe had followed the old woman's words.

"No, that was all I could tell her. I have no idea what became of Isaboe's children."

"Is there anything else ye can tell me, anything that might help me to find her?"

"Like what?"

"I dinnae ken. I'm just lookin' for any clues that might give me an idea of which direction she would've gone. There's more than one route to Orkney, aye?"

"So, it's your belief that Kaitlyn would go off to Orkney on her own? With no more information than what I just shared with you?"

"Aye, I think she would, and has."

The sister regarded Connor with a long, intense stare. "You know she's with child."

"Aye. She told ye?"

"She didn't have to." Sister Miriam paused and took a step forward. "I saw desperation in her eyes, as if she's struggling with something haunting her soul. Do you know what I mean?"

Connor couldn't answer, but knew exactly what she was referring to.

Though he didn't consider himself a particularly religious man, Connor bent down on one knee and kissed the old woman's hand. Looking up into her aged eyes full of wisdom and compassion, he saw what he needed to see—forgiveness for whatever role he had played in Isaboe's flight. Now, he desperately wanted her blessing. "Please, bless me, Sister. Please ask God to help me in my search for her. As I kneel here before you, let my life be sacrificed if I fail."

A smile broke across the woman's wrinkled, yet radiant face. "Well, I pray it won't come to that, but I'm sure our Lord is looking down on us and smiling at your passion." With her free hand, she touched the top of his head, and Connor left the Kirk with blessings from Sister Miriam and the Lord God All Mighty. He just hoped it was enough.

The walk back to the inn allowed Connor the time to put his thoughts together, wondering which of the two possible routes out of Edinburgh they should take. He had no plan other than to find Isaboe, and without knowing the route she took after leaving the city, they could waste precious time by choosing the wrong path.

Connor felt helpless. He had been up against odds that were not in his favor, but he would eventually figure a way out. This time, it wasn't just the odds that were against him. Isaboe's life was on the line. When a stranger bumped into him on the street, Connor realized how deep he was in his own thoughts. He was in the middle of a bustling city, full of people in motion, yet he had barely even noticed them. The nagging truth that he hadn't lived up to his obligation to protect Isaboe made it difficult to focus on anything other than holding her again.

Stopping to look around, he leaned against the cold stone of a small building and watched citizens going about their lives, pondering on how bizarre his and Isaboe's lives had become. Once, they were only strangers—two souls who were merged together in another time, in another world. Now he couldn't imagine his world without her in it.

Reaching into his jacket, he pulled out a pouch and opened it, dropping the ring into his hand. It was the silver band the wizard had given him to mark Isaboe during their time together in the other world, and he clasped it tightly in his fist, trying to pull her essence from the metal.

Maybe there was still enough magic in the ring to find her. He glanced up into the sky and muttered under his breath, "Demetrick, if there is any power in this ring, I could really use it now."

"Orkney Island!" Margaret exclaimed. "Do you really think she's going to travel *that* far? I have a hard time believing that Isaboe would go all that way to find sisters she hasn't seen in years. She doesn't even know if they're still alive, or if they have any information about her children. There must be something else she had to go on."

"Well if she had any other information, she didna get it from Sister Miriam."

"But that's not enough information for her to take off on her own. That don't make sense."

"Aye, not to a rational person, but Isaboe's state of mind is anything but rational right now, and she's not alone. Somehow Lorien talked her into leaving before I returned. She obviously convinced Isaboe that staying here to wait for us was not an option. What lies must that bitch have told her to make Isaboe believe she had no other choice?" he growled. "But the thing that has me most concerned is not that she's with Lorien, 'cause Lorien wants the child, and Isaboe must stay well till the child comes to full term. It's the fact that Lorien must ken we'll follow. Who knows which route she'll take? There's a lot of land between here and the coast, aye? With winter comin', we could waste valuable time if we dinnae take the correct route. I'm sure Lorien will try to keep one step ahead of us. I've tracked men on horseback before, but we're dealing with something very different. If only we had some other bit of information to go on."

"Maybe we do," Margaret said as she reached behind her pillow, cringing a bit from the tenderness of her wounds. Pulling out the envelope that held the crinkled letter from Isaboe, she reached in and slowly lifted out a beautiful blue stone dangling on a long green cord.

"What's that?"

"It's Isaboe's."

"So?"

"It has powers," she whispered.

"What kind of powers?" Connor asked suspiciously. After experiencing Lilabeth's powers, he was quite sure he'd had enough of fey magic.

"Remember the night at the tree when you asked what we were looking at, and we told you we were looking at fire flies? They weren't fire flies, Connor. They were *pixies!* And we communicated with them through this. They spoke to us, told us things. That was the first time I heard the name Lorien. I think the pixies were trying to warn Isaboe about her."

"I remember that night," Connor replied. "How did she come to have possession of this...pendant?"

"On our way to Inverness Isaboe told me about a strange old woman who had appeared in our coach while I was asleep. She said the woman gave it to her, and apparently the old crone also told Isaboe things that frightened her."

"What kind of things?"

"I don't know for sure."

"Did ye see this old woman?"

"No, like I said, I was sleeping. At first, I didn't believe her. But after seeing what it can do, let's just say that it's more than just good fortune that Isaboe left it behind."

Connor stared at the blue stone dangling in Margaret's hand. "If that thing has some sort of power to communicate with *any* type of fey creatures, I want *nothin'* to do with it!" he spat, rising quickly to put distance between himself and whatever magic the pendent held.

"They're *pixies*, and not all fey creatures are bad. These were good pixies. Weren't you listening just now? They were trying to *warn* Isaboe about Lorien. I can communicate with them using this...pendant, or amulet, or whatever it is. Maybe they know where Isaboe is, or at least can help us find her. It's worth a try."

Connor didn't attempt to hide his distrust. The sting of having been deceived by these Underlings, whether it be faerie, muse, or pixie, was still too fresh. He was not prepared to gamble with Isaboe's life and trust the very creatures they were fighting against. "How does it work?" he asked cautiously.

"I don't really know, other than if you are wearing this, or just holding it, you can see and hear the pixies. It really was incredible! If I hadn't seen 'em myself, I wouldn't have believed it. But it was real. They were real."

Connor sat back down and gazed intently at her. "So, ye're tellin' me that there are wee pixies fluttering all around us and we cannae see 'em unless ye're holdin' that pendant? Do ye see 'em now?" he asked mockingly.

"*No,* I don't see them now!" she snapped. "Why are you being so difficult? This works, I saw them, spoke with them. I heard them warn Isaboe about Lorien. The very fact that I have this, the fact that Isaboe left it behind, whether it was a conscious decision or not, is too big to ignore. This is a sign that Isaboe intended for us to follow her. You'll just have to trust me," Margaret said curtly.

His arms folded across his chest, Connor sat in the chair staring at Margaret. As the two of them locked gazes, he finally let out a sigh of resignation. "So, show me how it works, then. How do ye get the pixies to talk to ye?"

A week prior, Connor would've never believed that he would be asking such a question. But now they were up against the unexplainable, the indefinable. An event was taking place that went against all rational thought, and he, Margaret, and Isaboe, were caught up in the middle of it. Maybe it was time to play their game.

CHAPTER 5

THE PAIN OF
A BROKEN HEART

Weeks passed as horse and rider slowly made their journey north through the rough, and often dreary conditions of the Highlands. Though Isaboe McKinnon moved through the motions necessary for survival, it often wasn't a conscious effort. Each day the amount of light became shorter as winter moved in, bringing dark and seemingly perpetual rainclouds that rolled across the land. With fewer hours of daylight available for traveling, the amount of time that Isaboe was exposed to the inclement weather was shortened. Though during the long nights, even with decent shelter, it was a growing challenge to stay warm, and her sleep was often broken by miserable dreams.

Blurred by time and misery, warmth and human companionship had become distant memories. Cold, wet loneliness was all Isaboe knew as life became just a matter of existence. The only thing that kept her going was her drive to reach the islands before winter clutched the land in its frigid grip, making travel nearly impossible. She was determined to know the fate of her children before leaving this world.

And the knowledge of her looming fate was another misery altogether. To escape the pain of her reality, she mentally crawled into a dark hole just behind her heart and stayed there. It was her only escape from the deep ache in her soul, and her mind's only option for survival.

As promised, Lorien met up with Isaboe each night, making sure she had food, shelter, and any necessary supplies. She reveled in taking care of Isaboe, like a wet nurse to a small child.

And Isaboe never resisted. She took the Fey Queen's direction without question. Knowing she would live a loveless life if she stayed in this world made it easier for her to accept her fate, and Isaboe allowed her deceitful protector to dictate her every move. There was no fight left in her anymore.

Yet riding through the cold and bitter wind day after day was taking its toll. On this late, autumn afternoon, wicked gusts whipped through her heavy cloak and bit at her face, numbing her nose and stinging her eyes. Isaboe could no longer feel her hands as she held the reins, gripped in a frozen fist. The scarf wrapped around her neck and mouth offered little protection, and her freezing pain had turned to a numbness that ached and throbbed with every pump of her heart. Shivering violently, she felt the cold all the way to the marrow of her bones. Even in her disconnected world, Isaboe's sense of survival instinctively told her to find shelter, and soon.

As the swollen clouds let loose nature's fury, releasing their rain in torrents, the sky became dark and ominous. When the wind picked up, blowing the rain sideways, Isaboe pulled the cloak tighter around her head, but she was already soaked. Other than the horse's heavy breathing and the sound of its hooves as it squished through the mud, she could hear nothing over the howling wind and steadily falling rain. The darkening sky offered little guidance as to the time of day, nor could she see any shelter on the open plain, only rolling hills covered by low-hanging clouds whose wispy, rain-filled fingers reached down to soak the land.

Leaning forward over on her horse, Isaboe hugged its wet mane. "It's up to you girl," she whispered as she clung to the animal for warmth against the deluge that beat down upon them. With a frozen grip on her reins, she surrendered her fate to the survival instincts of her four-legged companion. Horse and rider were no longer separate beings as they struggled together in an attempt to survive the storm. Her eyes closed, Isaboe slipped in and out of awareness, completely oblivious to her surroundings.

She was only semi-conscious of her horse being led into the shelter, and it took a few moments for Isaboe's partially frozen mind to register that the rain was no longer plummeting down upon her. Though the wind still howled fiercely around the small barn, threatening to blow it over, it was no longer whipping across her frozen cheeks.

"Ye havta let go now. Come on, I've got ye."

Isaboe barely heard the woman's words over the chattering of her teeth, and though her body was stiff from the cold, she shook violently. It took great effort to make her frozen fingers release their grip, but she finally allowed herself to slip off her horse and into the arms of her rescuer.

"What in God's name are ye doing out on a day like this? And all by yerself! Here, let's get these wet clothes off before ye catch yer death of cold."

Allowing the stranger to strip off her rain-soaked outer-clothing, Isaboe tried to control her shaking. The blanket smelled musty, but it was dry, and she sunk into the embrace of the woman who briskly rubbed her frozen body, coaxing the blood to move again. Gradually, she felt the icy grip starting to release.

"There, I think ye'll live now. I'm gonna tend to yer horse."

Isaboe watched as the figure of a woman, dressed in a long, heavy wool jacket, unsaddled her horse and led it to an empty stall. Walking to the end of the barn, the woman picked up several good-sized logs from a pile of firewood. After placing them next to a small potbellied stove that stood in the center of the barn floor, she opened the fire door and tossed the logs in. The fire crackled and popped as it stirred back to life, and the smell of the seasoned wood filtered its way over to where Isaboe stood, encircling her in a smoky blanket of warmth.

The sound of baying was her first indication that she shared her shelter with a small group of goats. She looked around her surroundings and could feel her body starting to relax as warmth gradually returned.

"Ye better now?" the woman asked as she stood next to Isaboe, lighting an oil lamp that hung from a beam. "What's yer name, lass? Why were ye out in this weather with no more than a bitty cloak? Where ye goin'?"

"North," was all Isaboe could say before she started coughing.

"How far north?"

When the coughing attack finally stopped, Isaboe wiped her nose with the edge of the blanket. "I'm heading to Orkney Island," she said between sniffles.

"You're going all the way to Orkney by yourself on horseback, with winter coming on? Are ye mad girl?"

Looking into the baffled face of the woman, Isaboe held her gaze as she regarded the question. "Yes, most likely I am."

Scratching the side of her head, the old woman gave Isaboe a bewildered look as the wind howled and shook the small barn, causing the goats to bleat nervously as they shuffled around their enclosure. "I'm Gilda MacHanley, and I still haven't heard yer name."

"Isaboe McKinnon."

"Well, Isaboe McKinnon, 'twas lucky for you that I was out looking for my lost nanny-goat, or ye might just have died out there this day," Gilda said with a slight reprimand in her voice. "When's the last time ye ate?"

"Uh...I'm not sure, yesterday maybe."

Gilda turned and grabbed a pitch fork of hay, tossing it into the stall for Isaboe's horse. "I'm heading back to the house. My son Fergus will be fretting with this storm howling like it is. I should've been back by now. I'll have him bring ye some food and water. When the storm lets up some, he'll bring ye back to the house. Ye should stay warm enough here; at least it's dry." Gilda started for the barn door, but stopped and turned around.

"My boy, he don't speak, born deaf and mute. He'll probably be with me till I die. 'Tis just as well now that his pa is gone. He's a good strong boy, and, well, he's all I got." Though there was a tinge of heaviness in Gilda's words, they were rimmed with acceptance, and the look in her eyes said so much more.

"I'll have him bring ye some dry clothes," she added. When she slid open the latch that held the door, the wind rushed in, sending a whirlwind of dust and hay swirling about the barn. Throwing the lamb's wool hood up over her head, Gilda fought against the wind as she pulled the door closed before latching it from the outside.

Listening to the wind howl, Isaboe walked over to the wood stove and stood as close as she could without touching it. She soaked up the radiant heat, letting the smell of wood smoke embrace her and chase the last traces of chill from her bones. She held the tresses of her hair over the heat rising from the stove, but they were tangled and knotted.

Gilda had placed the saddle in the stall where Isaboe's horse munched on the hay, the beast also thankful to be out of the storm. After retrieving a brush from her saddle bag, she combed out her tangled hair and watched as her horse ate. She thought about how dependent she had become on the animal, how the two of them had developed a bond during their insane trek together. Her horse had been her constant companion, one she had relied heavily on, and Isaboe suddenly felt a jolt of gratitude.

Putting the brush away, she stroked the horse's neck. "I know we had a rough start, old girl, but I think we've become pretty good friends, aye?" As she continued to stroke the horse, her actions immediately caused the flashback to unleash. She couldn't stop it or slam the door fast enough before the memory of Connor wrapped around her mind, and the recall of when he taught her to connect with the animal burst into her thoughts. A week's worth of stubble from being on the road without a shave; the rough cadence of his voice that brought so much comfort; the gentle puff of his breath against her hair; and the warmth of his chest against her back as he held her hands, teaching her the right motions. Built up by weeks of determined misery, a floodgate of memories broke free.

Closing her eyes, she remembered Connor's kiss, an unpracticed thing, but so honest. She had tried to deny her desire, but when she embraced it, the feeling of being held in his arms had brought her such *joy*. As all the feelings seeped back into her mind, into her soul, it was as if the memory of him had driven out the cold—but it brought back the pain.

The renewed ache in her heart barreled down on her so unexpectedly and with such intensity that Isaboe clutched at her chest. With the memory of Connor also came the agony of knowing that she would never see him, never touch him again. She slid down to the floor, pulled her knees up, and let the tears run unabated.

A quick snort from her horse and a gentle bump against the side of her head brought Isaboe back to the present. She stroked the animal's muzzle and looked up into the large brown eyes staring back.

"What? You worried about me?" she said in between sniffles. "I'm alright girl, I just cry a lot. You should be used to that by now." As if agreeing with her statement, the horse tossed its head a few times before returning its attention to the pile of hay.

As she watched the animal's reaction, Isaboe felt the hint of a smile twitch across her lips. Pushing up off the floor, she rummaged through her saddle bag for a hanky, but pulled out a folded piece of crinkled paper instead. It was the letter she had written to Connor, but at the last minute decided not to leave for him. Sitting back down on the stable floor, she pulled the blanket over her still damp undergarments and leaned against the wall. Tentatively, she re-read the words she had written:

Connor,

There is so much I want to say to you, so many feelings I wish I could share. You have shown me that love can happen more than once in a lifetime, and for that, I will always be grateful. But unfortunately, it is a love that cannot be. If my circumstances were different, if my life was normal, I would want nothing more than to be with you. But they are not.

You are a good and honorable man. I am fortunate to have known you, to have loved you, and to have been loved by you, however briefly. I also know that you are a man of conviction, and you do not accept defeat easily. But please, you must let me go. I know that I promised to be here when you returned, and my heart breaks for not being able to keep that promise, but it is for the best. My life is in a downward spiral, spinning out of control, and there is nothing that anyone can do to stop it. Please trust me on this.

I wish you happiness and I wish for someone to love you as you deserve. Unfortunately, these things just aren't meant for some of us. Please forgive me.

Forget me.

Isaboe

The tears ran silently down Isaboe's face as she refolded the letter. All of the sorrow she felt at leaving Conner and Margaret suddenly overwhelmed her. "The pain of my broken heart hurts so badly I should surely die! Why do I still live?" She screamed out her unanswered question, but her only response was the howling of the wind, leaving her feeling empty and alone. When her horse once again nuzzled her gently, Isaboe reached up with both hands and hugged the soft, downy nose against her cheek while she sobbed.

CHAPTER 6

FERGUS AND
THE GOAT-MEN

The sound of the barn door creaking open brought Isaboe temporarily out of her misery. Quickly wiping the tears from her face, she stood up slowly and looked over the stable wall where she saw a young man standing soaking wet in front of the closed barn door. Holding two leather bags, he stared at her with wide, brown eyes.

Fergus appeared to be not much younger than herself, and though he wore a heavy wool coat and a wool hat pulled down around his ears, she could tell he was strong and fit. Years of farming showed in his large hands, yet he seemed almost frightened as he stood frozen, staring at Isaboe. Remembering what Gilda had said about him being deaf and mute, she pulled the blanket up around her shoulders and stepped out of the stall. After looking at him in silence for a moment, she gave him a meek smile.

Receiving no response, Isaboe walked over to stand a few feet from him. He never moved, never flinched, never took his eyes from her. "Are those for me?" she asked, nodding toward the bags.

Fergus instantly looked embarrassed, and he averted his gaze while nervously holding out the bags. Still clutching the blanket around her shoulders, Isaboe took the bags with her free hand and then quickly returned to the stall.

One of the bags held items of clothing. In the other was a jug of water, a small flask of something definitely not water, some dried meat, bread and cheese. Isaboe put on a man's shirt, pants, and a pair of wool socks. Though they were both quite large and she had to roll up the sleeves and the pant legs, she was grateful for the extra room. Over the last couple months her belly had grown in size, and the larger clothing fit comfortably.

Making his way to the stove, Fergus threw in a few more pieces of wood while periodically glancing in the direction of his guest.

Now dressed, Isaboe picked up the food bag and the blanket before walking over to the wood stove. Laying out the blanket, she sat down and pulled out the loaf of bread, the cheese, and a piece of dried meat, which she assumed was most likely lamb. Tearing off a hunk of bread, Isaboe ate quietly as she watched Fergus move nervously about the barn, as if he were looking for something to tend to. With an occasional uneasy glance in her direction, he made sure the goats were well fed, moved a pile of hay from one side of the barn to the other, checked on the wood stove one more time, until at last it seemed he had run out of activities.

Looking so uncomfortable in his own environment, Isaboe felt badly for Fergus, and knew she was the reason for his unease. Tearing off another hunk of bread, she held it out toward him, patting the ground next to her. At first, he waved off her offer, quickly dropping his gaze to his feet. However, Isaboe didn't accept this response and tried again. "Come on, you're making me nervous, too. Please, sit down and relax. I won't bite," she said with a smile. She knew he couldn't hear her, but hoped he could at least understand the sentiment.

It took a few more moments before Fergus finally gave in. He removed his hat and his heavy coat, hanging them both on a hook before taking a tentative seat next to Isaboe. His dark brown hair stuck to his head in a perfect mold of the hat he had just removed. When she again offered the bread, this time he took it. As he watched her with eyes that caught her every move, Isaboe wondered how many women, other than his mother, he had been exposed to. Surely he had to know women his own age, but his demeanor spoke of someone who had lived a simple and sheltered life.

Fergus bit into the bread, eating anxiously as his eyes darted around the small barn. When his attention became abruptly focused, Isaboe turned to see what he was looking at—a pile of hay in the back corner of the barn. Not seeing anything unusual, she turned back toward Fergus whose gaze was still locked on the hay. He slowly raised his hand and pointed, encouraging her to look again. Isaboe looked once more, but this time held her gaze and hoped to understand what he wanted her to see.

It was so slight and quick, if she hadn't been staring at the right spot, she would have missed the movement. But then it moved again, and this time Isaboe was sure she saw it, and heard it too. It was barely audible over the howling of the wind and rain, but it was a distinguishable sound, the undeniably weak cry of a small animal. At first, it was just a little pink nose and two round black eyes making their way through the hay, but they were soon followed by a tiny, furry gray paw, then another, until a little ball of fur made its way out into the light. Blades of hay poked out of the kitten's fur, as if one of its parents could have been a porcupine. Now that it had made its way completely out of the enclosure, the tiny animal stood on wobbly legs and meowed fiercely.

When Isaboe looked back at Fergus, he smiled for the first time. Forgetting her troubles for a moment, she returned the smile and got up, then slowly made her way over to the desperately-crying kitten. Though it tried to turn and run back into the hay, its little legs were not yet strong enough for it to get away. Quickly scooping up the frantic fur ball, Isaboe hugged it to her chest as it meowed loudly.

"Oh, don't cry, little one. I won't hurt you," Isaboe spoke softly as she held the kitten cradled in her arms and gently stroked the soft down of gray fur while picking out strands of hay. With the kitten nestled in the crook of her arm, still meowing, though not quite so loudly, she came back to sit down by Fergus.

As she held the kitten, Isaboe realized that she had not heard it cry until it made its way through the hay. But Fergus knew it was there, even before movement could be seen. Somehow he knew. Isaboe wondered what kind of special gifts someone like him could acquire that the rest of the world was completely unaware of.

"I see you've found shelter out of the storm." The sound of Lorien's voice drew Isaboe's attention from the kitten, and she looked up to see the fey woman standing directly behind her host. "What on Earth are you wearing, my dear? You look positively ridiculous! And what is that *thing* you're holding?" Lorien spat before turning her look of disdain on the boy. "Who's this?"

Now it was Fergus who turned to see what Isaboe was looking at.

Startled by the sight of another woman in the barn, the boy leapt to his feet.

"Yes, I have found shelter from the storm, no thanks to you," Isaboe snapped. She was in no mood for the Fey Queen and she didn't care for Lorien's tone. "This is Fergus. His mother found me riding blind out in this weather, and she led my horse here, gave us shelter."

The Fey Queen walked over and looked down at Isaboe before turning toward Fergus, whose gaze was locked on her in bewildered amazement. "Well, I guess we owe you and your mother a debt of gratitude. You will give her our thanks, won't you?"

"He can't hear you and he doesn't speak. He was born deaf and mute," Isaboe answered for him as she stood, still holding the kitten.

"*Oh really?* A broken mortal?" A wicked smile grew across Lorien's face as she slowly encircled Fergus like a predator examining its prey. "How delightful!"

Fergus turned his frightened gaze on Lorien as she closed in, never taking his eyes from the mesmerizing faerie woman.

"Lorien, what are you doing?" Isaboe asked, as she watched a horrible smile grow on the Fey Queen's face.

"It's been a long time since I've had a bit of fun," Lorien said, carrying a look of malicious whimsy in her eyes. "I think we should play."

"No. No Lorien. Just leave him alone. He's done you no harm. Whatever it is you're thinking, just don't!" Isaboe had no idea what Lorien meant or what she had in mind, but knew it couldn't be good.

"Oh, don't worry yourself about this one, dear. I won't hurt him." Lorien ran a delicate finger sensually down the side of Fergus' face. "We'll just have a little fun, won't we, Fergus?"

"Lorien, I mean it. Leave him alone. I'm warning you!"

As the Fey Queen turned her focus on Isaboe, a subtle but ominous change fell over her demeanor. Her eyes were dark and shadowed, and her pale skin seemed to almost glow, causing Isaboe to take a few steps back. "You're warning *me*? Have you forgotten *who I am*? You are in no position to be making threats, Isaboe. If it weren't for me, you would have been dead long ago!" Lorien's words came out vile and threatening.

Isaboe's heart pounded in her chest as she struggled to find the words to fight back. Lorien's power seemed to radiate off her like heat, but a glance at Fergus brought Isaboe a tiny burst of courage, and she stood her ground. "And if I was dead, you wouldn't have this child you want so desperately, would you? You *need* me alive, Lorien. I know that. So don't threaten me! Haven't you destroyed enough lives already? What's this boy to you? If you do this Lorien, I won't go back to Euphoria with you!" Her entire body shook as she spoke, but not from the cold.

But before Lorien could respond to her attempt at defiance, Fergus stepped in front of Isaboe. His eyes were wide with fear as the boy bravely faced the strange woman. Perhaps he couldn't hear the words, but Isaboe suspected that he knew body language better than anyone, and he could see that she was being threatened.

When she realized what he was doing, Lorien threw back her head and bellowed in laughter. "He's protecting you. How *wonderfully* pathetic! Oh yes—let's play!" Lorien said wickedly just before she suddenly vanished.

Turning in circles, Fergus's gaze darted around the barn trying to make sense of what just happened. He looked back at Isaboe, but she knew there was no way to explain, much less protect him. As she reached out to the confused boy, the kitten in Isaboe's arms suddenly lifted into the air, slowly spiraling upward on an invisible current of energy as she and Fergus stared in disbelief.

The small gray ball of fur floated above them just out of reach before coming to a stop. Looking down, it let out a small mew, and then suddenly began to shape-shift, elongate, and grow in size. The short, furry, gray paws metamorphosed into long, sleek, human legs and equally proportioned arms on the body of an idealized female torso. The gray fur on her back became long gray tresses streaked with black that tumbled down and around the length of the woman's body, encircling her as she floated back down to the floor. As the apparition stood in front of Fergus and Isaboe, her hair hung loosely around her like a striped gray and black cloak. She lifted her head, exposing beautiful, jet-black, cat-eyes set in a delicate and haunting face. Reaching for Fergus, she began purring, mewing, and rubbing her body up against his, but he stood stiff, trapped by fear.

Isaboe reached out to push the strange creature away, but the feline-woman hissed and swung at her with a clawed hand. As she took a step back from the lethal nails, Isaboe's attention was diverted by the restlessness of the goats.

Just as she had watched the kitten change before her eyes, the goats also began to transform in their appearance. As they stood up on their hind legs, each goat's fur split to reveal a man's torso. On their heads, the goat horns remained, but they now stood out against a man's face, chest, and arms that replaced the animal's upper torso. The lower part of the body retained its original form on stilted hooves, but now the hind legs were larger and more muscular. At first the goat-men seemed baffled by the change; their new skin and upward stature. But they soon became accustomed to their new forms, and as males of many species will do, they began strutting and parading themselves until shoving and grunting erupted between them.

When they noticed that they were not alone, the goat-men easily jumped one-by-one over the wall of their small enclosure to investigate Isaboe, Fergus, and the kitten-woman. Though no words were spoken, they communicated with small, guttural noises as they encircled the two humans clinging to each other, watching with wide, unbelieving eyes.

The goat-men began to sniff and touch Isaboe and Fergus, but when they discovered the feline-woman, she stole all of their focus. Turning their attention on her, they began licking, nipping, and pawing at her, tugging at her long, streaked hair. Encircling her, the goat-men grabbed at her soft skin and pushed their bodies up against hers. She tried to escape, but as soon as she pulled free from the grip of one goat-man, she would land in the arms of another, and the groping continued. Isaboe and Fergus watched in astonishment as the feline-woman hissed and scratched, trying to break free of the goat-men's torrid circle game.

With legs that seemed to be made of springs, she abruptly leapt into the air, landing in the rafters with all the grace and fluidity of a cat. But she wasn't high enough. The goat-men also launched off the floor on their own muscular hind legs, finding that they too could project themselves through the air, and the chase was on. The feline-woman jumped from one beam to the next, only to be seized by another goat-man. Groping, nipping, and biting at her face, neck, and breasts added to the frenzy as they began thrusting their groins against her. Hissing and scratching viciously, the feline-woman spat on their half-man, half-goat faces as she tried to escape.

Isaboe and Fergus could do nothing but watch in horror as the goat-men took turns terrorizing the feline-woman in the rafters overhead. The chaos taking place was escalated by the excitement of the chase. In their attempts to mate with the feline woman, the adrenaline rush of the goat-men began to create conflict, and before long they were fighting among themselves. The sound of head butts and clattering horns filled the barn, overpowering the rain and the wind. Attacking with their horns, they pushed each other off the rafters. Loud, guttural sounds shook the barn as the fight grew more intense. Their man-like bodies crashed wildly into one another, and the impact of their battle echoed throughout the building.

During the heated battle of horns and flesh, the frightened feline-woman made her escape. Jumping down to the barn floor, she ran over to Fergus and hid behind him as she watched the chaos taking place above.

Soon she was purring again, rubbing and pressing herself against Fergus, though he tried to push her away. And when the goat-men noticed that their prize had chosen a new suitor, they turned their attention toward the floor of the barn. An unspoken treaty seemed to emerge between them that would last just long enough for them to destroy Fergus. Isaboe could see the panic and fear building in the eyes of the traumatized young man as one-by-one, the goat-men dropped to the floor and began stalking him.

With wide, terror-filled eyes, Fergus ran toward the barn door, only to find it stuck closed. In a matter of moments, the goat-men were on him, ramming Fergus with their horns, tearing nasty gashes in his skin, and biting at his arms and legs. Fergus screamed in pain and terror as he tried to kick and push the goat-men away, but he was out-numbered, and a mere mortal.

"STOP IT! LORIEN STOP IT! I'LL DO WHATEVER YOU WANT, JUST MAKE THEM STOP!"

No sooner had Isaboe screamed the words when everything went suddenly still. There were no more goat-men, only small goats bleating softly in their pen. The feline-woman was also gone, and the soft bundle of gray fur could be seen running back into the hay. Whimpering like a whipped dog, Fergus huddled with his arms over his head to ward off the phantom attackers. There were no signs of injury, no bleeding wounds, no rips or tears in his clothes. There were no signs of what had just taken place with the feline-woman and the herd of goat-men, because it had only happened in their minds.

Moving carefully, Isaboe made her way over to Fergus. She reached out to touch his shoulder, but he lashed out at her, his eyes wide with terror. There was no way to tell him that what just happened wasn't real. There was no way to explain that it was an illusion brought on by a twisted and powerful Fey Queen, strictly for her own entertainment. Nor would there ever be a way for him to rid himself of this. Who could he tell? Even if he could speak, who would believe him? This would stay with him for the rest of his life, his own private secret that would haunt him in his dreams.

"Fergus, I'm so sorry." Again, she tried to reach out to the boy, but he jumped up and grabbed for the door. Finding it no longer stuck, he ran out into the night, leaving his coat, his hat, and a vivid, terrifying illusion behind him. Isaboe watched him disappear into the storm, wishing it would be that easy for her to run away from her own nightmare.

CHAPTER 7

A COLD TRAIL

It took another three days before Margaret was ready to ride, and still against her doctor's wishes. The wounds were healing well, but she was still weak and hadn't fully regained her riding strength. However, there was no way Margaret would let Connor leave without her. It took all of his patience to sit and wait, but he had promised not to leave until they could ride out together.

Yet, when the wait was over and the morning finally came when they were preparing to leave—their horses saddled and waiting outside the inn—Connor started out sullen and short tempered. As he leaned over the map sprawled across the lobby desk, his brow was more furrowed than usual. "This would be the most logical route," he said, running a finger up the center of the map, "back across the center of the Highlands. But that dinnae mean much. We're not exactly tracking a logical person."

Cringing slightly, Margaret pushed her arm through the sleeve and very gingerly pulled on her coat before looking over Connor's shoulder. "How 'bout this way?" she asked, pointing toward the coastline, the opposite direction of the Highlands.

"That route would add another three weeks to her trip. And since we've heard nothin' from yer *damn* pixies," he said, shooting her a glare, "I'm followin' my gut, and we're staying in the Highlands."

"And what if you're wrong?" Margaret asked defensively. "What if the pixies say she did follow the coastline north? What then?"

"Pixies, my ass," he grumbled. "You convinced me to wait for ye, so you and the *pixies* can lead us to Isaboe. But I've seen nothing that confirms ye can do that, and each day I've been waiting, that faerie bitch is taking Isaboe further and further away."

"Oh, so, somehow this is *my* fault?" Margaret asked with hands on her hips. "Yeah, I made you wait for me because Isaboe is *important* to me. And if the truth be told, Connor, if you really cared about her, you would've never left her alone in the first place."

"Ye already said that. Ye dinnae need to keep reminding me." Connor growled as he held Margaret's reprimanding gaze, knowing she was right. But that didn't matter now. His only focus was finding Isaboe and making it right. "If she did take the coastline," he said, softening his tone, "if the *pixies* confirm she went that direction, then we'll have to cross over the Grampain Mountains, and with winter fast approaching, that's something I'd rather not have to do."

"Then let's hope your gut's correct." Margaret scowled and then turned to pick up her bag before walking out to where the horses were waiting.

It was two days into their ride before Margaret finally made contact with the pixies. Connor still had reservations about putting his trust in Underlings, but he trusted Margaret. He couldn't help feeling relieved when the pixies finally revealed themselves, and grateful when they verified that he and Margaret were on the right path. The pixies, Tiena and Finn, confirmed that Isaboe and Lorien were only two days ahead of them, but their direction frequently changed. Lorien had sent Isaboe traveling on an erratic path, never keeping to a direct course. It was obvious the Fey Queen knew that Connor and Margaret were following, and she was doing everything she could to throw them off the track.

Days turned into weeks, and with the onset of winter, the safe daylight hours for traveling were swallowed up by bleak, dark nights. Trying to maintain the hope that they were tracking the right course was a struggle at best, and the pixies would make an appearance only when they chose, which was not often. When they did show up, Isaboe would often be heading in a different direction. Though it was encouraging to know that she was still alive, the frustration of never quite catching up, always just being a few days away, was maddening.

In one small town they hired a local artist to sketch Isaboe, as best as they could describe her. Though it wasn't a perfect likeness, it was close, and Margaret showed it to everyone. Unfortunately, her idea gave them no leads. After all, weren't the Highlands filled with redheaded women?

More than once, Margaret tried to coerce Connor into wearing the amulet himself and speaking to the pixies. Though he wanted to trust her, knowing that she truly believed what she saw and heard, he couldn't bring himself to find the same confidence. "I told ye that I dinnae want to touch that thing. I already feel like a goddamn bloody fool for taking directions from a couple of...*pixies,*" he spat.

"If you have any better ideas on how to find Isaboe, I'm open to hear 'em!" Margaret snapped back.

"We have no idea if they're leading us on the right course!" Feeling a sense of hopelessness, Connor lashed out. "For all we ken, they could've been sent by Lorien, and this switch-back path we've been takin' is nothing more than a ruse and a waste of our time."

"The pixies were not sent by Lorien!" Margaret shouted back. "They tried to warn Isaboe about her. Weren't you listening before?" She paused and sighed heavily before continuing. "It's no big surprise Lorien's one step ahead of us," she added defiantly. "Who knows what kind of faerie glamour she might use on Isaboe? We could walk right by her and not even recognize her. We have no choice but to trust the pixies. We'll catch up to her, Connor. It's just a matter of time."

"We're running out of time," he snarled, before turning and stalking off to his own corner of their camp. He knew it was frustrating for both of them, wandering a path that twisted and turned without reason, based only on guidance from invisible folk. But Isaboe's life was at stake, and the fear of not making it in time had left them both short tempered and lashing out.

Connor could feel the cold grip of dread wrapping around his gut. Though he never spoke the thought aloud, he knew there was a very real possibility that he may not reach Isaboe in time to save her.

CHAPTER 8

NOT YOUR FRIENDLY FAIRY GODMOTHER

The further north Isaboe traveled, the colder the nights became as winter eagerly swept across the Highlands, replacing the last warm days of autumn. Mounting up onto the saddle was becoming more of a challenge each day. The only thing that kept her moving was her determination to reach Orkney before winter arrived in earnest.

The night before she had found shelter in an abandoned farmhouse, but traveling by horseback and daily exposure to the elements were taking their toll. Though the morning started out under a cloud-filled sky, Isaboe made it through the entire day without getting wet. Her unmarked route took her up a hillside littered with mossy stones. The rocks that jutted out from the undergrowth looked as if they had been strategically placed in a straight line up to the crest of the hill. The steep slope of the ascent became more difficult for both horse and rider, but they finally reached the top where Isaboe saw the first remnants of jagged and decaying walls.

When she reached the peak of the hill, the massive sprawl of decomposing ruins came fully into view. Isaboe sat upon her horse looking out across what was left of a castle that at one time had stood on a grand scale. Though it must have been quite impressive in its day, all that remained now were crumbling walls and rotting timbers. The remnants of life that once thrived here now flowed through the open emptiness on a sorrowful breeze that swept across the ridge. Isaboe could feel the energy of the souls who had been there when the castle still stood. Souls that may have died on this very ground, leaving their essence forever etched into the memory of the stones.

In the middle of what may have been a great hall, she saw the cold remnants of an old fire. Soot blackened rocks encircled half burnt timbers and a pile of ashes. Obviously, someone before her had used these ruins as a resting place, and with the ebbing light of day, Isaboe decided to do the same. Using one of her last wood matches, she piled up the half-burnt timbers and coaxed a fire to life.

By the time darkness had engulfed the last light of dusk, a cold winter wind had picked up, blowing the clouds inland. The moonless night sky was clear and crisp, filled with stars. As the biting wind whipped over the ridge, Isaboe wrapped her blanket tightly around her shoulders. Without cloud cover, it would be a frigid night, so she sat close to the fire, trying to soak up as much heat as possible. The stones that had once defined a mighty fortress now provided a perfect artery for the unabated wind as it rushed through the ruins, spawning an eerie howl. Isaboe wasn't sure if it was the cold or the wailing of the night that caused shivers to run up and down her spine.

Having purchased a jar of brewed Chamomile tea in a small village she'd passed through a week earlier, Isaboe wrapped her hands around the last cup, trying to fight off the bitter cold that nipped at her fingers. As she stared into the glowing embers of her small campfire, an image of Margaret lying in her sick bed flashed across Isaboe's mind. She felt the sting of regret for leaving before her friend had fully recovered.

But if Lorien was right, and everyone who loved her was destined to die, then what choice did she have but to leave when she did? Isaboe felt justified at the time, but now she struggled to swallow her guilt for walking out on her only friend.

"Of all the places you could have stopped for the night," Startled by the familiar voice of the Fey Queen, Isaboe jolted in her seat before turning to see Lorien standing on a rock behind her. "You chose here, out in the open, under the cold winter sky with only a wee fire to warm you?" the queen asked with a disappointed glare.

"This was the path I was on when night fell," Isaboe snapped. "Look around. Do you see any grand hotels? I didn't have any options," she snarled before turning back to the fire. "I don't know why it matters to you anyway. You're not the one sleeping on the ground." Rubbing her hands together in front of the fire, Isaboe was tired, hungry, and cold. She didn't appreciate being lectured to by a being who had no concept of discomfort and no compassion for what she was feeling.

"A bit testy tonight I see," Lorien said as she stepped down and took a seat on a smooth rock before handing Isaboe a cloth-covered basket. "I brought you some hot stew and a loaf of fresh bread. Hopefully this will help with your attitude. Perhaps you ought to show me a little apprecia-tion once in a while. After all, I am providing you with food, protection, and company on your journey. You could be a little thankful."

"Thankful for what?" Isaboe snapped back. "Ruining my life?"

"Oh, are we going there again?"

"Yes, Lorien, we *are* going there again!" Isaboe put the basket down and glared at the Fey Queen. She had given up hope for a life of her own choosing, and her will to keep going was weakening. Yet, somehow, she found the strength to challenge her foe, her captor, and her only companion. "I can't keep traveling like this, Lorien. I'm tired, cold, and I ache all over. I have nothing to keep me going except the hope of find-ing Benjamin and Anna. Because I am with child, it's becoming harder to climb on that horse day after day, and if I continue on under these conditions, you and I may never see this baby born. I have to get off the ground and sleep in a bed, have some decent food and proper shelter, even if just for a few nights."

Seeing that her rant had no effect, Isaboe picked up her meal again. "You can just disappear whenever you want, whenever you're uncom-fortable. You could care less how I feel. So, if you think you deserve my gratitude, then you are sadly mistaken, and pitifully self-serving!" Isaboe spat, before turning her back to the narcissistic, but dangerous fey.

A few moments later, Isaboe felt heat on her back. The light around her brightened as the fire reignited. Over her shoulder, she saw Lorien staring into the embers with her arms stretched out over the flames. Hundreds of sparks shot out from her fingertips to join with those that rose from the fire as the Fey Queen performed a sort of mystical ritual, mumbling under her breath. Though Isaboe couldn't make out the words, she knew something magical was about to take place.

The tingle of faerie magic swirled around and through the open, dilapidated walls. Goose bumps rippled across Isaboe's skin as she watched heat spirals rising from the fire, sending thousands of tiny sparks into the sky. As each spark lifted and rose from the heat wave that gave it birth, it became an independent, living flame of light. Each light then began its own dance, until the air was filled with the sound of fluttering wings, wings that moved the astral lights with the grace and agility of hummingbirds. Isaboe sat in awe as the night sky turned into an amazing constellation of beings. Dancing and diving through the air, these beings seemed to consist of pure light, pure energy.

"I thought you could use a little cheering up, so I've invited some friends to entertain us tonight," Lorien said, looking quite pleased.

But Isaboe was not appeased, and she stood up, glaring at the Fey Queen. "I don't want more of your faerie glamour, Lorien. I don't need, nor want, to be entertained by you! What I want is to be with my own people, sleep in a bed, and eat at a table like a civilized person. I hate this life, and I HATE YOU!" Isaboe trembled as she screamed.

"I've already told you once, mortal, be mindful of how you speak to me." The Fey Queen's words were coated with indignation. Her small frame seemed to expand with each word she spoke. "You forget yourself, Isaboe. If it were not for me, you would be dead by now."

"I'm not a fool, Lorien. You need me alive because you want my child. So spare me the lecture, because I don't owe you a damn thing. I could've easily joined my dead husband more than once on this excursion. The only reason I haven't rode my horse off a cliff yet is because there's still a chance I can find out what happened to my children. That possibility is the only thing that keeps me going, the only reason we're having this conversation right now. So don't threaten me!" Though she had no idea from where the courage came—obviously from a place that had long been untapped—in that moment every nerve in her being screamed to be released from her fate.

However, Isaboe's short-lived boldness was quickly replaced by fear when the small beings of light began to morph in shape and size. From a distance, they appeared as beautiful dancing lights, but when two of them suddenly rushed toward her, she could see that they were vile and ghastly creatures. Misshapen faces, fangs jutting out of hideous mouths, and claws like talons forced her to jump back. When something landed on her cloak, she screamed at the horrid creature crawling up her side. The squat little being had the face of a rat, gray and wrinkled, with a long, pointy black nose. As it crawled up her cloak, the tips of its claws dug into her clothing. From between two tusks on either side of its curled-back lips, the creature hissed with a monstrous sneer. After quickly kicking it off, Isaboe ran from the campfire and the chaos taking place above the flames.

The space above and around the fire was alive with beings that swirled on a current of energy. Some were beautiful, delicate fey creatures with transparent wings and faces like angels. But others had morphed into creatures with long fangs and claws, and their wings of lace turned into black, webbed-appendages. Those who remained fragile and innocent were soon victims, viciously attacked by those who had changed into hostile predators. The attacks were brutal and rapid, and Isaboe couldn't tear her eyes from the horrific sight. Slowly backing away, she placed her hands over her ears, but still could not block out the awful sounds. The air was filled with blood-curdling screams as the snowflake-fine bodies of the dainty fey were torn to bits. What remained was nothing more than faerie dust drifting to the ground.

When there were no more victims to be found, the hideous beings circled around Lorien like pit vipers awaiting further instruction. Then, as one, they all turned toward Isaboe, who by now had taken several steps back away from the fire.

As Lorien watched the fear consuming Isaboe, she continued her threatening lecture. "You see, Isaboe, the weak are destined to be over-taken by the savage, the more powerful. It is the way of life, the way of nature. You cannot stop it. You can only accept it. Do you actually *believe* you have any control over your own fate?" She chuckled with a wicked grin. "Nature–life–destiny, I have the power; I choose your fate. I'm the one who has kept you safe from predators, including those of your own kind, threats you have been totally unaware of."

The fire returned to a low burn as Lorien stalked Isaboe. With the glow from the flames behind her, the face of the Fey Queen was cast in shadow, creating an eerie silhouette that made her appear even more sinister. Fear pierced Isaboe's core as she continued slowly backing away one step at a time, never taking her eyes from Lorien.

"It would be wise not to provoke me, Isaboe. Yes, I do need you alive, but you're testing my patience. If you cannot find it in yourself to pay me the respect I'm due, then you leave me no choice." Lorien casually swept her arm back toward the snarling group of vile looking creatures that hovered over the fire. "My children need someone to play with now and then, and though they won't kill you, their games are not kind."

The smile on Lorien's face made Isaboe take another step back, but she stopped abruptly when she felt the earth crumble beneath her foot. Looking over her shoulder, she saw nothing but blackness. The darkness called to her; *take one more step and it will all be over.* The wind whipped at her hair and tugged at her cloak, urging her to give in. All she needed to do was to give up the fight, let the wind take her over the edge and all of her anguish would be over.

When Lorien saw Isaboe's position, teetering on the edge of the crumbling ridge, the Fey Queen's face instantly changed, as did her demeanor. "It doesn't have to be like this, Isaboe," she said nervously. "You hold a place of great honor among my people. You are greatly loved! I'm sorry if my little display upset you. I was only having a bit of fun. Please, come away from the edge. You're making me anxious," she said with an uneasy smile as she reached out towards Isaboe.

"Don't touch me!" Isaboe snarled. Though she was almost paralyzed with fear, Isaboe found the mettle to push back. "I'm done with this, Lorien. I don't care anymore if I live or die. If I just let myself tumble backward, at least you don't win!" she shouted as another rock crumbled beneath her back foot, and she teetered on the rocks before regaining her balance. She literally stood on the brink of going over, both physically and mentally.

"Wait, Isaboe! This is madness! Alright, alright, you can have it your way. Tell me what you want, just please, come away from the ledge."

"I already told you. I want to sleep on a bed. I can't travel by horseback anymore. I want to be with my own people, not these hideous creatures that want to rip the flesh from my bones. I want to be free from *you!*"

"Oh, my dear, I'm afraid that I cannot free you from your fate. I'm sorry that my children's games frightened you, but I would never let anything hurt you. You must believe me." Lorien lifted her arm toward the creatures still hovering above the fire. As a bolt of energy shot from her extended hand, the ghastly Underlings were immediately engulfed in a mass of spinning light, and the whole area within the ruins was filled with a brilliant luminescence. Then, just as quickly as it had appeared, the light vanished. Once again, the two women were alone in the dark with only the faint glow of the fire.

"See, now they're all gone. There's nothing that can hurt you." Lorien waited for a response, but Isaboe gave her nothing. Something like fear twisted the queen's face, knowing how close Isaboe was to jumping. "There's a town not far from here where you can catch a coach," she said, inching closer. "You can ride in comfort the rest of the way. You don't have to travel by horseback any more if you don't wish. There's also an inn there where you can get a good night's rest and a hot meal too. Please, Isaboe, let me help you. Come, and warm yourself by the fire." Lorien was now only inches away.

"Stop! If you take a step closer, I'll jump. I mean it, Lorien!" For the first time in a long while Isaboe felt she had control. If it meant throwing herself over the edge, at least it would be of her own choosing. The look on Lorien's face told Isaboe the fey woman was afraid, and she found the strength to use that fear to her advantage. She watched carefully as Lorien stepped back tentatively and attempted an emphatic smile.

"Fine, but please, come away from the edge. I'm sorry, Isaboe, if I haven't been more understanding of your discomfort. I forget how fragile mortals are. It will be different now, I promise. Please, just come back to the fire."

Isaboe leaned forward slightly, but took only one step before she stopped. "I decide how I travel and where I stop to rest. I will spend the rest of my time on this Earth in the company of my own kind, not the nasty and vile creatures you call children. Do I make myself clear? Do we have an understanding?" Though every nerve in her body was screaming danger, every muscle was tense and ready to move her out of harm's way, Isaboe held her ground.

"Yes, I understand completely. Now please, step away from the ledge."

As the queen stepped backward, Isaboe made tentative steps forward, and when she was a safe distant from the edge, she watched the relief wash over Lorien. Isaboe slowly made her way back to the fire, took a seat, and picked up the basket with her now cold meal.

Though the howling of the wind made her jumpy, and she looked over her shoulder multiple times, Isaboe ate the rest of her dinner in relative peace. The fire crackled, throwing dancing shadows on the crumbling stone walls as Lorien slowly made her way back to silently take a seat next to her.

"Tomorrow I'll ride toward the next town where I can sell my horse for coach fare." Isaboe stared into the fire as she laid out her plan. "I will find out where I need to catch a ferry to the islands. So far all of your directions have not taken me any closer to the coast, so I'll be finding my own way. I should be able to get enough money from the horse to pay for a few nights stay and some decent food as well. I'm so tired of sleeping on the ground and eating this crap you bring me."

"I've conceded on the coach travel, as well as a stay at a hotel for a couple of nights, but don't push me, Isaboe. I may have been too hard on you, and if so, you were right to bring it to my attention. However, if you intend to be around other mortals, you need to limit your contact with them. It will only confuse you. There is no point in making this harder than necessary. Your time here is temporary. It would be best for you to remember that," Lorien spat out her warning before she disappeared in a flash of light, leaving Isaboe once again alone in the darkness.

CHAPTER 9

A KIND SOUL
AND A WARM BED

Late the following afternoon, Isaboe rode into the small town of Cullen under another cloud-filled sky. The community was small enough that it didn't take long for her to find its only livery stable. After an uncomfortable negotiation with the keep, she settled on a frustratingly modest amount for her horse and saddle, bringing up the memory of Margaret's poor trade for the horses she bought in Inverness. Though Connor had stepped in and made it right, Margaret had been furious with the man for taking advantage of her, just because she was a woman. Something told Isaboe that her case was no different, but after an amount was finally agreed upon, she didn't feel like fighting about it.

Turning to walk out of the stable with the few coins she'd made, the sound of a soft whinny made Isaboe stop. She looked over her shoulder to see the horse she had just sold tied to a post and staring at her with big, brown eyes. A lump rose in her throat, and Isaboe stood for a moment trying to rationalize her decision, but it was still painful. Walking back to the horse, she gently stroked its neck and rested her cheek against the side of its nose. "It has to be this way, girl," she whispered. "Thank you for getting me this far, but it's for the best. We've got too much history together, and you're a constant reminder of him. I need to forget you both." With tears threatening to spill, Isaboe turned and fled the stable.

The Cullen Inn and Cafe across the street offered Isaboe what she needed. When she entered the small establishment, the smell of meat cooking set her stomach growling. She approached the front desk only to find it unattended. After looking around and finding no one, she followed what sounded like the low roar of people talking all at once. Walking around a corner, she entered a hectic café that was filled to capacity with patrons at every table. In the center of the establishment, a low fire burned in a round, brick pit, and the heat from it radiated out into the room. Other muted lighting was provided by the few oil lamps attached to the walls, along with one low-hanging, candle-lit chandelier.

Glancing about the chaos, Isaboe finally spotted what appeared to be the only person working the floor. Looking frazzled, tired, and wearing a filthy apron, the woman was serving plates and picking up dirty dishes as quickly as she could. While addressing multiple requests going from table to table, she slapped at a hand that came too close as she maneuvered through the crowd, and Isaboe was impressed with her dexterity as she balanced a tray of plates and mugs, as well as her restraint from dumping the contents on the ill-mannered patron.

"Excuse me." Isaboe quickly caught the woman's attention on her return trip to the kitchen. "Can someone help me check in? I'd like to rent a room."

"Aye, but ye'll have to wait a bit. I'm short-handed," the waitress said as she disappeared behind a swinging door into the kitchen. No sooner had she gone in than she was right back out, balancing plates of food and mugs of ale.

"What does the room rent for?" Isaboe asked as the waitress rushed by.

"Ten shillings a night," the woman responded over her shoulder without breaking her stride.

Counting her money, she didn't have much, but it would have to stretch. She desperately wanted that bed, even for just a couple of nights. Clutching the few coins she had in her hand, Isaboe glanced up when the waitress made her return trip to the kitchen. Apparently, her need was written across her face, because the woman seemed to take pity.

"If ye're a bit short, lass, I could use some help here," the woman said, standing at the kitchen door. "The gal that was s'posed to be here this afternoon is sick in bed, and as ye can see, I'm slammed. If ye fancy, put on an apron, and ye can work for yer room. I'll throw in yer food, too. What do ye say, lassie? Can ye handle waiting on the likes of this rowdy and hungry group?"

Isaboe paused for a moment to look around at a room filled mostly with loud, rough-looking men who seemed to think they didn't have a moment to spare, or any common courtesy, for that matter. "Sure, I...I can do this," she finally said, her words stuttered. "But can I get something to eat first? I'm famished."

"Aye, but make it quick. Come into the kitchen and I'll introduce ye to Rufus. He's my husband and the cook. He'll feed ye and I'll get ye an apron. As soon as ye're ready, come back out here and I'll put ye to work. I'm Moya," she said, wiping her free hand on her apron before presenting it. "We own the place."

"Nice to meet you, Moya," Isaboe said, returning the greeting. "I'm Isaboe, and thank you for the offer."

"Don't thank me yet, lassie, 'specially with this group," she said with a smirk.

Isaboe soon learned that most of the patrons were workers coming off the day shift at the textile factory, though other tables were occupied by a less rowdy group. A few well-dressed couples and one young family helped to fill the small cafe. Moya first put Isaboe to work serving ale and clearing tables. When she had apparently proved herself competent, the room was split, giving one side to Isaboe. She scurried from one table to the next, taking orders and delivering slices of roasted pork, hot shepherd's pie, and mugs of ale. Though she had never waited tables in her life, it didn't take long for her to get into the swing of it. It also offered her a much-needed distraction.

After three hours on her feet, scampering to and from the kitchen, Isaboe had done her best to ignore the boorish statements made by the dirty laborers who had dined and left, but there had been a steady stream of the same uncouth cliental, and she couldn't help but read the looks she received as she pushed through the tables. She was unaccustomed to being the target of such brazen comments. They may have been frequent patrons at Rufus and Moya's establishment, but Isaboe was not on the menu, and it didn't take long before their vulgar behavior brought her frustration to a peak.

"There's no more pork, gents. All that's left is shepherd's pie or lentil soup. What'll you have?" Isaboe said, unable to deny the exhaustion in her voice. Holding two empty mugs in one hand, she brushed the hair from her face with the other as she waited for the three men's reply. While they eyed her with lewd gazes, she shifted her stance, trying to ease the cramp she felt building in her back.

"Ye blokes can have the shepherd's pie," said one grimy, bearded-man. He had dark, greasy hair, and the odor that surrounded him made it clear he hadn't seen a bar of soap in weeks. "I'll just take me a slice o' this wee tart!" He shot her a toothless smile as he reached behind Isaboe and grabbed more than a handful of skirt and petticoats.

That was it, the one that pushed her over the edge, and Isaboe lashed out without thinking. Slapping his hand away, she jumped back. "Mind your hand, sir!" she shouted, glaring at the crude man and feeling the heat of anger rising to her cheeks. But in the next second, a shriek and the sound of scooting chairs behind her had Isaboe spinning around.

"Oh, my good Lord!" said the man she had just served. Both he and his wife stood looking down at their clothes, which were now covered with thick, brown soup. When Isaboe jumped back from the rude man's advance, she had unknowingly bumped into the table behind her, causing the bowls of lentil soup to dump onto the couple's laps.

"What is wrong with you, wench?!" shouted the woman. The bodice of her rose-colored dress was now splattered with brown mush, and her face was contorted into a ghastly expression of disdain as she glared at Isaboe.

"I'm so sorry! Let me get that off of you," Isaboe said, trying to clean the mushy soup from the front of the man's white shirt using only the hem of her skirt, and not very successfully. Instantly she felt like a scullery maid—wiping up spilt soup and being the target of filthy men's advances—and wondered how her life had come to this. But her moment of self-pity was quickly squashed when the couple abruptly pushed her aside, announcing that they would not be paying for their meal. As they hurried toward the exit, they were soon accompanied by Moya, offering apologies and the promise of a free meal next time.

"I'm so sorry, Moya," Isaboe said as she followed her back into the kitchen. "But I hadn't expected your customers to be so crude! I've never been treated with such disrespect!"

"Put those dishes down," Moya said sternly, and waited until Isaboe had done so. "Now show me yer hands."

"What? Why?"

Moya grasped Isaboe's hands, turned them over and ran a thumb across the smooth ridges of her palms. "Ye've also never known a hard day's work, have ye? Ye have the look of one who's used to being waited on, not the one doing the waitin'."

Isaboe jerked her hands free. "That's not true. I know how to keep a home, do laundry, prepare meals for my fam…" she stopped and dropped her gaze to the floor. That was all past-tense. She didn't have a family to care for anymore. She didn't have anything, not even the ability to wait tables properly. Feeling the tears threatening to break free, Isaboe felt pathetically inadequate.

"But ye're in a family way, love, and ye're waitin' tables. That tells this group ye've got no man to look after ye. Any respectable gal wouldn't be working while she's with child, and this crowd dinnae miss much, 'specially with a wee, pretty thing like you." Moya gently led Isaboe back to the swinging door before pushing it open. Standing in the door frame, she nodded at the few working men still lingering over their meals. "Aye, they are a rough group, and they don't know how to behave proper around a lady. But they're also a lonely group. Got no one at home to cook for 'em; that's why they're here. I probably shouldn't have thrown ye out to this bunch, and I apologize for their boorish behavior, but ye helped me out tonight, love." When Moya paused, Isaboe saw the concern written on her face. Moving back away from the swinging door, she let it close, and they were once again removed from the view of the patrons in the cafe. "Where is the father, lass?" Moya asked rather pointedly. "Ye're not married, are ye? Do ye have anyone waiting for ye?"

The questions caught Isaboe off-guard, and she could only shake her head. There was no one waiting for her. Only a twisted Fey Queen and a life she didn't want and hadn't asked for. As much as she willed them not to, Isaboe felt the warm tears spilling over her cheeks before Moya pulled her into a hug.

"Oh, dinnae cry, love. It'll be alright." Drawing back, Moya shot

Isaboe a compassionate smile. "I think ye've done enough today, lassie. The crowd has thinned down, and I can finish up here. Rufus will show ye to yer room, and when ye get hungry again, just come on back and I'll take good care of ye."

After two days and nights at the Cullen Inn and Cafe, with the opportunity to sleep in a real bed and eat as much as she wanted, Isaboe felt comfortable for the first time in months. She would have been content to stay longer had her situation been different.

But on the second night, Lorien made an appearance in her room, just as she was getting ready for bed. "It's time to move on, Isaboe," the Fey Queen announced. "Your temporary reprieve has lasted long enough. Mid-winter is practically here. If you wish to make it to your destination before the weather turns even more unpleasant, there is no time to waste. You need to be on the coach out of town tomorrow, agreed?"

Though she couldn't argue with Lorien's reasoning, Isaboe wondered about the Fey Queen's true purpose for keeping her moving. Was it really in her best interest, or was Lorien simply continuing her self-serving ways and trying to impose her control? Isaboe knew the Fey Queen discouraged interaction with other mortals, and she sensed there was more to Lorien's expediency in continuing on with the journey than just the change in the seasons.

The following morning after the breakfast shift in the café, Moya walked with her to the coach station, even though Isaboe insisted it wasn't necessary. But now that the regular hired help was back on the job, Moya chose to take a few minutes to get away.

"Do ye have someone waiting for you in Orkney?" Moya asked, but Isaboe just shook her head and kept walking. "What about the father? Ye're not raising the child alone, are ye? I could always use some extra help, and ye could stay here for a while. For someone who hadn't waited tables before, ye picked it up right smartly."

Isaboe gave Moya a sideways glance but didn't break her stride. "I appreciate it, but I really can't stay. Don't worry about me, I'll be fine," she said with a forced smile. When the two women reached the station, Isaboe handed her bag to the coachman before giving Moya a hug.

"Thank you so much for everything. The bed, the bath, and a couple of good day's rest have been wonderful. I ate more than I had a right to, but the food was great."

"Ye helped me out in a pinch, lass. Ye earned it. I put together a little something for yer trip. If ye ever find yerself back 'round here again, ye'll always be welcome," Moya promised with a smile.

Taking the bundle, wrapped in a pretty checkered cloth, Isaboe returned the smile and gave her host another brief hug before stepping into the coach. With everyone onboard, the driver wasted no time, and the snap of the reins had the carriage moving north toward the coastline.

CHAPTER 10

A GLIMMER OF HOPE

Connor and Margaret always seemed to be just a day or two behind. The frustration of that knowledge and the gloomy winter weather was taking its toll on the tracking party, and any attempt to keep a positive outlook had long been abandoned. As they set out each morning, the feeling that their journey was futile continued to grow.

Not one day went by that Connor didn't mentally berate himself for falling into Lorien's plot, for being so easily fooled by Lilabeth. The sting of knowing that Margaret was right—that he should have never left Isaboe alone in Edinburgh—only added to his misery.

It wasn't until the pixies directed them toward a town called Cullen that Connor had his doubts put to rest. When they stabled their horses for the evening, Margaret asked the stable-keep to look at the sketch of Isaboe, just as she had done in every town they had stopped in, expecting the same unsatisfying result.

"Aye, I think I've seen this woman," the keep said, holding the sketch under a lantern. "Aye, a pretty girl, she was. 'Twas 'bout three or four days ago I think, matter of fact, I bought a horse from her." The keep pointed toward the back of the stable. "Still have it in the…" But before he could finish his sentence, both Margaret and Connor bolted in the appointed direction, looking for a familiar pony.

It was like finding a beacon of light in an oppressive fog. Connor looked at the horse for a few seconds and realized this was the break that they had been searching for. It was confirmation, something tangible that kept them connected to Isaboe, and evidence that they were on the right trail. When he walked over and gently stroked the horse's neck, it turned its head toward him, returning the greeting. "How ye doin' girl? It's been a while, aye? So, how was she? Did ye take good care of her? Aye, I'm sure that ye did." Connor whispered to the horse, stroking its coat and hoping he could somehow pick up Isaboe's essence from the animal.

"This is the sign we've been desperately looking for, Connor," Margaret said as she stepped up next to him. "Now we know for sure we've been following the right course. This proves that we're close to finding her. It also proves that the pixies *really are* trying to help us. So, can you just trust me now, and stop being so goddamn angry all the time?"

Connor turned to see the frustration on Margaret's face, and in that moment he realized the residue of his self-loathing had fallen onto her. It was a pain he hadn't meant to cast on anyone but himself. But he had, and instantly he felt the sting of regret. "I'm sorry, Margaret, and I do trust ye, honestly." Giving her a gentle smile, Connor placed a hand on her shoulder. "Ye're right, I'm not sure about the pixies, but this is proof they've been leading us in the right direction. Sorry if I've made ye feel badly, its, um...it's only myself that I'm angry with. I guess I've been a bit of an ass, aye?" he confessed.

"A bit? I'd say, the whole damn jackass!" With her hands on her hips, Margaret's expression morphed into defiance. "You've been sullen, you won't talk to me, and when you do, you lash out! I feel like you blame me 'cause we haven't caught up to Isaboe yet, as if it's somehow my fault. I want to find her just as badly as you do, Connor, but we have to work together. The pixies are all we have to go on right now. Since you refuse to even touch the *bloody* stone, that means I have to be the one talking to 'em. So you're going to have to trust me, trust them, and get over your *bull-headed* self!" Margaret's frustrated vent left her red in the face, and she snarled at Connor before turning her back and stomping off, leaving him alone with the horse.

"Hmm, she thinks I'm a jackass. Well, I've been called worse." Connor turned his attention back to the horse as it tossed its head up and down. "Oh, so ye think I'm a jackass, too? I cannae win. Two legs or four, females are all hard to please."

"I'm going across the street to the inn. The keep believes she went that direction when she left. Do you want to go with me?" Margaret asked.

"Aye, but I'm buying this horse back first. I'll meet ye there," he replied.

"Do you have any money left?"

"Enough. I'm sure the keep didna pay Isaboe a fair price, so I'll buy the horse for no more."

"How will you know how much that was?"

"I have my ways. Go on over to the inn and I'll catch up with ye."

Margaret regarded Connor for a moment, then turned and made her way across the street.

The sound of the bell above the door announced Connor's entrance, and both women glanced in his direction.

"Connor, she left here just two days ago!" Margaret exclaimed. "This is Moya. She and her husband own this establishment. She was just telling me that Isaboe stayed here a couple of nights."

Connor nodded in Moya's direction as he closed the door and joined Margaret at the desk.

"Aye, when Isaboe first arrived I was running ragged in the cafe," Moya said, holding the sketch of Isaboe in her hand. "It was the dinner shift and I was shorthanded. I could see she was tight on money, so I asked if she wanted to wait tables for her room and grub. She did a fine job, seemed like a sweet girl, if rather quiet. Why are ye looking for her? What's she running from?"

"It's not what she's running from that we're concerned about. It's who's running with her, and the danger that she's in if we don't find her in time," Margaret answered before catching Connor's glare.

"What kind of danger? In time for what?" There was an uncomfortable silence as Moya glanced from Connor to Margaret, waiting for an answer.

"How was she?" Connor asked, ignoring her questions.

"She looked frail and tired. I didn't even know that she was with child until she came out of the kitchen with an apron on. If I hadn't been so slammed, I wouldn't have asked her, but I really appreciated the help. The next two days she spent most of the time in her room sleeping, and I made sure she ate well while she was here."

"The keep told me she sold her horse for coach fare."

"Yes. She took a coach to Scrabster, and from there she intends to catch a ferry over to Orkney. I tried to get her to stay here, but she said she couldn't." Moya paused and placed the sketch on the desk before continuing. "Look, since ye seem to be worried about her, something seemed off. My brother-in-law did a bit too much fighting the British and it touched him in the head, changed him deep in his soul. She reminded me of him, and I saw no hope in her eyes. Do ye know what I mean?" Neither Connor nor Margaret answered her, but they both knew exactly what she meant. Connor turned to walk out, but stopped with his hand on the door knob. Turning to speak over his shoulder, he addressed Moya at the desk. "Thank ye for yer kindness to her. It's much appreciated." He then turned and walked out.

Margaret watched the door close before returning her attention to Moya, giving her a smile and a shrug. "Well, he may not care where he sleeps tonight, but I do," she said, placing coins on the counter. "One room please."

CHAPTER 11

SCRABSTER

The coach rolled to a stop, waking Isaboe from a restless nap. She rubbed her hands over her face, clearing the sleep from her eyes as the coachman opened the door, announcing their arrival in Scrabster. As she stepped out of the carriage, the smell of the sea enveloped her, and she took a deep cleansing breath of the salty air. Traveling the last few days by coach may have been physically easier, but the bumpy ride and confined compartment she shared with three other travelers—all of whom were in desperate need of a bath—had left her nauseous most of the time. She felt a wave of gratitude as the sea air instantly settled her stomach.

It was nearly dusk when they arrived in the quiet, little seaport. To stretch her legs, Isaboe took a lone, chilly walk down to the water's edge. A number of small fishing vessels were moored along the pier, along with nets and floats that lay haphazardly next to the boats.

Dropping her bag, Isaboe stood on the rocky shore looking out across the water as the sun dipped into the horizon. Another winter day was ending under a cloud-filled sky, when the sun could only be seen at dawn and at dusk. She watched the long fingers of sunlight streaking across the water in ripples of coral and lilac as the sun made its descent into the ocean.

The smell of the sea reminded her of Glasgow. Her life was simple then, but now all of who she had been was just a distant memory, as if it had been someone else's life. Loneliness and a broken heart were her reality now, her waking nightmare, and she fought back the tears that constantly threatened to spill.

Shivering in the cool evening air, Isaboe briskly rubbed her arms and picked up her bag before making her way back up the rocky bank. There was only one building near the shoreline, and in the dim light of dusk, Isaboe could barely make out the sign on the weathered storefront: Scrabster Inn, Bait, and Tackle.

The woman behind the counter looked up when she heard the bell above the door. "Evening Miss, I was just getting ready to close up for the night. What can I help you with?"

"I'd like to rent a room, please." Isaboe walked to the counter pulling a few coins from her bag, "How much?"

"For how many, and for how many nights will ye being staying with us?"

"It's only me, and just one night. I'll be leaving tomorrow for Orkney. Do you know where I could purchase ferry passage?"

"Oh, there'll be no ferry runs tomorrow. You'll have to wait till the day after."

"Why won't there be any runs tomorrow?"

"Because tomorrow is the first day of Yule, and the ferry tender has decided to take the day off, which is something I plan to do as well," she said pleasantly.

"Did you say...*Yule?*" Isaboe stuttered, staring wide-eyed at the woman while a flood of images rushed through her mind.

A slow look of empathy grew on the innkeeper's face. "Oh, ye were probably hoping to make it over to the island before Yuletide. You must have family there, aye?"

The sound of her coins hitting the floor did not register, only the innkeeper's question. Vivid memories of previous Christmases spent with Nathan and her children swept over Isaboe like a vicious wind, and each one carried emotions that felt so real, so tangible, that she grabbed at her chest, barely able to breathe. "*Yuletide? It's Christmas?*" Isaboe's words were barely audible as she felt the blood draining from her head and her knees buckled.

The innkeeper rushed around the counter just in time to catch Isaboe from hitting the floor.

"*I have no family...I have no one!*" Isaboe sobbed uncontrollably, her face buried in her hands as the woman helped her into a chair.

"There, there, dear, it'll be alright." The innkeeper cradled her crying guest in her arms. "Ye'll not stay here alone. You can come home with me and spend this night of Yule with my family. How's that sound?"

Though this person was a complete stranger, she was a kind soul, and Isaboe would have thanked her for her compassion, but she couldn't stop sobbing long enough to find her voice.

After quickly closing up the inn, the woman helped Isaboe into a small buggy. After they were settled in with blankets wrapped around them to protect against the bitter wind that whipped up off the sea, the innkeeper snapped the reigns, prompting the elderly pony into movement before stepping out onto a well-traveled path home.

"So ye brought her home, even with the family here? She looks a bit touched in the head." Frank Campbell questioned his wife's actions as he looked out from the kitchen at the despondent woman sitting in his front room.

"Shhh, keep yer voice down. I had to, Frank. You should've seen her. There was no way I was going to let her stay alone in that inn tonight, not on the first night of Yule. She's obviously suffered a great loss to have no family. What else could I have done? It was the Christian thing to do, aye?" Evelyn Campbell attempted to justify her spontaneous gesture.

"How long will she be staying?" Her husband's reply was a resigned grumble.

"She'll probably be leaving for Orkney the day after tomorrow. You can be a kind host for one day, can ye not?"

"We already have a house full. Where are ye planning on putting her up for the night?"

"She can have Richard's room, and we'll put the grandchildren on the floor in Nora's. They'll be fine, they're young."

"What's wrong with her anyway? She doesn't look well. Are ye sure it's safe to have her here with the children?"

"Oh, for God's sake, Frank! She's just a young woman all alone, and if ye haven't noticed yet, she's with child. What if it was Nora out there by herself? Wouldn't ye hope that some kind family would take her in?"

Shooting his wife a furrowed glare, Frank tore a hunk of meat from the goose his daughter had cooked for their holiday meal and stuffed it into his mouth, grumbling on his way out of the kitchen. No sooner had her husband walked out, when Nora walked in.

"Mother, she doesn't speak. She just sits there with that far off look in her eyes, like she's not really here. We don't even know her name. What do you want me to do with her?"

"Just be kind to her, Nora. She'll eventually come 'round, I hope." Evelyn put the dinner plates on the counter before looking at her daughter questioningly. "I did do the right thing by bringing her here, aye? You should have seen how distraught she was, and she would've been all alone tonight in that cold inn."

"Yes, Mum, you did the right thing. It'll all be fine." Nora gave her mother a quick hug. "I'll set the table for one more."

"This goose turned out wonderful, Nora. Thank you for cooking today."

"Oh, you're welcome, Mum. I'm just happy we could be here. Next year we'll have to be at Ethan's parents, and I'm already not looking forward to that. Ethan's mother is so demanding of his time, and she completely takes over Hanna and Sara. She constantly corrects me on how to raise my own children. It drives me to screaming, I do swear!"

"I'm sure she means well, Nora. Now let's go in and join the rest of the family. Maybe we can get our guest to open up a bit, at least find out her name. It'd be nice to know who we're sitting down to dinner with, aye?"

Evelyn and Nora walked out of the kitchen to see Frank and Ethan sitting on a sofa in the back corner of the room, holding their own private conversation. A rough rendition of *Silent Night* filled the small home, courtesy of Hanna, the seven-year-old who sat at the piano in her pink holiday dress. The golden braid of hair that hung down her back was tied with a matching pink ribbon. Younger sister Sara sat on a rug in front of the cozy fire, also adorned in her holiday attire. Her fair hair, not yet long enough to braid, hung in soft curls around her tender young face while a ragged doll in her hands danced to the music played by her older sister.

From the kitchen, the two women observed their unknown guest, who hadn't moved since she first arrived. The strange woman's blank expression showed no emotion as she sat in the chair next to the fire, staring into the flames. She seemed oblivious to everyone around her, as if she had crawled into some dark recess in her mind.

"What do you think I should say to her?" Evelyn asked. Nora offered only a shrug, but then she elbowed her mother as she saw Sara walk over to their guest, still cradling her doll in her small arms.

"My name's Sara. What's your name?" the little girl asked. Isaboe turned her eyes from the fire and looked at the child. It was the first time she had made eye contact with anyone in the house, much less acknowledged them. It was a slight shift, but in that moment something changed.

"Hello, Sara. I'm Isaboe," she said, even managing a weak smile.

"This is Sara, too." The child held up her doll. "She doesn't look so good 'cause I left her outside and Duke chewed off her head. Daddy was gonna throw her into the woodpile. He said she wasn't good for nothin' but to start a fire with. I cried. I didn't want Sara to be burned up. So Momma sewed her head back on, but she doesn't look the same no more."

"Maybe Saint Nicholas will bring you a new doll tonight, Sara," Nora interjected, looking pleased at her young daughter's kindness.

"That'd be nice, but I'm still gonna keep Sara. Just 'cause she doesn't look so good doesn't mean I don't want her any more. Even if someone's broken, you can still love them, don't you think, Isaboe?"

Isaboe looked down at her new little friend, and felt something stir deep inside. "Yes, Sara, I do think so," she said softly.

"Out of the mouths of babes," Evelyn pleasantly whispered to her daughter. "Dinner is ready, everyone. Isaboe, would you like to join us for a bite to eat?"

Though the conversation over dinner was light and casual, Isaboe's presence cloaked the family's gathering with an awkward tension that hovered over their holiday meal. Despite an occasional moan and cringe from Ethan's attempt at humor, there was a definite sense of unease. That was until an innocent question from a small child brought a hush across the table. "Isaboe, why are you here?" Hanna asked.

"Hanna, that was impolite," Nora reprimanded. "Apologize to Isaboe at once."

"I'm sorry, Isaboe," Hanna said obediently. "I was just wondering," she mumbled, staring down at her plate to avoid her mother's glare.

"It's quite alright, Hanna." Isaboe spoke up. "I've been traveling for a while in search of family members I'm hoping to find on Orkney. Though I really don't know what I'll find when I get there, they're the only family I have, if I even have them." She took a drink of water, leaving her wine untouched. "I've been traveling for so long it seems I've lost track of time. I didn't realize tomorrow was the first day of Yule, and it caught me by surprise. Your grandmother was kind enough to open her home to me, and I know that I've intruded," Isaboe paused and glanced at the faces around the table, "but I greatly appreciate your family's kindness."

"Oh, no, dear, you're not intruding," Evelyn said. "I invited you. You're our guest."

Isaboe forced a smile. "This is a very lovely meal, Evelyn, and I don't mean to seem ungrateful, but, I'm really tired. If you don't mind, could I please retire for the evening?"

Although Evelyn had said that her son Richard was unable to make it home, and it was just as well that she made use of his room, Isaboe was sure she had kicked someone out of a previously assigned bed. But she was grateful for it, and made sure to tell Evelyn more than once before her host closed the door and returned to her family.

The downy bed was in the second-story loft, and she could hear the low murmur of voices that floated up the stairs. Partial moonlight crept through a small, triangle window, casting a soft glow around the unfamiliar room. The scent of lavender wafting from the fresh bedding helped to ease the heavy weight Isaboe felt in her chest as weariness took its place. But just as she closed her eyes, beckoning sleep to take her away, Isaboe was jarred back to full awareness.

"What are you doing here?" Lorien's demanding voice jolted Isaboe upright, and though there was little light in the room, there was no mistaking her presence. "We agreed that you would be staying at the inn. Why are you in this house with these people?"

"*Shhh!*," Isaboe whispered. "Keep your voice down." She paused to calm her racing heart from Lorien's startling and abrupt arrival. "It just sort of happened. I didn't plan it."

"This is not acceptable. You must leave here at once."

"Lorien, I'm tired, and it's late. I just want a good night's sleep. Is that asking so much?"

"We've already discussed this, Isaboe. You are not to have any unnecessary contact with other humans. You know how confusing it is for you. I can't allow you to stay here. I demand that you leave with me, for your own good."

"For *my* own good? Don't you mean *yours*? Look, Lorien, I'm not going anywhere with you tonight, and I am staying here tomorrow as well." Isaboe didn't know if it was courage or exhaustion talking.

"What nonsense is this—staying here tomorrow? I thought you wanted to catch a ferry over to Orkney as soon as you arrived? You can't stay here. I won't hear of it!"

"*Shhh!*" Isaboe said again, this time with her finger held to her pursed lips as she shot Lorien a steely glare. "Tomorrow is Christmas, the first day of Yule," she whispered. "There will be no ferries over to the island until the following day, so there's really nothing I can do. This family has been nice enough to take me in and share their holiday with me. This is the last Christmas I will ever have, Lorien. Just let me stay. It's a small thing. Can't you just give me this one last gathering with my own people—mortal, human people like me?" Though her heart was pounding in her chest, Isaboe did her best to keep her voice down.

"But you're not like these people, Isaboe." Lorien softened her tone. "You know that. I don't think this is a good idea."

"Well, it doesn't matter. I'm not going anywhere tonight, or tomorrow. You'll just have to accept it." Isaboe snapped.

Lorien gave Isaboe a long hard stare. "It appears you're not giving me much of a choice, are you?"

"It's just one more day. What can it hurt?"

"Fine, but we leave early the day after tomorrow, understood? And I will be waiting for you just outside to accompany you back to the ferry. So don't even think of trying to leave without me."

"It's not likely that I could get very far without you, Lorien. You always seem to know *exactly* where I am. I don't know what you're worried about. Now leave me alone and let me get some sleep." Isaboe plopped back onto the bed, pulled the blanket over her head, and attempted to ignore Lorien, mentally willing her to disappear just as quickly as she had arrived. More than a couple of moments passed before she opened one eye and looked around the room. Seeing no sign of Lorien, Isaboe hoped that she had truly left. Now, if she could only make it through the next day without any extra surprises. It was very hard to know what to expect from a Fey Queen.

CHAPTER 12

AN UNEXPECTED GIFT

Christmas morning floated up the stairs on the wings of children's voices. The tantalizing smell of maple-smoked ham teased at Isaboe's nose, bringing her out of a deep sleep and causing her empty stomach to grumble. Evelyn had provided a robe the night before, and Isaboe pulled it snugly around her shoulders, grateful for its warmth on this cold winter morning. Silently making her way down the stairs, she stopped on the landing to observe Nora cooking breakfast in the kitchen. The girls were poking at packages under the evergreen swag that hung on the living room wall, trying to guess the contents. At the dining table, Frank's bald head was visible above the newspaper he held, and a crackling fire finished the scene, offering a warm, comfortable setting.

Observing from a distance, Isaboe couldn't help but recall similar scenes from her past life. But instead of feeling pain, gratitude had blurred her sorrow into a distant sadness. Though it felt good to be a part of something normal, something familiar, she felt like an intruder on this family's gathering. They knew nothing of her, nor her of them, yet they had opened their arms and welcomed her into their midst, and into the sanctuary of their family's home.

Isaboe's silent observation was broken when Evelyn walked through the kitchen door and glanced at her guest standing on the landing. "Good morning, lassie. I trust ye slept well." A brisk morning breeze accompanied her host's entrance, and a basketful of freshly-gathered eggs hung around her arm.

Evelyn's acknowledgment of her guest drew Nora's attention to the stairwell, and the young woman flashed Isaboe a warm smile. "Oh, good morning, Isaboe," she said over her shoulder. "I didn't see you there. I hope the children didn't wake you. I've been trying to keep them quiet, but that's rather difficult to do on Christmas morning."

Nora turned back to the stove and flipped the pancakes on the hot griddle. "Are you hungry, Isaboe? You didn't eat much at dinner last night. I'm making some pancakes for Ethan, but he's still out filling the wood box. Got some nice ham slices here, too."

"Plus, we now have fresh eggs," Evelyn added in a lively tone as she placed the basket down on the kitchen table. "I'll go wash up, Nora, then I'll be back to give ye a hand."

"That's alright, Mum. I've got it."

Stepping down from the landing, Isaboe made her way over to the table.

"Can I offer you a few pancakes, Isaboe?" Nora asked.

"Yes, actually I am quite hungry, thank you." When she took a seat opposite Frank, he lowered the paper long enough to give her a quick nod of acknowledgement before returning to his reading.

As Isaboe quietly ate her breakfast, the family's morning activities bustled around her. Hanna and Sara were still in their nightclothes sitting on the floor under the evergreen swag and bubbling with excitement as they tried to read the names on the packages. Their anticipation of tearing off ribbons and bows was palpable, and they didn't even seem to notice Isaboe as they got up and began rushing around the house.

"When is Daddy coming in?" little Hanna asked excitedly for the third time. "We want to open presents!"

"I already told you—when he's done and ready," Nora said firmly. "Now take Sara into the wash room and clean her up. She's all sticky. When you're finished, maybe Daddy will be back in the house. Go on now, and no more pestering." Nora shooed off her anxious daughters. "Children can be so trying at times," she said as she took a seat next to Isaboe and sipped on her cup of tea.

"And yet, what would you do without them?" Isaboe placed a hand on Nora's arm and held her gaze. "You have a beautiful family, Nora. Don't ever take that for granted."

Nora placed her own hand over Isaboe's, and without saying a word they shared a silent moment of understanding.

Gift bags, ribbons, and bows lay strewn about the floor. Hanna and Sara sat blissfully in the middle of it, absorbed in their newly-acquired wealth. A miniature tea set, a new doll for Sara, beautiful new bonnets, dresses, and shoes lay abundantly around them as parents and grandparents sat back, remembering the joy of Christmas through the eyes of children. Though Isaboe enjoyed watching the girls tear into their gifts, more than once she had to fight back tears when the event triggered a memory.

"Let's get this picked up, girls," Nora said as she began gathering up wrapping and ribbons. "You've been lollygagging in your nightclothes long enough."

"Look what grandpapa has here—a wee storybook." Frank, who hadn't said much all morning unwrapped his previously hidden gift. "Who wants to sit on my lap while I read it?" he said, offering the invitation to his grandchildren. Both Hanna and Sara jumped up, squealing with delight at the counter option.

"Dad, what are you doing? I want the girls to get cleaned up and dressed. I promised Aunt Della that I'd bring the girls by for a visit."

"What's a few more minutes gonna hurt, Nora?"

"Oh, Mum, can't we just stay here today?" Hanna whined.

"Yeah, we don't wanna go see ol' Aunt Della," little Sara added with a small frown, never looking up from the new doll she held dancing on her lap.

"Sara, don't be rude!"

"Oh, come on, Nora," Frank said. "It's obvious that they don't want to go, and your Mum and I don't get to see them that often."

Looking over at Ethan and seeing no support in that direction, Nora finally conceded. "Alright fine, but they have to pick this mess up and change their clothes first. Then you can read them the book."

As Hanna hurried to follow her mother's directions, little Sara walked over to acknowledge Isaboe for the first time that morning. "What did Saint Nicholas bring you, Isaboe?"

Once again, a statement from a small child brought a hush over the room, and all eyes turned in Isaboe's direction where she sat in a chair next to the fire. She forced a grin, but before Isaboe could respond, a sudden jolt in her abdomen stole the smile off her face.

"Isaboe, what is it? Are you alright?" Nora was immediately at Isaboe's side.

"I just felt the baby move, for the first time!" Isaboe looked up at Nora, and in that moment the two young women shared something that only an expectant mother can appreciate. Another quick, small movement under Isaboe's hand indicated the stirring of life inside of her. "There, I felt it again! My baby just kicked me!"

"You have a baby in your tummy?" Sara asked with a bewildered look on her young face.

"Yes, Sara, I have a baby." Isaboe turned her tear-filled eyes from the curly-headed child down toward her rounded belly. She caressed it softly, as if she were already holding the infant in her arms. "I have a baby," she whispered.

This child was hers, and was more important than anything Isaboe would ever do on her own. Lorien wanted her to hand this child over—this precious little human—and Isaboe, in all of her misery, was preparing to do exactly that. In her moment of awareness, a subtle shift took place, but it was a crucial change nevertheless. What the Fey Queen had her believing suddenly felt muddled, as if Lorien's truth might not be truth at all.

Isaboe carried the precious life of her unborn child, and for the first time in many months she had a reason to live. Tears ran freely down her face, but this time, they were tears of joy.

"Saint Nicholas brought you a baby, Isaboe! Don't cry." Sara smiled as she put her pudgy little hand on Isaboe's belly, apparently hoping to feel movement of the small, unseen life. Fearing her daughter was being too bold, Nora reached out to move Sara's hand away, but Isaboe stopped her.

"Nora, it's alright. Sara, put your hand right here and be patient." Waiting to feel something move, the fair-haired child locked gazes with Isaboe. For someone so young, she was quite patient, and her wait paid off. Isaboe and Sara both broke out into a smile as they felt the quick movement roll across Isaboe's belly.

"I felt your baby move!" Sara exclaimed as her older sister came running over, unwilling to be left out. After both girls had been satisfied by feeling the new life move under Isaboe's rounding middle, they returned to the task at hand, and to the anticipation of being read a book by Grandpapa. But before Nora could lead Sara off to change her clothes, the inquisitive child walked back over to their guest. "How did Saint Nicholas get that baby in there?" Sara asked as she pointed to Isaboe's belly.

"That's a story for when you're much older," Ethan quickly interjected. "Now go with your mother and do as you're told." As Nora led the children from the room, Frank and Evelyn quietly chuckled.

CHAPTER 13

RECOGNIZED

By the time Connor and Margaret made it to the final hostel on the route to Scrabster, dusk was quickly swallowing the last hint of daylight. Though they had stayed dry on this day's journey, there was moisture in the air, and the sky held the threat of snow the further north they traveled.

After introductions, they found Ian Buchanan, the young hostel keep, more than accommodating. He had shelter and a hot meal to offer for a reasonable price. A warm fire snapped and crackled in the large stone pit that sat in the middle of the spacious sitting area. Hovering above it was a matching stone chimney, directing the smoke up and out through the roof while both heat and light radiated out into the room below. The space was just large enough to accommodate a small group, but on this night, the hostel was void of other guests.

"The cook stove is cold. We weren't expecting visitors this late," Ian said, filling two bowls from the steaming kettle that hung over the open fire. "But the pork and pea soup has been simmering all afternoon. It's good and hot; should warm ye right up."

"Thank you," Margaret said before digging into her meal. "Mmm, this is very good!"

"Glad ye like it. I grew those peas myself this last summer. Da' and I butchered a pig last week, and the ham hock adds a tasty bit of flavor, don't ye think?"

"Oh, aye! It adds a great flavor," Margaret said, and though Connor was too busy eating, he eagerly nodded in agreement. "Oh, I just remembered." Margaret put down her bowl and opened her bag. Pulling out the sketch of Isaboe, she handed it to Ian, explaining their situation.

"I dinnae recognize her, but she may have come through. A coach left here just two days ago for Scrabster, but my Da' usually deals with the guests, so I didna get a good look at any of 'em. I'm really just the laborer 'round here, if ye ken what I mean," the young man said with a wide smile. As he handed the sketch of Isaboe back to Margaret, the jolt of a slammed door turned everyone's attention toward the back of the building.

"Damn it, Ian! How many times do I havta tell ye to make sure the latch on the gate is closed so the bloody cows cannae get out!"

The loud, bellowing voice announced his entrance long before the strapping, full-bearded man made his appearance. Upon seeing that his son was not alone, he stopped abruptly and his demeanor instantly changed. "Please forgive the outburst. I didna realize we had company." The barrel-chested man walked over to his son and cuffed him on the back of his head.

"Ow!" Ian grimaced as he rubbed the offended spot. "So, did the cows get out?" he asked timidly.

"Aye, a few, but I rounded em' up, no thanks to you." The older man leaned in towards his son. "Ye could've come and told me we had guests," he growled quietly.

"Aye, I could've, but then I would've had to round up the bloody cows myself, and gotten twice the lecture." The reproach on his father's face told the young keeper that he'd spoken too boldly. He dropped his gaze to the floor, avoiding his father's scowl, but a slight smirk lingered on his lips.

"Well, at least my son has done something right. How's the soup?"

"It's very good, thank you. It was just what we needed after riding in this cold weather all day," Margaret replied, trying to lighten the mood.

"Ian, go fetch us some ale and a few mugs," the father barked as he reached out a strong hand in greeting. "William Buchanan. Ye can call me Will, and ye have already met my son, Ian. Welcome."

"Margaret MacDougal," she said, shaking Will's extended hand. "And this is Connor Grant." Connor tore himself away from his meal and stood to shake his host's hand. Nodding quickly, he turned away and returned to his seat.

"So, where are ye bound on this cold, winter evening?" Will took a seat on the wide, stone hearth encircling the fire and rubbed his hands briskly in front of the flames.

"Scrabster," Margaret answered. "Do you know how much farther it is?"

"Ye're almost there, 'bout half-a-day's ride."

Ian returned with a pitcher of ale and four mugs. Placing them on a table, he filled two of the mugs and set them in front of his guests as his father continued. "Most folks en route to Scrabster are headed for Orkney. Is that yer destination?"

"Aye. I just hope the weather holds till we reach the coastline," Margaret said as she took her first sip of the ale. "Feels a bit like snow in the air."

"It's been a few years since we've had snow 'round here," Ian piped up with a grin. "I'm ready for it."

"Oh, ye are now, aye?" Will said, scrutinizing his son. "Ye won' be so excited when ye havta push a barrow through it."

"Why would I havta push a barrow through it?"

"How else are ye gonna bring in the firewood? Speaking of which, ye better get out there and fill this fire box before ye find yerself with a new lump on yer worthless head."

While Margaret observed the debate between father and son, she couldn't help but notice Connor's withdrawal. Though he had been quiet and sullen for most of their trip, he usually opened up around others, but not tonight. He appeared restless, almost anxious as he kept his head bent down over his bowl, shoveling in bites of soup between gulps of ale. Margaret had spent enough time on the road with Connor that she'd become pretty good at reading his body language, and it was obvious he was trying to avoid not only conversing with, but also making eye contact with their host. Concluding that he was either very hungry, or simply not inclined to engage, Margaret ignored his aloofness, but found it curious when William Buchanan gave Connor a long, interrogating glare.

"Oh, Mr. Buchanan, I'd like you to look at this." Margaret handed him the sketch of Isaboe.

"Ye can drop the formalities. Call me Will, or William, if ye prefer."

"Alright, William," Margaret said a slight smile. "Do you recall seeing this woman? We think she may have been on a coach that stopped here a few days ago."

The large man examined the rough image of Isaboe before handing it back. "There was a group that left a few days back on their way to Scrabster. I don't recall a woman like this, but she may have been with them. Who is she?"

"Her name is Isaboe McKinnon. She's a friend of ours."

"Why are ye following her?"

"We believe she's in trouble. We're trying to catch up to her before she reaches the coastline."

"So, ye think yer friend is heading to the island?" Will asked as he glanced at Connor, whose face was still hovering over his bowl.

"Aye, that's what we believe." Margaret supplied the answer.

"The shipping lanes will be closing for winter soon, and the bay gets a bit rough this time o' year," Will said, returning his attention back to Margaret. "I'm not sure the ferries will be runnin' this week."

"Because of the weather?"

"No. Because of the holiday."

"What holiday?"

With bushy brows that framed his dark, brown-grey eyes, Will sat back in his chair and crossed his arms against his wide chest, looking a bit puzzled. "Today is the first day of Yule. Ye do ken that today is Christmas, do ye not?"

"It's Yuletide? I had no idea we've been traveling that long. I guess we've kind of lost track of time. Connor, did you hear that?" Margaret asked and waited for a response, but Connor had no reply. "Are you not feeling well tonight? You seem a bit more quiet than usual." Margaret made no attempt to hide the slight sarcastic edge to her voice.

Not having missed Margaret's obvious rub, Connor shot her a sideways glare.

"Ye say yer name is Grant, aye?" Will asked. "I cannae shake the feeling that I've seen ye somewhere before, but the name dinnae seem to fit. Do ye have family in these parts?"

Connor suddenly looked uncomfortable in his own skin. Walking over to the table, he poured another mug of ale before replying. "No, no family this far north," he said over his shoulder. After filling his mug, he walked away from the group before stopping to lean against the window frame, looking out into the darkness. His evasiveness had not gone unnoticed, and it left an awkward tension in the room.

"Dinnae mean to be intrusive, friend. I must have been thinking of someone else," Will called out.

Connor only nodded, but didn't reply.

"Sorry for intruding on your holiday," Margaret said, turning the attention away from her aloof and annoying traveling companion.

"Oh, it's no intrusion at all," Ian piped up. "It's a pleasure to have ye here, and it's better than spending another Christmas with just this ol' man for company."

The older Buchanan scowled at his son and silently shook his head. "Do ye have any ungrateful children, Margaret? If not, I can give ye one hell of deal on this one."

Margaret only chuckled.

"I never said I was ungrateful, Da," Ian defended himself. "It's just nice to have company tonight. We're usually alone on the first night of Yule, and Saint Nicholas hasn't made a stop here for a long time." The rejection on Ian's face didn't go unnoticed.

"And he ain't comin' tonight, either." Will lightly cuffed Ian on the back of the head, but then he pulled the boy in closer before resting a large hand on his son's neck. A small grin grew across the older man's face, partially hidden by his beard. "But when ye go out to fetch another load of firewood, ye might find something stashed behind the shed."

Instantly, the look on Ian's face brightened. He had obviously been expecting a lecture, and his guarded look melted into one of pleasant surprise. "Oh, well, we need firewood now!" Ian jumped up and bolted toward the back of the hostel before he stopped and turned, as if suddenly remembering they had guests. "I mean, if you'll excuse me, Miss Margaret. Is there anything I can get for ye?" he added, before shooting his father a nervous glance.

"No, thank you," Margaret replied with a smile.

"Well, ye can fetch that good bottle o' whiskey that I've been saving for a special occasion," Will said without looking at his son.

"Uh...sure. Where do ye keep it?" Ian asked.

The older Buchanan's face suddenly grew stern. "Dinnae insult me, Son. I ken that ye've been stealing sips from it. Now, just bring me the damn bottle!"

Looking a bit embarrassed, Ian dropped his gaze, but the smirk on his face gave him away as he turned and slipped out the back door.

Shaking his head, William looked back at Margaret. "I give the boy everything and that's the thanks I get; stealin' my whiskey." Will picked up the pitcher of ale and approached Conner, who was still pacing around the small building and staying conspicuously aloof. "Can I refill yer drink, friend? I apologize if I offended ye in any way," Will said as he poured ale into Connor's mug.

"No offense taken," Connor replied, avoiding Will's gaze.

"I dinnae mean to beat a dead horse, but, any chance ye have some MacPherson blood running in yer veins? I think that's why ye look so familiar. Ye look like someone I used to ken, uh, but that was ages ago, at least twenty years, but it could be longer."

Connor shot his host a glance and hesitated before answering. "Not that I ken. Now, if ye'll excuse me, I think I'll go for a walk before retiring." Connor put the mug on the table and walked out into the night, closing the door behind him.

But he didn't get very far before Margaret was on his heels. She grabbed him by the arm and stopped him in his tracks by glare alone. "So, you know our host, huh? And it seems he knows you, as someone by another name, someone he knew *twenty years* ago." When Connor didn't respond, she continued. "Twenty years ago you couldn't have been more than just a boy, but that man recognized you. A bit more than just a coincidence, I'd say."

Turning away from her piercing gaze, Connor didn't answer and kept walking, but that didn't stop Margaret from continuing her interrogation. "What else haven't you told me? What happened up in Lochmund Hills? What's the rest of the story, Connor, if that's your *real* name?" She stepped into his path, making him stop.

Connor's face hardened, but again, he gave no answer as he turned and continued walking.

Not easily thwarted, Margaret was on his heels again. "I've got a long history with lyin' sacks o' shit, and I know how to handle 'em, so consider real carefully what you say next." Margaret's voice dipped, becoming low and dangerous. "If you've been lying to Isaboe and taking advantage of her, I'll slit your throat myself. So you better start talking, *Mr. Grant*, or I'll leave you tied to a log floatin' down the river, and you can get to the island on your own personal ship!"

Perhaps it was the threats or the insinuations against his honor, but Connor finally spun and faced Margaret, furious and half-shouting. "Alright! Aye, Buchanan knows me as Braden MacPherson. That is my name, or it was, until I was given a new identity."

Hands forming fists and nails biting into her palms, she stood silently and waited for more information. "Why were you given a new identity, and by whom?"

"By a man named Demetrick. Twenty years ago he saved me from a British execution."

All at once it became clear. Having spent time conversing with the pixies, and knowing what Isaboe had gone through, Margaret knew first-hand the power of fey magic. "You disappeared too, just like Isaboe. No, wait! You were *with* Isaboe, weren't you? That's why you connected like you did."

He hesitated, but quietly answered, "Aye."

"And you never bothered to mention this before? Don't you think this is an important bit of information, something I needed to know?" Standing in front of Connor with her hands on her hips, Margaret felt her protective anger growing.

"I had my reasons for not telling ye."

"Oh, really. And what were those? You said a sorceress claims that you were chosen to be Isaboe's protector. I want to know the *real* reason you want to find Isaboe. What do you know about those missing twenty years that you haven't told me?" Margaret's glare turned vicious as she crossed her arms. "You better start talking, Connor, or Braden, or whatever the hell your name is, 'cause right now I don't trust you as far as I can throw you. If you don't give me one hell of a good reason to believe you, I'll find Isaboe on my own!" Margaret wasn't simply being melodramatic; she meant every word, and knew Connor could tell she was serious.

"Come walk with me, and I'll tell ye. Though it'll sound unbelievable, I swear it's the truth."

As they walked back and forth on the dirt road with only the lights from the hostel to illuminate their path, Connor shared with Margaret how the sorceress had helped him to remember what took place in the land of Euphoria and his experience there with Isaboe.

"Before that incredible event took place, I was sitting in prison, waitin' to die." Connor spoke with his head down as they strolled, and Margaret noticed his voice was laced with a distant sadness. "Will and I are Jacobite Rebels. We were comrades in Prince Charles' campaign against the Brits. As ye ken, it dinnae end well. But Demetrick not only spared me from death at the hands of the bloody Brits, he gave me a second chance. He wasn't just an ordinary man; he was a wizard. It was his magic that sent me through to the other world."

Perhaps there were details he left out, but Margaret could hardly fault Connor in the face of everything she'd just learned. When he finished his story, they were standing back in front of the hostel. She watched him closely, not quite sure what to make of it all. "So, you're the father of Isaboe's child."

"Aye."

"I guess now I understand why you've been so upset. Between Isaboe and the child, you have a few precious lives at stake. But I have to ask." Margaret took a step closer. Standing a head shorter than him, she looked up, her eyes demanding Connor's attention. "Look at me, 'cause I have to know the truth. What's the real reason you want to find Isaboe? Is it out of love for her, and your unborn child, or are you just fulfilling some sense of obligation? You made a hefty promise to a man 'cause he saved your life. Are you just fulfilling a commitment to a dead man, or do you really care about her?" Margaret knew she was staring him down, looking straight into Connor's soul, and it took him several moments before he spoke.

"Up until Isaboe entered my life, I thought I knew the purpose of my existence and I was prepared to die for a free Scotland. Now, I want to live for her, and our child. With Isaboe I can see a future where I never did before." He paused, shifting his stance. "Aye, I'm a committed man. It's how my mind works." Holding her stern gaze, Margaret saw a subtle shift cross Connor's face. "But regardless of what I promised to Demetrick, my reason for searchin' for Isaboe is purely selfish. I want her back!" he almost shouted, and Margaret saw the serious intent flash across his blue eyes. "Neither of us has a life to go back to, Margaret. We've both lost our peace of mind. Together, we can build a life better than what we had before. But I have to find her first, and the hope of findin' her is the only reason that keeps me going each day. So if my search for her also happens to fulfill my commitment, what does it matter my reason?"

"It does matter. And it will matter to Isaboe."

"The only thing I'm telling Isaboe when I finally hold her in my arms again is how much I love her. The truth can wait."

"What the *fuck* does that mean? You have to tell her the truth."

"Why?"

"Because she has the right to know, especially if you're the father of her child!"

"That's how ye see it, aye?"

"Aye, the truth is the only thing you can tell her. Don't you realize that her pregnancy has been frightening for her, having no memory of what happened and no idea of who the father is? Maybe the idea of trying to get by in society being an unwed mother was part of the reason Isaboe left with Lorien in the first place."

Connor shifted his weight and cocked his head to one side. "Alright, so I'll say; "Isaboe, I was in faerie world with you. We fucked like rabbits and I am the father of your child." How's that for the truth?"

"You're such an ass!" Margaret growled. "You think that she's just gonna fall in love with you and be too stupid to ask questions? Is that what you want in a woman?" She turned on her heels and started back toward the hostel. "I'm not talking to you anymore. You're an *infuriating* man!" she shouted over her shoulder.

"Margaret, wait. Just hear me out."

She stopped and took a deep breath. Turning back to face him with her hands on her hips, she shot him a blistering glare.

Running his hands through his hair, Connor heaved a heavy sigh as he walked over to stand in front of her. "When Demetrick laid this at my feet, I really didna think I could do it," he said, staring down at Margaret. "It was all too incredible to believe, much less to be a part of. But the old man saved my life. I owed it to him to at least hear him out. I had no life to go back to, and he was offerin' me a new identity. What could it hurt to just go along with the old man's deluded fantasies, aye?"

Connor took another deep sigh before continuing. "When somethin' like this happens, a man questions his grip on reality. When I walked back into Demetrick's home and found nothing to be the same as it had been that mornin', I knew then I was dealing with more than just an old man's delusions. But the most incredible part of all of this has been Isaboe. Her courage in the face of all that's happened, and her beauty and passion are more than I ever imagined I could ask for in a woman. Maybe it was because I'd been with her before, even though I had no memory of it. But there was somethin' about her the moment I laid eyes on her. I've been with a few lasses in my time, but never lost my heart 'til now, not like this. Isaboe is everything to me."

With her arms crossed, Margaret glared at him. "That don't explain shit."

Connor sighed in frustration. "Look, I just told ye the truth, and ye have to admit, it's a bit hard to believe. It happened to me, and I hardly believe it. What if she rejects the truth, and me?"

"Do you have so little faith in her? She's been through the same, Connor. Why would she reject you for being the only man who'll ever be able to understand what she's been through?"

Connor felt the muscles in his jaw clinch, but he forced himself to remain calm as he attempted to explain his reasoning. "Just for a moment, put yerself in Isaboe's shoes. Ye've lost twenty years of yer life in the blink of an eye. Ye've lost yer husband, yer children, everything ye held dear, and now ye're on the edge of losing yer sanity as well. Ye have an evil fey with ye at all times, telling ye lies, manipulating and twisting yer mind so that ye no longer ken what is truth anymore. If I tell her what I just told ye, do ye think she's gonna believe me? She's in a very fragile state right now. I havta be careful what I say to her. I dinnae want to push her over the edge, or worse, lose her again. First and foremost, she has to trust me, and when the time is right, I'll tell her. I decide when the time is right, not you. Look Margaret, I trusted ye regarding the pixies, and you were right. I need ye to trust me on this." Connor's look was intense.

"Then what are you gonna tell her?"

"Same as I told ye; that I was chosen to be her protector." Connor let out a deep breath before dropping his head and casting his forlorn gaze to the ground. "Though so far, I've completely failed."

Margaret placed her arm through his and gave him a little squeeze. "Well, whether you're doing this out of obligation or love, and that I'm still not completely clear on, I do think the wizard chose wisely. You're as stubborn as an ass and don't give up easily. I'm glad we're on the same side," she said with half a grin. "Come along, let's go back in. It's cold enough out here to freeze the devil's tail in hell," she said, rubbing her arms and shivering.

Walking back in silence, they reached the steps of the porch when Margaret stopped. She turned and looked up at him. "Fucked like rabbits? Ha!" She shook her head with a chastising glare.

"Merry Christmas, Margaret," he said with a sly smile. Wrapping his arm around her shoulder, Connor escorted her back into the hostel, and back to the warmth of the fire as the first snowflakes fell behind them.

CHAPTER 14

THE CRONE

Lying awake in the warmth of her comfortable bed, Isaboe reflected on the events from the previous day. Having been accepted and welcomed into the home of the Campbell family made her feel somehow different, almost normal this morning. Her mind was alert and clear, and she noticed a new feeling residing in her chest. It felt a little like hope—a sensation she had not experienced in months.

It was still pre-dawn and the house was quiet. Though her room was gradually becoming less dark, full daylight was still an hour away. As Isaboe snuggled into the soft bedding, she contemplated getting up to prepare for Lorien's arrival, but wished she didn't have to face the Fey Queen. Yesterday was the first time she had felt the life of the child she carried; her *mortal* child, and that new life reignited her own desire to live. A familiar, nagging voice warned her not to let the fragile flame of hope grow, that it would only be futile, and she could never love, never have a family. But a distant whisper urged her not to let go.

Did she dare to think she might have a say in her future, and in the life of her unborn child, or had it already been written in stone? She had taken Lorien's word on faith, even though it was based in fear, and in doing so she had given up any hope to choose her own path. Life had handed her a complex basket filled with tattered pieces of an existence she once knew. It was a life that had carried on without her for twenty years, with no hope of being rebuilt. Now she faced a future as The Mother Alaina, living with people that she couldn't recall in a land that she couldn't remember. But was that really her only option? Maybe she did have another choice, and life still held the possibility of another outcome. *Lorien be damned!*

The sound of the kettle whistling in the kitchen jarred Isaboe from her thoughts. Shaking off the onslaught of questions that raced through her mind, she rose and quickly dressed. Making sure she had everything in her bag, she tiptoed downstairs.

"Good morning. I hope I didn't wake you," Evelyn whispered her greeting after seeing Isaboe on the landing.

"Oh, no, I was already awake. I was hoping it was you down here. I want to thank you, Evelyn, for everything. You have no idea what being here with you and your family has meant to me," she said, continuing down the stairs.

"Are you leaving?" Evelyn asked, glancing at Isaboe's bag and cloak. "The sun's not even up yet."

"Yes, I want to be on the earliest ferry, and the walk back to the dock may take a while," Isaboe replied, wrapping her cloak around shoulders and fastening the clasp at her neck.

"Don't be silly. I was just heading out to milk Lucy. It should only take about an hour, and then I'll drive you there after we have a bite to eat."

"No, really, I want to walk. I have a lot on my mind this morning, and the cool air will do me good."

"Isaboe, its cold out there, and you haven't eaten yet. Are you sure you want to do this?" Evelyn asked, and worry showed in her eyes as she gently touched Isaboe's arm.

"Yes, I'm sure." Isaboe smiled and placed her hand over Evelyn's. "But thank you for your concern, and for inviting me into your home. You are a good woman, Evelyn, and you have a beautiful family. I will never forget your kindness." Giving her host a hug, Isaboe turned toward the door.

"Well, at least take a loaf of apple-bread. You can eat it on your way. It looks like the sun is just starting to break the horizon, so it's lightening up a bit." Evelyn hurriedly wrapped the bread in a white-muslin cloth and handed it to Isaboe, giving her another quick hug. "Take care of yourself, lass. If you're ever back this way again, know that you will always be welcome."

Isaboe only smiled, then turned and walked out into the early morning mist. The sun was visible only briefly at the horizon before the sky encased it under another blanket of clouds. Though she hadn't been walking long, the sea air had already worked its way through, and Isaboe shivered from the chill. Pulling her cloak tighter around her shoulders, she lifted the hood over her head.

As she walked, Isaboe recalled Lorien's words from the night before. Knowing that the Fey Queen could appear at any time, any place, she felt her old anxiety bubbling in her stomach. Spending time with the Campbell family had pulled her from the long, dark months of misery she'd been lost in, and it gave her a small bit of confidence. Regardless of her situation, she longed for that family unity again. The small life she felt move within her had jolted open a closed door, allowing the promise of that possibility. Though still uncertain, a small grain of hope lingered, however delicate and fragile it might be, and Isaboe clung to it.

Hearing footsteps and voices behind her, Isaboe glanced over her shoulder and saw two men walking in her direction. Each man had a bag slung across his back, and by their clothing, they appeared to be dressed for a day at sea. Their longer strides soon brought them abreast of her, but the seamen gave her no notice. As they walked on past, another person came into view, but this time walking directly toward her.

Short and hunched-over, Isaboe watched the cloaked figure with a cane, and she could see white hair poking out from under the hood of what appeared to be an elderly woman. Her bent spine and gait held the tell-tale sign of an aged and crippled soul. Instantly, a flash of recognition fluttered in Isaboe's chest, bringing her to a stop as she stared at the figure coming ever closer. In another few steps, the woman was near enough for Isaboe to see her face, and a jolt of remembrance had her heart pounding.

The old woman walked right on by, and Isaboe turned, watching her take every step before she finally stopped. Turning around, the old crone looked at Isaboe with a strange grin that made her skin crawl. "So, how's yer journey been so far?" she said, in a familiar, raspy voice.

Isaboe felt her jaw drop, and she stuttered to find her voice. "It's you, isn't it? You're the strange old woman from the carriage, aren't you?"

"And you still be a half-witted lil' fool."

"*Excuse me!?*" Isaboe boldly took a step toward the woman. "I'll have you know that my life has been *hell* ever since you appeared to me that day, telling me all that frightening gibberish!"

"And ye didn't listen, did ye? Now look at the mess ye're in, lil' fool."

"Listen to what, your cryptic babble? All you told me was that I and everyone around me are in danger because of this child I carry. You certainly didn't offer any advice on how to put my life back together. And what is *left* of my life has been a nightmare ever since you showed up!" Isaboe shouted.

"Only 'cause ye didn't heed my warning." The crone took a step forward. Her bird-like eyes were squinted, and her brow was furrowed. "I told ye not to listen to the poison in yer head, but ye ain't smart enough to know when ye're being lied to. Lorien is *using ye*, little human, you and your spawn." Softening her tone, the old woman paused. "But it's time to see clearly, child; wise-up and listen to the voice in yer heart." The crone raised her cane, touching the tip lightly to Isaboe's chest, "here," she said, before lifting it and tapping the tip a few times against Isaboe's head, "not here," she grumbled.

Startled at being thumped by the woman's walking stick, Isaboe stepped back, rubbing her head. "What do you want with me? What are you trying to tell me?"

"Lorien's become over-confident. Been spinning a web of lies, she has. Her poisoned words keep ye trapped, like a fly in a spider's web, spinning tighter and tighter. She be using yer past to convince ye that ye ain't got no future, 'cept what she offers, but that be a lie, too. Ye've been caught, lil' fool, and ye best get yerself free, or ye'll lose the child and yer life."

"I may not trust Lorien, but why should I believe you? I've lost twenty years of my life, my husband, and my children. If everything Lorien's told me has all been lies, then why have I suffered so much?"

"Oh, my apologies, I'd not realized ye were the only mortal to have suffered." The old crone's earthy eyes glared in her reproach. "Ye think yer loss be so unique? If so, then ye're truly shallow and ignorant. Open yer eyes, girl! Ye've lived too long a life of privilege and paid no mind to the less fortunate. Ye've been so caught up in yer own misery, wallowing in self-pity that ye ain't given proper thought to the unborn life ye carry. So, if ye think ye deserve sympathy, poppet, well, ye'll be disappointed. I only speak the truth, and how ye feel about it matters not."

Isaboe already had words on her tongue to argue, and tears in her eyes at the crone's criticism and cruelty, but her mind froze before she could let them loose. Had this ancient creature come only to tear her down? But the crone's message held more than criticism, and it only made sense that she was speaking the truth. Isaboe was selfish and privileged. Knowing these things, Lorien had used them to manipulate her into doing terrible things against herself, and threatening the life of her child. Isaboe had fallen for Lorien's lies and deserted her friends because she was too afraid to do otherwise. Perhaps the crone, with her cruel truths, did in fact have the answer.

"Lorien told me that anyone who loves me would die. Are you telling me this isn't true? If so, what about my father, Nathan, and…Margaret." She hated herself all over again for abandoning her friend, never knowing if she had recovered.

"Mortals die, Isaboe. That's how it works in this realm. Yer papa's demise was by his own poor health. Foolish Nathan made the same mistakes as ye did, but no one be there to pull him from his grief. Took his own life, he did. Aye, these deaths hurt, but ye weren't responsible for 'em. Lorien used their deaths to twist yer mind, to control and manipulate ye. Don't ye see that, child?"

"Why didn't you tell me this before? Why have you waited so long to bring this to me? I left the people I love and let them think I had abandoned them because she said I had no other choice!"

"Ye had to find a reason to live first. And yer child granted ye that inspiration, something ye've not felt in a very long time. Lorien and the weight of yer loss drained it from ye. But this child's future is bigger than ye, and if ye continue on this path, Lorien will use this child's abilities to spread a dark plague over the Earth that will affect the lives of beings from both worlds. It's up to you to decide what kind of life she'll have. Ye have a choice to make, Isaboe. Ye can accept Lorien's truth, or ye can take back yer life and yer child."

As Isaboe fought back the tears, she refocused on the woman before her. "But how do I do that? Lorien gives me no peace. She'll never let me be."

"Humans can be amazingly resilient, even in times like these." The crone's tone and eyes softened, and she offered Isaboe a smile that was missing a few teeth. "Don't lose spirit, little one, there's still time to change the tide. Choose now to break free. If ye wish to change what is written in yer book of life, ye must make a choice and then do so. I know ye've suffered and lost yer spirit to fight." The hag placed a wrinkled hand on Isaboe's arm and held her gaze. "Do ye recall what I told ye in the carriage? *You* decide on how the magic is used, and thus far, ye've allowed it to be used against ye."

Isaboe jerked her arm from the old woman's grip. "I can't stand up to Lorien's magic. I'm only a mortal!"

"Those are her words," the hag hissed.

"But you have no idea of how helpless she makes me feel!" No longer able to hold them back, Isaboe's tears broke free. "I don't know how to stand up to her."

"I gave ye a gift the last time we met. Where might that be?"

Isaboe's chest fell knowing that she no longer had it. "The blue amulet," she whispered, dropping her gaze. "I…I left it with Margaret," she mumbled shamefully.

"Fortune smiles on ye this day, poppet. 'Tis a good thing yer friend is smarter than you. She's wisely used it to follow ye, along with the soldier boy."

Isaboe's eyes snapped opened. "Soldier boy? Do you mean, Connor? Are you telling me that Margaret and Connor have been…*following me*?" Isaboe's heart jumped. Her dear friend was not only alive, but the man she thought she could never love hadn't accepted her abandonment, or her broken promise. For all of her mistakes, they had still come for her. He had come after her.

"Aye, and ye can be reunited with them this day if ye do as I tell ye."

"This day? They're that close?" The thought of being reunited with Connor and Margaret sparked an avalanche of hope Isaboe hadn't allowed herself to feel in months. But now with the promise of freedom being so close, she wanted it badly, no matter the cost. "Please, what is it? I'll do anything to be free of Lorien!"

"That's exactly what ye need, little one; yer fighting, human spirit. Lorien's assumed ye've lost yers, that she's sucked it out of ye, but it's the very thing that will cast her out of yer life."

"I don't understand."

"When ye see her next, stand up to her and be strong, for ye'll need to denounce her."

"Denounce her?"

"Aye." The crone took Isaboe's hand, and the woman's strange eyes bore into her soul. "When ye see her next, say these words to her: *Lorien Nicnivin Rankish, Queen of Euphoria; I denounce you, and no longer believe in you. I vanquish your control over me and banish you from my life forever.* Repeat this to her thrice, and after the third time, she will be forced to leave, never to appear to ye again. But be prepared. She knows this magic is strong and will try to stop ye."

"That's it? I just utter a few words and I can be free?"

"These are not just a few words!" the crone shouted, just before her face eerily shifted and she leaned in closer. "Names have power," she almost whispered. "Don't ever forget that. And know this—ye must never call upon her again, for if ye do, she will return, and once back under her control, ye cannot denounce her a second time. Do ye understand my meaning this time, lil' fool?"

"If I can truly be free from her, why would I ever call her back?"

"Because, along with all the lies, deception, and trickery she has used to control you, she's also kept a veil of protection around ye, keeping ye from danger. Think on it, little one. A lovely young woman traveling alone these many months, yet no harm has ever come to ye. That good fortune has not been of yer own doing. Once ye denounce Lorien, the veil will no longer protect ye, and ye'll be vulnerable to all the evils of yer own mortal world."

"So, then, what do I do? Where do I go after I denounce her?"

"Go to where the land ends and the sea begins and wait there. Connor and Margaret will come for ye before the sun sets. They travel the same road that brought ye here." The crone's expression turned serious. "Now, prepare yerself. I feel Lorien approaching. Remember the words. Ye must denounce her thrice, using all three of her names. Believe in yer strength. Look into yer soul, Isaboe, and ye'll find yer courage. Do ye understand the importance of the action ye must now take?"

"I understand, and I'm ready." Though every nerve in her body urged her to run from what she now had to face, Isaboe was ready. It was the beginning of the end of her long, dark journey. Though she was still shaking on the outside, from somewhere deep within a voice screamed out; *this is the truth. Listen and be free!*

"Take heart, little one. Ye can still have a beautiful life if ye make a choice to take it back. This here be the tipping point, lil fool. Which way ye gonna fall?"

Suddenly, a gust of wind, dirt, and leaves swirled around them, and Isaboe shielded her eyes from the flying debris. When the dust settled, the crone was gone.

"May the Goddess keep ye safe and give ye wisdom." The old woman's voice sounded distant, fading away in the morning breeze.

"Connor and Margaret will come for ye this day!" The hag's words played over in Isaboe's mind, fueling her excitement. The idea that she could hold them both in her arms before the day was over was almost too good to be true. Giddy with delight, she imagined the reunion, and her gait quickened into a light skip. The smile on her face turned to a joyous giggle of anticipation, and in the next few steps, she was running in the direction of the harbor.

"Where are you going in such a hurry?" Isaboe's happiness snapped to an abrupt halt at the sight of Lorien, who suddenly appeared on the road in front of her. "Did I not tell you to wait for me, and we would go to the ferry together?"

Now confronted by the Fey Queen, panic shot through Isaboe like a dart, but she knew what she had to do. She quickly reminded herself of the words the crone had given her, though she wasn't sure the restriction in her throat would allow them to come out.

"What's wrong with you?" Lorien asked. "Have you swallowed your tongue?"

Isaboe took a deep breath, and out of sheer willpower, forced the words out. "Lorien Nicnivin Rankish, Queen of Euphoria, I denounce you, and I no longer believe in you. I vanquish your control over me, and banish you from my life forever!" Though it was a bit shaky, and not totally convincing, she managed to speak the words.

The look on Lorien's face was pure shock, and it was then that Isaboe knew the words were powerful. The Fey Queen hadn't expected what she just heard, but her look of surprise was followed by fury. In a blink of an eye, Lorien was standing before Isaboe, as wind, cold as ice, swirled around them, fed by Lorien's powerful faerie glamour. The frightening energy that Lorien created was more ominous than Isaboe had even seen or felt from her before. "WHO GAVE YOU THOSE WORDS?"

Lorien's shriek and threatening glare made Isaboe's bones quake, all the way down to her toes. Her first instinct was to turn and run, but she found the courage to stand her ground. Her desire for this to be over was greater than her fear. *Just two more times!*, she thought to herself as Isaboe struggled to summon the courage and force the words out.

"Lorien Nicnivin Rankish, Queen of Euphoria, I denounce you, and I no longer believe in you! I vanquish your control over me and banish you from my life forever!" This time Isaboe shouted the words with conviction as Lorien took a couple of steps back.

With wide, frightened eyes, and her threatening demeanor draining, Lorien held up her hand to stop what was happening. "Isaboe, you don't know what you're saying. I don't know who convinced you to do this, but you are making a terrible mistake! I'm the only one who really cares about you. YOU NEED ME! I offer you a place of honor in my world, to be held in the highest of regard—the Mother of my people—and this is how you repay me?" Lorien desperately pleaded, but Isaboe saw her target was wounded. Drawing strength from that, she took another deep breath and went for the kill.

"LORIEN NICNIVIN RANKISH, QUEEN OF EUPHORIA, I DENOUNCE YOU, AND I NO LONGER BELIEVE IN YOU!" she shouted, even as her body quivered in fear.

"NO! No Isaboe, don't do this. Don't you realize that without me you would already be dead?"

"I VANQUISH YOUR CONTROL OVER ME..."

"After all I've done, you can't do this to me!

"AND I BANISH YOU FROM MY LIFE...FOREVER!!"

Isaboe screamed the final words behind eyes shut tight. Hardly able to breathe, she stood on the road shaking. After a few silent moments, she slowly opened her eyes. Seeing that Lorien no longer stood in her path, she quickly spun around, half expecting to see the Fey Queen behind her, yet she saw nothing but the empty road. Lorien was gone. Not only visibly, but Isaboe no longer felt Lorien's presence as she had so many times before. Could it really have been that easy? Did just the utterance of a few words really take the Fey Queen down? Was she really free of Lorien's control? If she was to rejoin the living, she had to believe it. Isaboe made a choice, and chose to be free.

As if reading her thoughts, the crone's voice whispered in the wind; *"Turn and leave this place. Don't look back."*

Taking a slow, controlled breath, Isaboe slowly turned toward the direction of the sea. Her pace was tentative at first, but with each step, she felt strength and courage replacing her fear. More than once she had to fight against the urge to look back over her shoulder. But soon her pace quickened, and it wasn't long before she was running—running to start living her life anew with the man she loved and the truest friend a woman had ever known.

CHAPTER 15

FREEDOM COMES
WITH A PRICE

By the time Isaboe reached the coastline, the docks were filled with the shouts of men throwing nets and gear into their various-sized fishing vessels. Seabirds screeched overhead as they dove at the boats, their frenzy fueled by the scent of the fishermen's bait. Powered by the men at their oars, some of the vessels had already left the docks, and she could see them heading out to sea, bobbing in the water. Pulling her hood over her head, Isaboe walked to the end of the pier and silently watched the rhythm of the seaman preparing for a day at sea.

"Can I help ye, lass?"

Startled, Isaboe jumped at the sound of a voice behind her and spun around to see a man in a black wool coat with a bag casually tossed over his shoulder. Standing so close, she could see the deep lines in his face under his dappled-grey stubble and dark eyes that spoke of hard living. The tangy smell of sweat and sea that wafted from him caused Isaboe to take a few steps back.

"Are ye lookin' for someone?" he asked again.

"No." Isaboe finally found her voice. "I was just passing by, and…,"

"Ye out here by yerself?" he asked, glancing around.

Suddenly feeling vulnerable, Isaboe pulled her cloak tighter and took a few more steps back. Out of the corner of her eye, she spotted two other fishermen dropping their gear and starting in her direction. Apparently, a woman on the dock alone was an unusual sight, and she was attracting attention.

"Where ye goin', lassie? Dinnae run off!" The fisherman reached out for her, but Isaboe pulled away, briskly walking back up the pier. "Ah, come on back!" he shouted. "I could use a little luck this mornin'. Come on back and rub my pole, aye?"

Hearing the sound of laughter, Isaboe glanced over her shoulder to see the three men now standing together looking in her direction. She picked up her pace and sprinted to the road.

The further she traveled from the coastline the colder the air became and the sky thickened with clouds. Pulling her cloak tighter around her shoulders, Isaboe rubbed her hands together as she blew into her cold fists. The old crone had told her to wait for Connor and Margaret where the water meets the land, and now, shivering and feeling her hunger building, Isaboe wondered if she should have done just that. Justifying her actions, she reminded herself that this road was the only way in and out of Scrabster, and felt confident that their paths would soon cross, bringing them together at last.

The rumble in Isaboe's stomach triggered her realization that she'd already eaten the small loaf of apple bread Evelyn had given her and had no idea when her next meal would come. Despite the anxiety bubbling in her stomach, the thought of being reunited with Connor and Margaret, *on this very day*, fed her with so much hope, she knew she could hold out for a little longer.

However, it wasn't just her empty stomach that made her feel uneasy. She recalled the old woman telling her that Lorien had cast a veil of protection over her, and there had been times when that veil had kept her from harm's way. What did that mean? Had she been so absorbed in her own misery that she had been completely oblivious to her surroundings? Over these last three months, Isaboe felt as if she'd been traveling in a fog, and she had followed Lorien's directions without question. Now that her mind was clear, she realized that she really was on her own, at least for the moment. Until her reunion with Connor and Margaret, she would have no protection. Digging into her bag, Isaboe found the dirk Connor had left for her at the hotel back in Edinburgh. She first slipped it into her cloak pocket, but then pulled it back out. "Hmm, if I'm not wearing my cloak, then I'll have no weapon," she said to herself, tapping the dirk on her palm. Bending over, she carefully slipped the knife down the inside of her boot, as she had seen Connor do, and took a couple of tentative steps. Finding that it made no difference in her gait, and that the weapon in her boot wasn't too uncomfortable, she felt a little braver, but at the same time, hoped she would never have to use it.

Suddenly, the smell of bacon cooking interrupted Isaboe's thoughts, and she stopped to gauge the location of the teasing smell. The side of the road was dense with underbrush and slender birch trees, but when she focused she also noticed the sound of voices. Stepping quietly off the road, Isaboe crept forward to get a better look. Carefully pushing the overgrown ferns aside, she peered through and saw three men sitting with their backs to her, focused on a small campfire. In the middle of the fire, a grill supported the pan cooking the bacon that had drawn her in. As Isaboe's stomach continued to rumble, she contemplated whether she could possibly find a way to share the men's food, but it seemed too great a risk for the reward. Finding no logical way without putting herself in danger, she reluctantly opted to ignore her hunger pangs.

When she heard the sound of horses riding up fast on the road behind her, Isaboe quickly crouched down in the brush. A group of men dressed in the uniforms of British soldiers galloped by her hiding place behind the ferns. She counted at least six as they rode by on their heavily-breathing steeds and entered the large clearing around the campsite.

When she moved closer to get a better look, Isaboe saw that the soldiers had set up camp to accommodate a small troop of men. The perimeter of the campsite looked much the same as the land she had been wandering through all morning—sparsely wooded with Scottish Pines and low underbrush. Three tents dotted the campsite, along with at least the same number of campfires. Watching through the brush as the riders brought their mounts to a stop, she could hear the men talking but couldn't make out their words. She did see that the abrupt appearance of the soldiers on horseback had brought the three men around the campfire to their feet at attention. When one of the riders barked out an order, the men on the ground went scrambling, each one running off in a different direction as the horsemen turned and rode back out the way they had come.

After a few minutes, the activity in the camp seemed to die down. But the men did not return to their campfire, or to the food they'd left cooking. *It really would be a waste to let the meat burn up, or to leave it for the crows,* Isaboe thought to herself.

Looking through the underbrush, she noticed a path that would provide an easy way in and out of the camp, without being noticed. The soldiers were nowhere in sight, and the campfire was only a few steps away. She could run in, grab the food, and run back out before anyone returned. Hearing distant voices gave her pause, and she felt her heartbeat quicken at the thought of what she was preparing to do for a few bites of bacon. But her hunger made her brave, possibly foolish, and she decided to take the opportunity.

Scrambling through the brush, Isaboe took a quick look around. Seeing no one, she dashed over to the fire and snatched a piece of the sizzling bacon from the pan. "Ouch!" she hissed, dropping the meat onto an abandoned tin plate and sucking on her fingers. A bowl of biscuits sat on a log not far from the fire. Grabbing one, she shoved it into her mouth before going back to the bacon. Finding it now cool enough to eat, she quickly devoured the greasy meat while scanning the perimeter of the camp for any movement. Returning to the bread bowl, she stuffed the pockets of her cloak, only to jump when she heard a sound behind her. Spinning around, Isaboe came face-to-face with a British soldier.

"Hey, what're you doing?" he asked, looking surprised. Isaboe immediately ran back toward the green brush, but didn't get far before the soldier grabbed her arm. "Are you stealing my food?"

"I didn't take much. Please, just let me go!" Isaboe pleaded as she tried to break free from his hold.

"Not so fast, lassie." The soldier reached into her cloak pocket and pulled out a biscuit. "Stealing food from the British army is a crime." As he yanked her closer, a wicked smile grew on his face. "But I'm sure you know a good way to keep my mouth shut, aye?"

"Let me go!" Isaboe squirmed and fought to break free, but the soldier's grip was too tight. He chuckled briefly before his attention was drawn by the sound of horses riding back into camp.

Turning to look, Isaboe saw that their uniforms were decorated and realized that the two horsemen were officers. Instantly, she felt her anxiety spike. "Please, let me go!" she begged. Struggling for freedom, Isaboe's nails tore at the soldier's hand, but he only squeezed her arm harder. Shooting her a sideways glare, he turned his focus to the officers as they dismounted.

Panic struck as Isaboe watched the men casually walk in her direction. Though they appeared to be having a discussion, both kept their attention on the scuffle between the soldier and a woman in their camp. Again, Isaboe tugged against her captor's locked-tight grip, but he remained at attention as the officers advanced.

Knowing she was trapped, Isaboe glanced around nervously. But it wasn't until she looked into the face of one of the officers walking toward her that her fear morphed into complete terror. Throwing her hood over her head, she hoped that Lieutenant Jonathan Blackwood wouldn't recognize her.

In a flash, Isaboe relived the horrific event when the British officer had accosted her months before in Inverness. He was drunk on liquor and his over-inflated ego when she and Margaret had unfortunately crossed his path. Blackwood had thought he could seduce Isaboe into spending the evening with him by winning a hefty wager on an impromptu boxing match held in the street. But what he hadn't counted on was being caught in the act of cheating, or Isaboe being the whistleblower who had called him out in front of everyone. Pursued by an angry crowd, the officer had dragged her through the busy streets of Inverness, threatening to make her pay for his losses—one way or another. After being cornered by his pursuers, the angry officer was knocked to the ground by a drifter named Connor Grant. Blackwood was then cuffed and led off to jail, but Isaboe had never forgotten his words or the look on his face when he made his threats.

"What's going on here?" Blackwood stopped short of where the soldier held Isaboe like a scared rabbit. "Corporal Fortner, tell me why this woman is in a military camp?"

"I caught her stealing food, sir."

"A thief, aye?" The Lieutenant stepped in front of Isaboe and tossed her hood back.

Instantly, Isaboe turned her face to the ground, but Blackwood lifted her chin so that their eyes met. "Ah, and a pretty thief, too," he said with half a grin before dropping his hand. "Do you know it's a crime to steal food from the King's army?" He started to leave, but stopped and turned back. His gaze fell over Isaboe's face with a scrutiny that made her quiver inside. "Have we met before? You look familiar."

"No." Again, Isaboe cast her eyes down, turning her face away.

"That answer came awfully fast," Blackwood said, still regarding her. Slowly, he tore his gaze away and walked over to address the other officer who had been watching from behind.

"I heard that General Saxton just returned from Kirkwall, came in this morning," Blackwood said casually. "That's why he's at Fort Langley, to hold a briefing. Any idea what that's about?"

"Colonel Hawthorn said it has something to do with a pocket of resistance in the Orkneys and his plan to address it."

"Do you know how long the ol' buzzard will be here?"

"Not sure, but I don't think it'll be long. Hawthorn mentioned that the General wanted to get back to Inverness before winter makes travel impossible."

Blackwood spun on his heels and pointed at Isaboe. "Inverness! That's where I recognize you from." As he strolled back over to her, the grin on his face made Isaboe's skin crawl. Taking her by the arm, the officer yanked his frightened captive a few steps away, out of hearing range. "You're that wench who caused me to lose a good deal of money, *and* spend a night in jail," he sneered, his face only inches from hers.

"I reported what I saw," she snapped. "It wasn't my fault you cheated." Isaboe tried to control the fear she heard in her voice.

"You should have kept your damn mouth shut." His eyes grew dark, and his gaze was paralyzing. As he leaned in closer, his grip tightened on her arm, and Isaboe winced in pain. "On top of a night in jail, I was demoted because of your loose tongue."

"None of that would have happened if you had left me alone. You can't blame me for your mistakes. Please, just let me go!" Though her words came out shaky, she hoped that with Blackwood sober and in the presence of his fellow soldiers he would do the right thing. She was wrong.

"Hold her," Blackwood ordered, as he thrust Isaboe back into the soldier's charge. He then walked off with his fellow officer toward the horses, talking quietly. After the other officer mounted and rode off, Blackwood returned.

"Do you know what the punishment is for stealing from the British army?" he asked, standing smugly in front of Isaboe as he pulled on his riding gloves. He then reached out and grabbed her right hand, examining it closely. "It would be a pity to cut off such a *pretty* hand."

Isaboe gasped as she jerked her hand from his. But Blackwood only chuckled before turning to address the soldier. "I have a meeting with General Saxton at Fort Langley, so I won't be back until after dark." He looked menacingly at Isaboe. "Take the woman to my tent and restrain her. I'll deal with her when I return."

"NO!" Isaboe screamed. "Let me go, please!"

"But, Captain Blackwood, it was only a biscuit." For reasons Isaboe didn't understand, the soldier spoke up in her defense. But his attempt to intervene on her behalf was short lived.

"Are you questioning my orders, corporal?" Blackwood's reprimand was quick and sharp as he stepped up to face the younger man.

"No, sir. But it seems extreme to punish the girl for only a biscuit."

"That's not your call to make," Blackwood snarled, staring down the man. "The next time you question my order, it will be the last time before I have you court-marshaled. Do I make myself clear?"

"Yes, sir."

Feeling queasy, Isaboe watched the fear growing on the young corporal's face as he swallowed hard. His moment of empathy had disappeared, replaced by his commitment as a soldier and self-survival.

"I'll expect a hot meal when I return," Blackwood said sternly, then turned to shoot Isaboe a snide smile. "The lady will be dining with me. We have some unfinished business," he said smugly, before turning and walking toward his horse. Mounting, he snapped the reins and quickly rode out of camp.

"Please, don't do this. I can pay for the food. I have a couple of schillings! Please, I'm begging you, just let me go!" But Isaboe's cries fell on deaf ears. As he'd been ordered, corporal Fortner walked his struggling prisoner across the camp, doing his best to ignore her desperate pleas.

Isaboe renewed her attempt to make him see reason. "Don't you know what Blackwood will do to me? He's a monster, and he'll probably kill me, after he's done his worst! Please, have mercy!"

"Blackwood is not going to kill you, nor is he going to cut off your hand, miss."

"Then why must I be held captive? You could just let me go, say that I escaped."

"Not likely," he chuckled.

"Please, you must listen to me." Isaboe grabbed the soldier's jacket, making him stop to face her. "As afraid as you are of not following his orders, you know what he's capable of. I can see it in your eyes. Please, just let me go!"

Isaboe could see the confusion and doubt in the corporal's face. The man was young and possibly innocent, but she was right about his fear of retribution. Giving Isaboe a quick jerk, he led her toward the opening of a tent.

In one last, panic-stricken attempt to escape, Isaboe jabbed her elbow hard into the soldier's mid-section, and for a moment, he lost his hold. She turned to run, but he quickly recovered and grabbed at her cloak, ripping it from her shoulders to reveal her swollen belly.

Instinctively, Isaboe wrapped her arms around her middle as the young corporal stood staring, eyes wide with fear, for both his prisoner and himself. "I'm with child. If what he does to me in this tent doesn't kill me, it could very well kill my unborn child. Please, I can see in your eyes that you're a good man. Don't let this happen! Please, just let me go!"

Gently, yet firmly, he led Isaboe into the tent. Sitting her on the cot, he tied her hands behind her back, binding her to the tent's center post. After replacing her cloak around her, he turned to leave, but paused at the opening. Taking a long deep breath, he spoke over his shoulder, but didn't turn to face her. "I'm sorry." In a rush of cold air, the corporal was gone, leaving Isaboe frightened and alone, waiting for the horrid inevitable.

CHAPTER 16

ILLUSIONS, INTRODUCTIONS, AND STRATEGIES

The previous night's snow flurry had been short-lived, and the ground was only lightly dusted in white when Connor and Margaret set out that morning. The air was winter crisp, but the wind remained calm while the land quietly awoke under a cold, grey sky.

Being on the road so early hadn't won him any favors with Margaret. She had grumbled and growled when Connor woke her before the sun was up, and her mood had been sullen ever since. Glancing over his shoulder, he could see Margaret shivering as she sat in the saddle, her cloak tight around her neck with the hood pulled up over her head. Though he couldn't hear what she was saying, he could see her mumbling to herself as she glared at him. When she kicked her heels into her slowly-moving horse, the reluctant animal refused to go faster. It appeared that Margaret wasn't the only one who didn't want to be traveling so early on a cold, winter morning.

Ignoring his cranky traveling companion, Connor turned his attention back to the road and came up short by what he saw. When Margaret caught up to him, he had stopped at a Y in the road. "What's wrong?" she asked, as she looked at his puzzled expression.

"Buchanan didna mention a fork in the road," Connor mumbled.

"He must have forgotten about it."

"This isn't the kinda thing Will would've forgotten to mention," he said, examining the road that split into two. "The man has given these directions a thousand times. Coming to a fork in the road is somethin' he would've mentioned. It dinnae make sense."

"You were in such a hurry to leave this morning; maybe you weren't paying attention. You did everything you could to avoid the man. You probably just didn't catch this part."

Margaret's flippant tone wasn't well received, and she turned away from Connor's angry glare. More than a few moments of uncomfortable silence passed when a young boy, clothed in a fine woolen cloak and shiny leather boots turned the corner of the left fork, walking in their direction.

"Good morning!" Margaret called out to get his attention. "Say, young man, can you tell us which of these roads leads to Scrabster?"

"Good day to you, my lady, sir. Aye, it would be this one, the road that leads to the west. That will take you directly." The well-dressed youngster was fair of face, had a pleasant smile, and was quick to answer.

"Oh, thank you. It was fortunate for us that you were passing by." Margaret returned his smile with equal pleasantries before heeling her horse into movement. Heading in the direction the boy had indicated, she hadn't gone far when she realized Connor hadn't joined her. She stopped and looked over her shoulder. "Connor, are you coming?"

He didn't respond or acknowledge her. Connor's dark-blue eyes were narrowed into a deadly stare while he studied the boy suspiciously. As the well-dressed boy continued walking in the direction that Connor and Margaret had come from, he seemed to sense the eyes on the back of his head. Glancing over his shoulder, he nodded, shooting Connor a quick smile. But that was a mistake.

Jumping off his horse, Connor caught up to the boy and threw him to the ground. Planting his knee in the young man's chest, he held a dirk to his throat. "Take the illusion away, *now!*" he growled as the thrashing boy tried to escape the Scotsman's hold.

It all happened so fast that Margaret could only look on with disbelief, but after finally dismounting, she ran over to join the scuffle. "What in the hell are you doing? Get off him!" she shouted as she tried to pull Connor off his seemingly innocent victim.

"Drop the illusion, or I'll slice ye from neck to nuts!" Connor's threat sounded lethal and genuine.

"Connor, stop it! You're gonna hurt him! What's wrong with you?" Margaret seriously feared for the young man's life. But just as fast as it started, it was over. The captive, who had been struggling under the weight of Connor's knee, suddenly vanished as the tip of Connor's dirk slid through empty air and into the dirt.

Margaret stared at the ground with her mouth agape as Connor stood, brushed off his clothes, and sheathed his weapon.

"What…what was that? What just happened?" she asked, pointing to the ground.

Connor nodded in the direction they were bound. "Take a look for yerself. There's yer explanation." Where two roads had laid out before them, there was now only one.

"I told ye Will wouldn't have forgotten to mention something as important as a fork in the road."

"But…how did you know? How did you know what we were seeing wasn't real? How did you know that boy wasn't real? What are you not telling me?" Her questions flying, Margaret followed Connor, even as he mounted his horse.

"It was just too convenient the boy happened to show up when he did, and I didna like the look o' him."

"You didn't like the *look* of him? Bullshit. What was he? How did you know he wasn't a real boy?" Margaret asked, scowling up at Connor.

"Margaret, how many weeks have we been dealing with magic? Did ye not expect this? Ye have no idea what Lorien is capable of. She'll be using illusions and magic trying to stop us from catching up to Isaboe. But she wouldn't have tried to send us off in the wrong direction unless we were close. So get on yer horse, and let's be on our way."

"Oh, no, you're not getting off that easy. You know something you're not telling me, and I want to know what it is!"

Connor pulled on the reins and kicked his heels hard into the sides of his horse, jolting it into action. Margaret quickly climbed up into the saddle and tried to push her reluctant pony into catching up with Connor's quick pace. "That story you told me last night was missing some details, wasn't it?" Though she continued badgering him with questions, Connor didn't respond. He kept a safe distance, a gap large enough that he could pretend not to hear her.

However, he became suddenly interested when he heard her mention

Isaboe's name. Bringing his horse to a halt, he turned to look over his shoulder. Margaret had stopped her horse and her brow was twisted in confusion. She appeared to be having a conversation with someone only she could see. "What? I don't understand. Slow down and speak one at a time!"

"What is it?" Connor asked as he rode up next to her.

"It's the pixies. They're trying to tell me something, but they're talking over each other, and I can't understand. Something about Isaboe denouncing Lorien, and she's now free from her control."

"What does that mean? Where's Isaboe now? "

"I'm trying to find out," Margaret said before returning her attention to the pixies. "What do you mean, painted men? You're not making any sense. What do they have to do with Isaboe? I don't know what you're trying to tell me!"

Connor listened as Margaret carried on her one-sided conversation. "What about painted men? Is Isaboe in danger?" he asked anxiously.

"I'm not sure. They're saying something about painted men with shiny bright stars all over 'em, and I think they have Isaboe."

"Here, hand me that thing. Let me talk to 'em." Connor held out his hand to take the amulet.

Margaret looked slightly shocked. "Are you sure?"

"Just hand it over!" he growled.

As soon as Connor held the amulet, he looked up, unsure what he would see. Hovering just above him, two small balls of light came into view with wings beating so fast they were barely visible. But what he did see were the delicate faces, tiny arms and legs, and the miniature bodies of the two pixies who floated in the air like hummingbirds. Though he had hoped that the pixies were in fact real, Connor was still taken aback by the sight of them, and for a moment, he stared in astonishment.

"Pretty incredible, aren't they," Margaret said quietly.

"The chosen one?" he asked.

"They mean Isaboe."

Connor readdressed the pixies. "Who are the painted men holding Isaboe and where are they now?" His tone was firm, but he forced himself to have patience as he listened. "I think Isaboe's being held by redcoats—British soldiers," he recited what he thought the pixies were trying to explain.

"Why?"

Focusing on the small creatures, Connor had a bad feeling building in his gut. "Who are these painted men? Did ye hear any names?" When the pixies uttered the one name Connor wished he hadn't heard, the uncomfortable feeling in his gut exploded into fury. *"Fuck!"* he shouted. "Blackwood has her!" Connor snarled through gritted teeth. The memory of what had happened in Inverness flashed through him like a cold knife, as did the threat the officer had made should he ever cross paths with either of them again. Connor suddenly felt sick. He was confident that if Blackwood had found Isaboe alone and vulnerable, the British officer would not hesitate to make good on his threat.

After chasing Isaboe across the country for months while she was held captive by a Fey Queen who cast magic to keep them off her trail, the thought that it was a mere man threatening her now was almost baffling. But at least Connor knew how to deal with mere men. He also knew that he had been chosen to be Isaboe's protector, and up until now, he had failed her. If he were to make things right, now was the time to act.

"Teina and Finn, listen to me very carefully. Isaboe's life is in danger. Ye must lead Margaret and show her where the painted men are holding her, but dinnae let Margaret be seen. Then bring Margaret back on this road to find me. Do ye understand?"

"Where are you going?" Margaret asked with a tinge of fear in her voice.

"I'm going back for help. Please, Margaret—ride fast, be careful, and stay out of sight. I dinnae want to rescue the both of ye."

"Will, I ken how hard this must be to accept, but ye havta believe me. I *am* Braden MacPherson."

With his arms folded across his chest, William Buchanan sat back in his chair. His steely glare and lack of reply told Connor that trying to convince his old comrade of his true identity would be no easy task. The two men had been friends, fought and bled together, but it had been a lifetime ago for the elder man, and he wasn't accepting Connor's strange story.

"I said ye resembled someone I once knew, but I never thought that ye *were* him. Yer bums out the windae if ye think I'd believe that whopping tale. Only a crazy man would go round saying he was someone who died years ago." Studying Connor closely, Will paused. "Aye, ye may look like Mac, but there's no way on God's green Earth ye *can* be. So take yer mad, crazy arse out of my establishment and be on yer way." Will planted his meaty hands on the table and pushed himself up. He turned to leave, but Connor reached out to stop him.

"Ye were a good friend to Braden MacPherson, and on the memory of that friendship, will ye at least let me have my say?" Connor held the burly man's gaze, hoping that William Buchanan might at least give him a moment. "What can it hurt for ye to just listen?"

Will sat back down, but it was clear that he had no patience for foolishness as he spoke again. "Yesterday ye told me that ye ken nothing of any MacPherson, and now ye want me to believe that ye *are* Braden MacPherson—a man who supposedly died in prison twenty goddamn years ago. Is that what ye're telling me?"

Connor had little time, and he needed to convince his old friend as quickly as possible. "Aye, but obviously, I didna die, cause, here I am!" Connor replied with a quirky smile and threw his arms out wide, playing the bit of a showman as he tried to hide his anxiety.

"Alright, let's just say that ye are Braden MacPherson, and somehow ye did escape from prison. How in the hell can ye be so damn young? Ye look like a twenty year-old kid. If ye really were MacPherson, ye'd look like me; a fat old man with grey, thinning hair and wrinkles!" Will patted his rather stout midsection.

"Well, that part's a bit hard to explain, and I promise to tell ye when we have more time. But right now, I really need yer help, so ye have to believe me."

"No. I dinnae, and I dinnae havta help ye either. Now, be off with ye mad self or I'll throw ye out!"

When Will stood to leave, Connor spoke up. "A couple of nights before the battle of Lochenbrough, we knew that we were gonna be outnumbered, and pretty sure we were gonna die in the skirmish. We snuck off together to that little town... what was the name, uh... Dalwhinnie it was, and we got stinkin' smashed. Ye met a woman in a bar and did everything ye could to bed her. Do ye remember? She said that she'd fuck ye if we both agreed to get tattoos from her friend, so we woke up the next morning with these." Connor pulled back the collar of his shirt to reveal a cross tattooed on his chest just below his left shoulder. "Ye never got laid and we were out twenty schillings apiece. Ye made me swear that I'd never tell the others, so we created some bullshit about the tattoos being symbolic—the cross we bore in our fight for freedom. We even made up a chant to go with it: *Forever it shall be the right for Scotland to be free. We will give our blood, we will hear the call. We'll fight for freedom. May our flag never fall.*"

With his mouth agape, Will stood staring as recollection flashed through his eyes. *"Forever and true, Bonnie Prince Charles, we pledge our loyalty to you."* Will recited the last line in unison with Connor as he placed his hand over his left shoulder. "Mac?" he asked astonished.

Connor sighed in relief. "Aye, yer captain, and yer friend, and as both, I need to ask for yer help,"

"But how is that ye haven't aged? Did ye find the fuckin' fountain of youth?" Will asked, gawking at Connor in astonishment.

"Like I said, it's hard to explain, and I promise I'll tell ye. But right now I'm in great need of yer help. The woman that Margaret and I have been tracking is being held by a troop of British soldiers near Scrabster. I've met the officer holding her and he's a right bastard. I dinnae ken what we're up against, but I'd rather not go in alone. Will ye help me, man?" Connor was desperate, knowing he didn't have much time, and the urgency came through in his voice. He knew it was an impossible story to believe, but the facts were hard to ignore. At one time, William Buchanan had been a true friend, and Connor hoped that he could count on that friendship now as he stared at the man.

"Oh, what the hell!" Will finally conceded. "It's been a while since I've had the opportunity to raise some ruckus and mess with the redcoats to boot. So, tell me, what do ye need?"

chapter 17

BLACKWOOD – BLACK NIGHT

By the time Connor and Will met up with Margaret, the sun was making its descent, and mid-winter's daylight was waning. Thick, dark clouds billowed in the grey sky, and the wind whipped across the open coastal plains. A distant, low rumble of thunder held the promise of a storm brewing.

All three riders had been traveling hard and fast, and they were surrounded by a cloud of steam that rose from their horses as Margaret told the men of her observations. "A dozen or so soldiers have set up camp just this side of Scrabster." She stopped to catch her breath and shot a glance at Will before continuing. "There are three tents in the camp, and I'm pretty sure Isaboe's being held in one of 'em."

"Any sign of Blackwood?" Connor asked anxiously.

"I didn't see him, and I don't think he was there. The soldiers were too relaxed, so I don't think any officers were around. And there were no horses in the campsite."

"How far is it from here?"

"Not far, maybe an hour if we ride hard and fast."

"Hopefully we'll make it by nightfall," Connor said as he heeled his horse.

"Wait! This is it? This is your help?" Margaret demanded as she gestured toward Will.

"I ain't exactly a teatless sow," Will replied defensively.

"Did you not hear me say there could be at least a dozen of them?" Margaret asked riding up beside Connor. "And you're gonna ride into a soldier's camp, just the two of you?"

"Will and I have faced greater odds before. Dinnae underestimate a couple of Jacobite rebels. Besides, I've seen ye handle a pistol."

"Well, yeah, but, please tell me your plan doesn't require me having to shoot someone."

"Right now, my only plan is to get there as soon as possible, and we dinnae have time to waste while ye flap yer geggie! I'll figure out the rest when we get there. Now take the lead and let's go!" Connor barked as the three rode off toward the coastal town of Scrabster. He knew that rescuing Isaboe would probably end in bloodshed, but with Will at his side, the odds were greater that it wouldn't be Scottish blood.

An hour later, after leaving the horses tied up on the road, ready for a quick getaway, Isaboe's would-be rescuers inched their way quietly through the brush. Distant murmuring voices, the smell of smoke, and the dancing light of the fire provided perfect beacons to the soldier's campsite.

Hunched down behind the hedge that overlooked the camp, no one said a word as they examined the scene. Connor knew they would have only one opportunity. He also knew it would be a risky attempt, and someone might be wounded, or worse. Whatever his plan was, it had to lay heavily in their favor so it wouldn't be any of them, or Isaboe.

"Alright, so what do we do now?" Margaret whispered as she stared at Connor, her large eyes revealing her anxiety.

"When ye were here before, ye said there were no horses in camp," Connor murmured, noticing a single black horse.

"Aye, that horse wasn't here before."

"Blackwood must be in one of those tents—with Isaboe." Connor growled as his gaze danced across the campsite. He knew that if anything went awry in their rescue attempt, Blackwood could easily take Isaboe's life. This had to go off perfectly and quietly.

"So, captain, what's yer plan?" Will whispered.

Connor looked at Margaret. "We need a diversion."

"Who? Me? Oh, God!" she hissed. "Now what do I have to do?"

With a quick nod of his head, Margaret and Will followed him out from their hiding spot, quietly making their way back toward the road.

The air inside the tent was as cold as it was outside, and Isaboe couldn't stop trembling as she sat at the end of the cot with her back pressed against the tent's center post that she was tied to. Although the corporal had replaced her cloak, Isaboe still shivered, and it wasn't just from the cold, but the horrid realization she was being held captive by a man who had haunted her dreams.

Daylight was waning, and as evening grew closer, the temperature inside the tent grew colder. Isaboe's shivering made her jaw ache and her nose run. Pulling her legs up to her chest, she tried to preserve her body's heat, but it didn't help. Since her hands were bound, she leaned over her knee and wiped her nose on her skirt, but the hair that hung down around her face stuck to her cheeks. When a nagging cough began to burn at her throat, Isaboe felt the familiar feeling of fever tingling on the surface of her skin.

Isaboe had been cold and hungry many times over these last few months while traveling alone, but Lorien would eventually appear with food and safe shelter for the evening. This time there would be no magical rescue by the Fey Queen. She was gone, denounced and vanquished by Isaboe's own words. The old crone had offered her the key to free herself, but now it seemed that she had only traded one captor for another.

She silently chastised herself for not taking the hag's advice and waiting for Connor and Margaret at the pier. If she had just done what she'd been told, she wouldn't be here now. If she had listened to Margaret twenty years ago, she certainly would not be living this nightmare.

"I brought you something hot to eat." Corporal Fortner appeared through the tent opening, holding a bowl. "It's not very good, but it's something." He knelt down in front of Isaboe and tried to spoon-feed her, but she turned away, refusing to eat. "Not interested, aye," he said as he brushed back the hair stuck to her face. "If you won't eat for your own sake, you should at least eat for the child."

Isaboe grimaced at his touch. "What do you care?" she snarled. "We'll both be dead when he's finished with me!"

The corporal stood and took a blanket off the cot, wrapping it around her shoulders and pulling it snug. "This should help some," he said sheepishly, but Isaboe wouldn't look at him or acknowledge his token attempt. "Your bag was discovered in the bushes. Petty Officer Lewis assured me he thoroughly checked it and found nothing in the way of a weapon. I don't need to search you for one, do I?" he asked, glancing in her direction.

The knife was in her boot! But she kept her face stoic and snarled back at the man. "Do I *look* like I have a weapon? If I did, I wouldn't be held captive with my hands bound behind my back, would I?" she held his gaze, hoping her retort cast enough doubt. Apparently, it was good enough, and Corporal Fortner only nodded at her before walking out.

Night had fallen, and Isaboe had been sitting on the cot shivering for hours when Blackwood suddenly entered the tent. How he strolled past her casually, as if it was just a normal evening, was perhaps what scared Isaboe the most. After removing his damp cloak, he hung it on the hook attached to a corner post, then tossed his gloves onto a small table before turning up the lantern that hung above it. Pulling out a chair, he retrieved a few documents out of the breast pocket of his coat and took a seat, attempting to review them by the dim light. The officer had not acknowledged her presence, and it made Isaboe feel like captured prey. It was a game of cat-and-mouse, and he would play with her for a while before striking.

"Your supper, sir," said a voice from outside the tent. Blackwood stood and walked around Isaboe to meet the soldier at the tent flap. After mumbling a few words to the man, he pulled the flap closed.

"You must be hungry." Breaking the silent tension, Blackwood finally spoke, almost too politely. "Corporal Fortner tells me you refused food earlier." With his back still to Isaboe, he placed the tray on the table. When he turned around with a knife in his hand, she felt her panic spike. He walked behind the post that bound her hands, and with a quick slice, she was free. Cupping her frozen hands to her chest, she sat shivering on the cot watching Blackwood as he walked back to the table and poured two cups of tea. The intense fear from the scenarios that had been running through her mind all afternoon was quickly becoming tangible.

"Please, join me," the officer said as he pulled out another chair on the far side of the table. But Isaboe didn't move, only sat and stared at him. "The whole reason you're here in the first place is because you were caught stealing food. Now, I'm offering it. Don't be stubborn." Blackwood finally forced her to the table and sat her down in the chair before taking a seat opposite her.

Pulling the blanket tightly around her shoulders, Isaboe stared at the ground, trying to stop her body from shaking as Blackwood placed a bowl of steaming stew and a spoon in front of her. She glanced quickly at the bowl, and the smell of the hearty meal made her mouth water, but she still refused to eat.

"Come now, you must be famished," he said, swallowing his own spoonful. "This is warm and it'll help stave off the cold a bit." He picked up her spoon and forced it into her hand. "*Eat.*" Isaboe glanced up, catching his demanding gaze. "That's an order," he said, before taking another bite of his own meal.

She was trapped, and it would be foolish to turn down a meal when she didn't know when the next one would come. She prayed it wouldn't be her last. Giving in, Isaboe took a small bite. The stew was hot, and had the circumstances been different, she would have considered it tasty, but her fear made it taste like ash. Silently, she ate a few more spoonfuls and felt it start to warm her some, but she still shivered.

"So, tell me, why are you traveling alone? If I remember correctly, when we last met, you were in the company of another woman." Blackwood said casually as he picked up the loaf of bread from the tray. Tearing off a piece, he placed it in front of her before tearing one off for himself.

Isaboe glanced up from her bowl and watched as Blackwood placed his spoon down and wiped his mouth. "What was her name? Mary, Madeline...Margaret! That was it. So, what became of Margaret?"

At hearing her friend's name, Isaboe again dropped her gaze. The crone had told her that Connor and Margaret were tracking her, that they were on the same road she had been traveling before coming across the soldiers' camp. But by now, they had probably already ridden past the campsite, completely unaware that she was being held captive in a tent just off the road. She was on her own, and no one was coming to save her now. As that horrid thought slammed into her heart, she fought back the tears.

"Hmm, by the look on your face, I can only assume that relationship ended poorly, aye? That's too bad. If I remember correctly, she was rather entertaining."

"Why are you doing this?" Isaboe finally asked. Her voice was shaky, but her words were firm. "You sit there making casual conversation, yet you're holding me captive. Why the mind games? What do you want?" Though she was afraid she already knew the answer.

Blackwood dropped his hands into his lap and leaned back in his chair, shooting her an uncomfortable stare. "Since we last met, I've had time to think about what would happen if I ran into you again." He looked down at his fingernails before continuing. "I went through a great deal of humiliation being demoted from lieutenant colonel down to captain." When he looked back at her, his gaze was vile. "Instead of being in front of a warm fireplace back in my quarters at the fort, I'm on maneuvers out here in the cold with this ragged band of worthless idiots. There was a time when I led a regiment of hundreds. Now I'm trudging through the mud with a handful of foot soldiers who can't follow orders." Blackwood leaned forward, "And that is all thanks to you," he snarled.

"What happened in Inverness was not my fault. You abducted me! You dragged me through the streets threatening me because you got caught cheating! You can't hold me accountable because you were punished for *your* actions." Isaboe knew she was trying to speak logically with a man who had no intent of listening, but she had to try. She had nothing else.

"Oh, but I do hold you accountable," Blackwood sneered. "Any sensible woman who would be benefitting from my win would have kept her damned mouth shut. And I've had plenty of time to think about my revenge." Blackwood leaned back and crossed his legs, casually laying his hands in his lap. "Fortunately, it seems that fate has smiled on me this day and delivered you to me." He reached out to touch her face, but she turned away. When Blackwood grabbed her roughly by the arm, Isaboe instantly froze. "I told you then that you would pay one way or another. Tonight, I'll be taking that payment," he sneered, releasing her as he leaned back in his chair.

Isaboe hated herself for crying. He didn't deserve to see her weakness.

"I suppose that encounter in Inverness has tainted your opinion of me. Unfortunately, liquor can sometimes bring out the worst in us." The officer stood and placed his hand under Isaboe's chin, forcefully turning her face up. "But if you cooperate, maybe tonight I can change your opinion."

She slapped his hand away. "The only way you could ever change my opinion is to let me go, *now!*" she snapped, eyes filled with both fury and fright.

Grabbing her forcefully by both arms, Blackwood yanked Isaboe to her feet. He held her so close that his dark, beady eyes were only inches from hers. "Do you know how long it takes to move up in rank in this King's army? Being demoted down to captain was a painful disgrace. So, I can't let you go—you *owe* me," he snarled, his mouth only inches from her cheek. Isaboe struggled to free herself from the officer's grip, but only managed to bruise her arms. He chuckled cruelly before continuing. "You only make this worse for yourself. I will take what's mine, whether you're willing to give it or not."

Releasing her, Blackwood turned, unbuttoning his jacket as he continued. "I've been told by many a satisfied woman that I am a very astute lover. Cooperation on your part would certainly be to your benefit." He stopped and looked back at her with vile intent, "but it's not necessary."

Isaboe sat back down and dropped her head, tears dripping onto her skirt as she squeezed her eyes shut. But right next to her growing fear was a burning anger, and she certainly wasn't about to be a willing participant. He would be in for a fight.

The opportunity presented itself when Blackwood sat on the cot and leaned over to unlace his boots. Silently, she slipped the dirk out of her boot before sitting up straight and looked directly at him. "What makes you believe that *you* have the right to inflict pain on *me*?" Though her voice was shaky, the weight of the dirk—Connor's protection in spirit—gave her a burst of courage. "What horrible thing must have happened in your life to make you believe that control over me is *your right*?"

Blackwood stood and stared at her for a moment. "A bad childhood, perhaps," he said, shooting her an odd grin as he stepped up to the table. A small, decorated wooden box sat next to the documents he had carelessly dropped earlier, and he lifted the hinged lid. Reaching in, he pulled out two shot glasses and placed them on the table. He then pulled a flask from his jacket pocket and poured an amber liquid into the small glasses. Picking one up, he tossed the liquor back in one easy gulp before licking his lips, then glanced down at Isaboe.

"I have to say there is one thing the Scots do well; they make a *damn* fine whiskey. May I interest you in a shot?" He picked up the second glass and held it toward her. "It would be to your benefit, and hopefully mine."

Isaboe stared at him, knowing if she was going to use the weapon, he had to be closer. She also knew there would be only one opportunity. If she missed, he would quickly disarm her. The thought of plunging a knife into a man's flesh was horrid, but knowing what he had in store for her was even worse, and it gave her courage.

Keeping the dirk tucked into the folds of her skirt, she dropped the blanket from around her shoulders and stood slowly. "I curse the day our paths crossed. There's no way I'm letting you lay a hand on me." Though every muscle in her body was tense and her insides shook violently, her words were firm.

Still staring at her, the former lieutenant colonel tossed back the second shot of whiskey before placing the glass on the table, harder than necessary. "Those are some pretty brave words, considering your situation." He stepped in front of her, only inches away. "But you forget yourself. There's no angry mob outside. It's just you and me, my dear, and a handful of my soldiers following orders," he sneered as he began to slip off his jacket.

When Blackwood pushed the jacket off his shoulders, exposing his white shirt, Isaboe knew this was her moment. But she had never before used a knife to defend herself, and she wondered if her heart was beating too fast for what she was about to do. In her next breath, she made her move. Reacting from a primal sense of survival, she swung the dirk toward him, letting out a scream that matched the adrenaline pumping through her veins.

Blackwood dodged the tip of the knife, and it missed his chest, but not his upper arm. Isaboe saw the steel slice through his skin before he could recover. But he did recover, and quickly ripped the dirk from her hand.

"You filthy bitch!" he snarled, tossing his jacket onto the ground. As he came at her with her dirk in his hand, Isaboe stumbled a few steps backward. She saw the blood from the cut rapidly soaking into the fabric of his shirt sleeve before catching the look on his face, twisted with depraved hatred.

"You got this past my men," he growled, waving the knife at her. "I'm impressed. Someone will answer for this." He placed the dirk on the table before grabbing Isaboe by both arms, jerking her hard. "So, apparently you don't intend to make this easy for yourself, aye? That's just as well with me. It makes my conquest that much more *satisfying*," he sneered, ripping off her cloak before throwing her down on the cot.

But just as quickly, Isaboe jumped back up, swinging her fists recklessly. "NO! NO!" she screamed as Blackwood restrained her flaying arms. Seizing her around the neck with one hand, he squeezed her throat violently.

"I've had enough of this!" he growled through gritted teeth.

Terror spiked in Isaboe's chest when she saw him raise the other hand in a closed fist. Trying to prepare for what she knew was coming, she closed her eyes as she continued to scratch at his hand that dug into her throat. But before Blackwood could launch his blow, the sound of the tent flap being pulled aside distracted him. "I gave strict orders I was not to be…" but his tirade was interrupted by the sound of a solid strike across his face. Isaboe's eyes shot open when Blackwood released his grip, and she saw him flying backward, landing with a loud crash as the small table shattered under his weight.

In a moment of complete astonishment, Isaboe saw the face of someone she thought she'd never see again. She stared in disbelief as Connor stood over Blackwood with the tip of his sword at the officer's throat. But she was quickly startled when another large man stormed into the tent.

Now that Blackwood was restrained, Connor gave Isaboe his full attention. "Are ye alright?"

It all happened so fast she could only nod. The shock of Connor's abrupt and unexpected entrance, along with the tenderness she now felt in her throat, prevented her from speaking.

"Isaboe, this is Will," Connor said without releasing his stance. "I need ye to go with him."

"No, not without you!" Isaboe pleaded, but Will gently directed her toward the tent opening. "No! Please, Connor, come with me!"

"I'll be right behind ye," he said, pausing to glance around the tent. "Will, grab her cloak and bag."

Quickly retrieving the items, Will wrapped Isaboe in her cloak and placed an arm around her shoulder. As he encouraged her toward the tent opening, she glanced back to see the lethal look in Connor's eyes as he stared down at the man pinned under his weapon. Although she couldn't make out the words Connor mumbled to the officer, she didn't miss the horrible sound of Blackwood taking his last breath, gasping and gurgling as the metal sliced through his throat.

CHAPTER 18

REUNITED

What happened after Isaboe was hurried from the tent was a blur. Dodging trees and running through brush, she followed Will blindly through the mud and darkness. In the distance she could hear thunder, and the smell of rain was in the air. It felt appropriate that a storm should be brewing as they made their escape. In the next few steps, they were on the road, and two breaths later, Connor was at her side.

Isaboe threw herself into his arms, and he wrapped her in his embrace, burying his face in her hair. Clutching each other, he held her tight, and though she felt safe for the first time in months, Isaboe couldn't stop crying. She breathed him in, afraid to let go lest it be an illusion and he might not really be here.

Connor drew back and looked down at her. "Are ye injured? Did he hurt ye?" he asked.

Isaboe could see the concern in his eyes. "No," she said, shaking her head. Grabbing onto the front of his jacket, she let the tears run freely as she looked up into his face. "I can't believe you're really here," she whispered, her voice shaky. "I can't believe you came for me." Even though it was dark, she could see the love in his eyes.

"Of course I did," he said, cupping her face and wiping her tears as a smile crossed his lips. "There was no way I was letting ye get away so easily. I'd follow ye across the whole damn world if I had to. I love you, Isaboe."

When he kissed her, his lips were soft and warm, and she sank into his arms, knowing this was where she belonged. As he pulled back, she felt the first drops of rain on her face and looked up, holding his gaze.

"I'm so sorry I didn't wait for you." Though she had broken her promise because she thought she was protecting him and Margaret, it now felt shallow and without merit.

"I should never have left ye in the first place. But that's behind us. We're together now."

"Hey, Mac, we need to get movin'," Will said in a hushed tone, breaking the moment.

"Wait. Where's Margaret?" Isaboe asked anxiously, donning her cloak.

"We'll take ye to her. Can ye ride?" Connor asked.

When Isaboe nodded, Connor lifted her into the saddle, and then mounted up behind her. Kicking his horse into a fast gallop, they rode hard into the night with Will bringing up the rear.

They hadn't gone far when the winter storm unleashed its fury and the sleet began to bite at Isaboe's face. Fortunately, it wasn't long before Connor brought the horse to a trot and turned onto a wet, grassy path. The frozen rain had turned wet and heavy, and mud sloshed under the horse's hooves. Stopping in front of a dark, desolate-looking barn, Connor dismounted and then helped Isaboe down.

Hanging in place by two rusty hinges, the old barn door complained loudly when it was pried open. As soon as they were inside and out of the drenching rain, Isaboe found herself wrapped in Margaret's arms. "Isaboe, my dear, sweet Isaboe! Thank God!" Margaret's hold was so tight that Isaboe could barely breathe. But she felt such comfort in the embrace, something she thought she would never feel again, that she returned the hug tenfold. Exchanging wet kisses and tearful smiles, she cried into her friend's arms.

Pulling back, Margaret rummaged in a saddlebag and lifted out a dry blanket. "Here, wrap this 'round you. I'd offer you something hot to drink, love," Margaret said in hushed voice, "but we've decided it best not to risk attention with a fire." Isaboe took off her wet cloak and pulled the blanket around her shoulders as she glanced to where Connor and Will were quietly talking. She was barely able to make out their figures in the dark.

The barn was cold, and the rain leaked through the deteriorating roof in a chorus of splatters, but Margaret had found a place under the loft that offered shelter. "Here, come over and sit down. At least it's dry." Leading Isaboe to sit on a soft bed of musty hay, Margaret began rubbing her back. Isaboe wasn't sure if she was shaking from the cold or from fear, but she tried to control her shivers as she listened to the low murmur of the men's voices.

"It was a surprise attack." She heard Will say. "We knocked the soldiers out before they saw us coming."

"But they saw Isaboe and Margaret," Connor grumbled. "When those soldiers come round and find Blackwood's body, this coast will be overrun with redcoats by morning, if not sooner."

"When's the last time you ate?" Margaret's question took Isaboe from her focus on the men's conversation. "Here, have some cracker bread."

"No. No thank you." Isaboe pushed it aside.

"You need to eat, Isaboe. Even if only for the child."

The child! The words jolted her, and Isaboe instinctively placed a hand over her belly before looking at Margaret with wide eyes. "Does Connor know?" she whispered.

After a few tense moments, Margaret nodded.

"Did you tell him?"

"No," Margaret said quietly. "He already knew."

There were so many questions, but she had no idea what to ask. *Connor knew!* Yet he had come for her anyway. How much did he know? She would eventually find out, but even with all the reckless and foolish choices she had made, it hadn't mattered to him. He loved her that much.

"Can we hold up at yer place for one night?" she heard Connor ask. "We'll be long gone and on our way south by morning."

His statement had Isaboe on her feet, and she quickly walked over to where the two men were talking in the dark. "We can't go south," Isaboe said forcefully, planting herself next to Connor. "We have to go to Orkney!"

"Isaboe, I killed a British officer tonight. There'll be redcoats all over the coastline searching for us. We have to head south. That's our best option."

"No! I've come too far to turn back now. We have to go to the island!"

"Connor's right, Isaboe," Margaret said putting an arm around her friend's shoulder. "We have to go south now. We have to get away from the damn Brits."

"NO!" Isaboe shrugged off Margaret's arm. "We have to go north to Orkney!"

"Isaboe, there'll be no ferry till morning, and the Brits'll be all over the harbor by then," Connor said. "Now's the time to flee, and in the only direction we can. That's south on horseback. If we ride hard and fast, we can get a head start before the Brits can organize."

Isaboe took a step closer and looked up at Connor, holding his gaze. "I've come too far, gone through too much not to go on." Though she had no idea how they would flee from the British over water, going back wasn't an option. "Going south is exactly what the British would expect. They can guess we have horses, and they'll expect us to go south." Though her throat burned, she ignored the pain and spoke hurriedly, knowing she had little time to convince them to see it her way. "If we head north by sea, they'll have a much harder time tracking us."

"Actually, she has a point," Will interjected. "I know a fella who owns a fleet of ships here in Scrabster. He owes me a favor, and I'm sure I could coerce him into lending us a ship tonight."

"It must be one helluva favor to get him out on a night like this." Connor guessed.

"Aye, it is. His wife's family owns most all o' the kelp fields on the coast from here to Whitefield. But the Missus ain't much to look at—married her for the family money. He brings his lady friends to my establishment and pays me well to keep my geggie shut. I think he can pay a little bit more."

"Do ye ken how to find this fellow?"

"Aye, I know where he lives. If ye and the women want to wait here, and I'll go see him about a ship."

"No, we're not waitin' here. If ye can commandeer a ship tonight, I want us all to be at the dock, ready to board." Connor turned back to Isaboe and Margaret. "Are the two of ye ready? There's no time like the present, aye?"

"Just let me gather our things and we'll be ready to ride," Margaret said as she and Isaboe returned to the bale of hay and began to repack their bags.

"Is she gonna be alright?" Will asked quietly as he nodded in Isaboe's direction. "She looks frail, Mac. Margaret mentioned earlier that she's with child. Is it yours?"

"Does it matter?"

"If it dinnae matter to ye, it dinnae matter to me."

Connor only nodded in silent agreement. "She'll be alright. She's stronger than she looks." Connor tried to sound positive, but knew that concern was written across his face. "Uh, Will, dinnae mention to Isaboe anything about our history; keep it to yerself. She dinnae ken everything about me yet."

"Then that makes two of us. When are ye planning on telling me what's going on here, Mac? Why haven't ye aged a lick?"

"I promise I'll tell ye, but I owe it to her first, when the time's right. So for now ye're just gonna have to trust me, aye?"

"Ye were my captain, and always will be my friend. Of course I trust ye. I'm just goddamn bloody confused."

"Then ye're in good company," Connor said with a smile as he clapped a hand on his friend's shoulder.

The ride to the dock was short, but they were soaked by the time they arrived. After securing the horses, the four late-night travelers found an empty fish shack on the shoreline. They made sure everything was clear and quiet before Will disappeared into the night.

The storm's winds tested the continuity of the small shelter, and the pattering of rain as it dripped through the patched roof only added to Isaboe's discomfort as they waited. Though she tried to stop her shivering, even with Margaret's hugs and continued rubbing, it seemed the longer they waited, the colder she became.

A distant lantern swinging in the wind allowed a faint illumination to shine through the slightly ajar door, and it cast half of Connor's face in shadow as he stood watch in the foul-smelling shack.

"May I stand next to you?" Isaboe asked, stepping up to him. "The smell in here is making me nauseous and I need some fresh air."

"Aye, but ye might get wet."

"It doesn't matter; I'm already wet."

As Connor pushed the door open wider, a fresh breeze rushed in, and Isaboe took a couple of long, deep breaths. Feeling the ache in her stomach begin to calm, she could feel Connor's eyes on her. Swallowing hard, she turned to face him. "What became of the other soldiers? You didn't kill them too, did you?"

"No. Margaret helped us with a diversion, so Will and I were able to take 'em out. Those boys'll have a helluva headache when they come 'round, but they'll live to tell about it."

"So, because of me, you've killed a British officer, and now you'll be hunted by the British Army." Even though it was what she had tried to do herself, Isaboe was now riddled with concern.

"Isaboe, had I not, we'd never be free of him. Not after tonight. Do I really have to justify killin' that bastard?" He paused and softened his tone. "It's not yer fault, and it's not the first time I've had the bloody redcoats on my arse—probably won't be the last. Ye dinnae need to worry 'bout me. I can take care of myself, and you as well." Connor brushed a lock of hair from Isaboe's face before wrapping his arm around her waist and pulling her close. They stood that way for a few silent moments, arms around one another, embracing their brief minutes of peace.

But Isaboe could feel her swelling belly pressing against him, and she knew Connor could feel it too. "So, do you know *everything* about me?" she asked tentatively, choosing not to look at him.

"Oh, I'm sure there's still a lot about ye I dinnae ken, but I look forward to finding out," Connor said as he drew back to give her a coy smile, which Isaboe returned shyly. "But, aye, I do ken what has happened to ye. I know ye were taken by the Fey, that ye've lost twenty years and yer family. I also ken that ye're tryin' to locate yer sisters on Orkney Island in hopes of finding yer children."

There was an uncomfortable silence before Isaboe spoke. "Obviously, you know I'm with child. You're alright with that?" she asked, looking deeply into Connor's eyes, longing to see the answer she was hoping for.

Connor brushed an affectionate hand across her hair before letting his palm rest on her shoulder. "Isaboe, I love you, and I'll love the child, too."

"But, I don't know..."

"It dinnae matter. I'll raise the child as my own." Connor paused before reaching a hand out to Margaret who had been standing in the corner, quietly staying out of the way. It took a moment, but Margaret finally conceded. Taking Connor's hand, she allowed herself to be pulled into their circle.

"But from here on, no matter what happens, we all stay together. We can face whatever the future brings, but we have to do it together, agreed? No one goes off on their own anymore, alright?" Connor said, looking directly at Isaboe. Before either of the two women had a chance to reply, the sound of a quick, low whistle drew their attention. Connor turned toward the door and responded with a matching whistle. Will was back.

chapter 19

midnight crossing

Apparently Will was so persuasive that he not only managed to commandeer a ship, but the ship's captain as well. Though the rain had let up some, the sea was still rough and choppy, and the captain was not pleased to be taking his ship out at night in inclement weather. He informed them, as if he were trying to scare them off, that the trip to the island under good conditions took a couple of hours, but at night and on rough seas, it would be a long and unpleasant voyage.

However, it had been made clear by his employer that the captain was to do whatever Mr. Buchanan asked. After they had loaded the horses into the hold, and the four human passengers were on board, the captain slipped his Argosy quietly out into the black, icy waters under the cover of darkness. After the dock was out of sight, Connor found Isaboe and Margaret huddled under a canvas, taking shelter from the wind and rain. "Let's go under," he said as he grabbed the women's bags.

Darkness enveloped them as they entered the stairwell that led to the cargo hold. Unable to see her footing, Isaboe stumbled when she took the last step off the stairwell, almost knocking her friend over. Fortunately, Margaret caught her, and was able to help Isaboe to regain her balance.

The sound of a match strike cast a yellow glow as it flared to life, and Connor lit the swinging lantern that hung from a beam above his head. Isaboe shivered as she examined the damp, filthy hold. Empty wooden boxes, mostly broken, lay haphazardly along the length of the ship's hull, scattered amongst piles of dirty straw that stank of urine. A number of bottles clinked as they rolled back and forth with the lilt of the ship, and

Isaboe had to grab a vertical post to keep from falling over as the ship rolled first one direction, then the other.

"Not exactly the Ambassador Hotel," Connor mused. "Must have been used for livestock. Smells like the backend of a mule."

"Well, at least it's dry, and we're out of the bloody rain," Margaret said as she wrapped a blanket around Isaboe before throwing one over her own shoulders.

"Where's Will?" Isaboe asked.

"He's helping the captain. He'll be down shortly," Connor said, before rummaging through the boxes. Finding a few more stable ones, he stacked them so they wouldn't have to sit in the filthy hay. "Here, sit down before ye fall over." Connor helped Isaboe take a seat and sat next to her, beckoning Margaret to join them.

Though they were out of the wind and the rain, the empty hold was frigid, and Isaboe couldn't stop shivering. "I'm so cold," she said before being interrupted by a fit of coughing. When it passed and she could finally draw a breath, Isaboe sat up straight, but could feel the fever tingling on her skin.

After digging through her bag, Margaret pulled out a small brown bottle. "Here, take a swig of this. It ain't hot tea, but it ought to warm you some."

Isaboe took a small sip and cringed at its taste. "What is that?" She could hear the scratchiness in her voice and felt the tonic burn all the way down her throat.

"Before we left Edinburgh, nurse Pritchard gave it to me. She and the doctor both felt I was leaving too soon, but there was no way I was letting Connor go without me, whether I was ready or not. When the nurse handed me this, she said not to mention it to the doctor. Apparently, she and her husband make their own brew. It has a little extra something, not sure what it is, but it makes you feel better. It may not taste very good, but it warms you up on the inside."

Isaboe took another sip before handing the bottle back. As Margaret reached out to take it, Isaboe placed a hand on her friend's forearm. Touching the red, ragged scars just above Margaret's wrist, she asked, "Does it hurt much?"

"Not so much. Every day's a bit better. It took a while to get full use of my hand, but it's nearly back to normal. The scars look nasty, and they itch like hell, but I feel damn fortunate. Attacked by a wolf and living to tell about it—I think I have a lot to be grateful for, and it's quite the story, aye?"

"Oh, Margaret, I prayed every day for you! I felt horrible about leaving you. I'm so sorry I left, but I really didn't think I had a choice. Lor..." Isaboe stopped herself before the denounced Fey Queen's name crossed her lips. "She told me things, made me believe that everything that had happened was my fault. Because I was the Chosen One I couldn't know mortal love. She said that everyone who loved me would die. If leaving you would spare your life, what choice did I have?"

Isaboe turned to Connor with the same pleading eyes, trying to justify her actions, to impress upon them the fear that had made her run from them. "I'm so sorry that I left you both. When I promised to wait for you, Connor, I meant to keep that promise, I did. But I was so scared that it might be true. I left because I love you." Looking back, she was embarrassed by her rash action, even though it made sense at the time. Now, in hindsight, she knew it was all based on fear, real or not.

"Darlin', you never get to make that kind of decision for us again," Margaret couldn't keep the chastisement out of her voice. "If you'd just told us, you would've known we were willing to take that risk with you. My God, girl, don't you ever do somethin' stupid like that again." She couldn't keep the scowl off her face.

"The pixies told us about the lies Lorien told ye," Connor said as he ran an affectionate hand through her hair. "We ken how manipulative she is. So, ye dinnae need to apologize. Ye were alone then, but not anymore, and we're all in this together. We didna come all this way and not be prepared for a fight."

Isaboe nodded with a weak smile, only to have it interrupted by another coughing fit, which reignited the uncontrollable shivering. When she finally stopped coughing and was able to take a few deep breathes, her throat felt like it was on fire and her body ached.

"You're burning up, lass," Margaret said, as she placed her hand up against Isaboe's forehead.

Glancing at her, Isaboe saw the concern on her friend's face, and saw the same worry in Connor's eyes as Margaret handed her a cup. "Here, take a drink of water. When was the last time you ate?"

The water cooled Isaboe's irritated throat, and after a few more breathes she finally answered in a raspy voice. "Uh...other than the little bit I ate at the soldiers' camp, I think it was early yesterday, but I don't really remember. This day has lasted an eternity."

"I have some bread. Would you like it now?" Margaret began rummaging through her bag, but Isaboe stopped her.

"I'm not feeling so well, and I don't think I'll be able to keep anything down. Maybe later."

They sat in silence for a few moments, trying to adjust to the rolling of the ship before Margaret finally broke the quiet. "Isaboe, the pixies told us that you denounced Lorien and freed yourself from her. What does that mean, and how did you do it? Are you really free from her now?"

"The old crone told me what to say."

"What old crone?" Connor asked.

"It was a woman I met before, but I'm pretty sure she wasn't human. You remember, Margaret. It was the same old woman I told you about who appeared to me in the carriage."

"You saw her again?"

"Yes, on the road back to the coastline. She just appeared, walking toward me."

"What did she tell you this time?"

"She told me what a fool I've been for listening to the queen's lies. The old hag said that if I ever wanted my life back, if I didn't want to lose my child, I had to realize that she was using my past to keep me trapped in fear. It was the crone who gave me the words to free myself. She disappeared right before the queen materialized in front of me. It was like I cast a spell!" Isaboe paused, recalling the moment, "When she heard me start to recite the words, the queen became horribly threatening because she knew what they meant. I was so frightened. I didn't think I could say it, but I did."

"What did ye say? Are ye really free from Lor...?"

"Don't say her name!" Isaboe pressed her fingers against Connor's lips, preventing him from finishing his question. "Names have power." Her eyes were wide, full of fever and fear. "The crone told me never to call on her again. If I do, I'll never be free from her. I don't know if just uttering her name would bring her back, but I won't take the chance."

Connor took both her hands in his. "You're safe now, *Breagha*. She cannae hurt ye anymore."

"Connor, I saw things—hideous things I can't explain. I don't know if they were illusions, but they seemed so real," she whispered, her eyes rimmed in red as the fever took hold. "I saw goats turn into men and viciously attack an innocent boy. I saw ghastly creatures do horrible things, and she did it all for fun; to torment me and anyone else she could get at." Isaboe then turned to face Margaret with the same expression. "There was one point when I almost threw myself off a cliff. I didn't think I could take it anymore, Margaret. I felt like I was losing my mind!"

Margaret's face twisted with misery and compassion. "Well, thank God you didn't go through with it." Her lips twitched into something of a smile, albeit forced, before she resumed rubbing Isaboe's back. "But that's all behind you now. You look like you could use some rest, love. Why don't you drop your head on my lap and rest until we get to the island?"

"Wait, I have to ask something." As Isaboe turned to look at Connor, she could feel the beads of perspiration on her brow and upper lip, even as she shivered. "How did you know what happened to me? Margaret said she didn't tell you. So, how do you know?"

Connor shot Margaret a quick glance before taking a deep breath. "Do ye remember me telling ye about the man I made a promise to, the man who released me from prison?"

Isaboe nodded. "Yes, and you said that you had to see a woman in the Lochmund Hills about helping you to fulfill this promise. Did you find her?"

"Aye, Rosalyn, and she's a sorceress. Demetrick, the man who paid my way out of prison, was a powerful wizard. He knew what this Fey Queen was planning, and he chose me to stop it. He needed someone who could fight, someone he could trust, and someone he could count on to find you. He offered me life and a new identity, so I owed it to him to at least try. But even Demetrick had no idea of who it was that I was to protect.

That's why he sent me to see Rosalyn. She performed a ceremony, and though I dinnae quite ken what happened, I remember waking up seeing yer radiant face in my mind's eye." Connor paused and ran a hand affectionately down her hair.

"It was you all along, Isaboe. The woman I was traveling with, who I'd fallen in love with, was the same woman I was looking for, and I didna even know it!" Connor's eyes sparkled in the low light. "Isaboe, can ye ever forgive me for not being there when ye needed me? I ken I've not been much in the way of a protector, and maybe Demetrick made a mistake in his choosing, but Isaboe," he whispered, gently taking her hands as he looked longingly into her fever-laden eyes, "I promise that I'll lay down my life to save yours, and I'll never let anyone or anything ever hurt ye again." His gaze held hers, as if searching for acceptance.

Isaboe ran a hand over his cheek, covered with a good start on a winter's beard. "You were chosen for me," she whispered. Absorbing what Connor had just revealed, Isaboe looked deeply into his blue eyes. "I think the wizard chose wisely," she said with a weak smile. "But why were you in prison? What did you do?"

"I was accused of crimes against the crown, fighting against the Brits. As I mentioned earlier, I'm used to havin' redcoats after me."

Isaboe pondered this new information before giving him an odd look. "You said the wizard gave you a new identity. So, Connor Grant isn't your real name?"

"No."

"What is it?"

"Braden MacPherson."

"Braden MacPherson." Isaboe spoke his birth name for the first time and it felt odd. It didn't seem to fit the man she had lost her heart to. "That explains why Will calls you Mac. Can I still call you Connor?"

"Ye can call me anything ye like, my love," he said with a smile as he brushed a stray lock from her face and let his palm rest against her cheek. Though she was still shivering, Connor's hand felt cool against the heat that radiated off her face. "But enough talk. Ye need to rest now."

Connor stood and picked up his makeshift seat, placing the box between Margaret and Isaboe to create something that resembled a bench.

Pulling off his jacket, he turned it inside out, making it into a small pillow. Margaret immediately took the jacket and placed it on her lap. "Lay your head down, love," she said to her sick friend. Pulling her blanket up around her shoulders, Isaboe made herself as comfortable as possible while resting her head in Margaret's lap.

The roll of the ship slowed to a gentle rocking as the storm finally passed over. With his feet planted wide and his arms crossed, Connor stood with his back pressed against a wooden post. It had been an exhausting day for all of them. Though sleep danced at the edge of his consciousness and his eyes felt heavy, he refused to give in. It would still be dark when they reach Orkney, so finding a warm, dry place for Isaboe to rest till morning would be difficult at best. At one time, the islands had been a stronghold, one of the last places of refuge for the Jacobite rebels. But the British had squashed all attempts to rekindle the rebellion and Connor had no idea what to expect twenty years later. He decided that staying on the ship until dawn may be their best option.

He glanced over at Margaret who still had Isaboe's head in her lap, and noticed that both ladies had opted not to fight sleep. Margaret's makeshift seat was pushed up against a post, and though it supported her back, her head still rolled side-to-side, reflecting the ship's movement. The low, rhythmic snoring coming from her direction made Connor smile, if only momentarily.

Heavy footsteps on the stairwell announced Will's entrance, along with a fresh gush of cold marine air. Margaret stirred and brushed the sleep from her eyes as the big man looked over their accommodations.

"Not the best traveling arrangements, aye?" Will said, standing next to Connor. His stance was wide, and he swayed with the lilt of the ship to maintain his balance. "This was the best I could get under the conditions. I insisted that the owner make no record o' this trip in his ship's log. He assured me the captain would also keep his geggie shut, but ye never ken." He nodded towards Isaboe, "How's the lass?"

Connor shook his head. "Not good. She's sick with fever, exhausted, and malnourished. We need to get her someplace warm and dry where she can rest and recover."

"I saw lights from the island. We should be there within the hour. What's yer plan when we land?" Will grabbed a post, swaying with the tilt of the ship as he looked at Connor for direction.

"I dinnae have one. I have no idea where Isaboe intended to go, but I'm sure she must have some information on the whereabouts of her sisters. That was why she was coming here in the first place. When we get to the island, I'll see what she kens. Right now, she needs rest."

Connor motioned for Will to follow, and the two men took a few steps further back in the hull. "I didna think this through, Will." Connor murmured, keeping his voice low. "My only focus has been on findin' her, and I've got no idea where to go, especially now that we'll havta be on the run."

"We weren't seen, Mac. As long as ye keep her hidden, we should be fine, but the sooner ye can get away from here, the better. Is there no place ye call home? Or is there some reason ye can't go back? "

"There's no home for either of us. I've been on the road so long that wherever I drop my bedroll is home, but that's no life for her, or the child. She's been through so much already. With all the madness she's lived through, she deserves better. But this ain't yer problem, Will. When we land, go back with the ship. I couldna have done this without ye, and I'll forever be in yer debt. But ye have a life and a son. Go back to him. Ye dinnae need the Brits after ye, too."

"What're ye talking 'bout? I haven't had this much excitement since the rebels disbanded. As far as my boy, Ian can handle the hostel himself. There's not much in the way of travelers this time of year, so he can manage for a while longer without me. Dinnae think ye can get rid of me that easy, Mac. Ye still owe me an explanation on why ye haven't aged, and that's gotta be one hell of a story. I'm not leavin' without it."

Connor placed a hand on Will's broad shoulder and gave him a crooked smile. "Thank ye, friend. I think it'd be best if we stay aboard till dawn. Can ye get the captain to dock somewhere away from the main port so we can lay low for a few more hours?"

"Consider it done." Motioning toward Margaret, Will asked. "What's Margaret's story? How's she connected to the two of ye?"

"She's just the best friend anyone could ask for. Isaboe would be in a lot worse place if it wasn't for Margaret. We owe her everything."

"She's definitely got spunk. I'll give her that. When she ran into that circle of soldiers, screaming and carrying on about a husband trapped under a carriage, they were fuckin' shocked. Somehow, she convinced every bloody redcoat to follow her. If she was afraid, she covered it well."

"Aye, she's a Godsend," Connor said as he eyed Will. "Ye sound interested. Been a while, aye?"

"Ach, no!" Will growled, but then his faced softened. "Well, maybe." Will looked oddly uncomfortable before giving Connor a quick elbow in the ribs. "I'll go talk to the captain about findin' a good place to dock," he said as he headed back up to the deck.

Standing alone in the dark, Connor wondered what his next move would be. Whatever it was, caring for Isaboe's health was first and foremost. He would not accept that they had traveled this far, endured both Lorien and Blackwood, only to watch her die from a fever.

She just needs food and rest, and she'll be fine. She's a fighter. Connor tried to reassure himself, hoping that Isaboe could find enough strength to make him right. But her body was weak, frail, and drawn from months without proper nourishment and exposure to the elements. The bizarre excursion had certainly taken its toll.

CHAPTER 20

COMING OUT
OF THE DARKNESS

The first fingers of dawn were stretching across the land when Connor and Will unloaded the horses. The western shoreline on the main island of Orkney was rocky and treacherous, but the captain, who knew the area well, had located one of the few perfect landing sites. Most ships made anchor in the natural harbor of Stromness, a safe inlet between the North and Atlantic Seas, but docking this vessel required obscurity and no witnesses.

Margaret managed to get Isaboe to eat and drink a little before disembarking, but her fever and cough had not improved. Concern was etched in Margaret's face as she helped her sick friend put on additional layers of clothing, hoping to protect her from the cold winter wind while they pushed forward on horseback.

Though Isaboe insisted that she could ride her own horse, Connor quickly offered an alternative. "I've been lookin' forward to holding ye for a long time, *Breagha*. How 'bout ye ride with me and I can wrap ye up in my arms? It'd make me feel better," he said with a quirky grin.

Since he offered so sweetly, what could she do but oblige? Much to her silent embarrassment, he swept her up in a blanket and helped her to settle in side-saddle onto his horse. After making sure Isaboe was well covered, Connor mounted up behind her and wrapped his arms around her before grabbing hold of the reins.

"After everything I've been through," Isaboe murmured, "It'd be rather ironic if I should die of a fever." Her bitter laugh was hoarse.

"None o' that kinda talk, love." Connor eased her closer to offer more of his warmth. "We'll find a town with a warm bed for ye. Everythin'll be fine."

"I just want you to know, I mean, you've come so far to find me, and I'm deeply grateful that you did." When Isaboe stopped for a moment to cough, the effort left her shivering and exhausted. Connor attempted to shush her, but she kept going. She needed to say this. "It's not your fault. I didn't leave with her because you left." Isaboe struggled to finish. "It was my decision to make, even if it was the wrong one. I don't want you to feel guilty, whatever happens." Her throat burned, her head throbbed, and every part of her body ached, and she knew Connor was sick with worry for her.

"It dinnae matter what ye say, I still should've been there. But I'm here now, and we're in this together." He paused and softly stroked her hair. "I just traveled across the whole damn country lookin' for ye, and it'd break my heart if ye died on me now. So unless ye're alright with me being a lonely, broken-hearted man, ye best not die." The grin and twinkle in Connor's eyes brought a brief smile to Isaboe's lips before she leaned back into his chest, allowing him to cradle her in his arms.

The ground was covered with a fresh layer of snow, a gift from the previous night's winter storm. Glistening in the morning sun, rugged cliffs jutted high above the crashing waves, looking as if they had been dusted with spun sugar. The sea air was crisp and the sky was clear, but a vicious wind whipped across the landscape, making travel by horseback much more uncomfortable for the four riders.

As the travelers ventured east, signs of civilization began to appear, and when Stromness finally came into view, the winter sun was already moving low across the horizon. The route to Stromness had taken them around the southeast tip of the island so they could enter from land and not sea, just in case the British soldiers had already made it over from the mainland. Connor had little doubt that Blackwood's body had been found by now, so it was just a matter of time before the island would be covered with redcoats. Finding a secluded place to let Isaboe recover was top priority.

Built into the rocks above the shoreline, The Harborview Hotel was one of the newer inns in Stromness. The collaboration of rock, wood, and sandstone ensured that it was in harmony with life by the sea. The interior décor carried the ocean theme with elegantly framed paintings of maritime vessels lining the hotel walls. In the lobby, a large, overstuffed sofa sat behind a massive wooden table, which featured a beautifully polished tree stump as its base. The intricate model of a ship—complete with masts, oars, and rudder—sat regally in the center.

Connor assisted Isaboe onto a bench next to the front desk and took a seat next to her. Wrapping his arm around her, she rested her head on his shoulder while Margaret and Will stepped up to the counter.

"Good day folks. How many rooms?" asked the hotel clerk.

"I assume ye ladies will want to share a room?"

Margaret responded to Will's question with a nod and a yawn.

"Three," Will said as he pulled a pouch from his jacket and laid coins on the counter. Margaret placed her own coins on the desk, but her large companion silently slid the money back toward her.

"What're you doing?" she asked with a hard stare.

"I got this."

"I can pay for my own room," Margaret said, slightly annoyed as she pushed her coins forward.

"Aye, I can see that. But, how 'bout ye let me take care of this? Ye've been traveling for a while now, probably a bit short."

"I'm fine, so you don't need to pay for me. Anyway, you should probably keep your money. Best not to owe you more than we already do. We don't know what's coming."

Examining Margaret's stern expression, Will paused, but then gave her a soft smile. "Tell ye what; I'll take care of the room and ye can buy me dinner."

Margaret was tired, they all were, and all she really wanted to do was crawl into a bed. But the way Will smiled at her, so confident that she would jump at the offer, only added to her annoyance. "Fine. Pay for the damn rooms," she sighed heavily, taking her coins and the room key before swooping over to Isaboe. "Come on, love, let's getcha' up into bed. We'll get you cleaned up, and then you can sleep it off, aye?"

After helping Isaboe take a warm bath, Margaret fed her chamomile tea with ground cinnamon and a shot of whiskey to chase out the fever before tucking her into bed. The next few days were spent the same, Connor and Margaret taking turns playing nurse and holding vigil over their patient. Not infrequently, Margaret had to chase Connor off to go get some sleep himself.

Isaboe's fever continued in waves, leaving her dripping wet and kicking off the blankets, or freezing cold and shivering. Though she managed to keep food and water down, and the feverish attacks gradually began to subside, it wasn't uncommon for Isaboe to wake up screaming, thrashing at some unseen enemy that haunted her dreams.

Margaret had decided two things. First, that whatever Isaboe had been through while they chased her up and down the Highlands had been absolutely horrible. Second, that she was not going to relax until Lorien met the same fate as Blackwood. When she expressed this to Connor, instead of trying to dissuade her as she had expected, he only set his mouth and nodded grimly.

On the morning of the fourth day, Isaboe's fever finally broke. Though still weak, she directed Margaret to the marriage certificate she had brought with her from Edinburgh. Yellowed with age, it was tattered and torn from being carried across the country tucked in the bottom of her bag, but legible nonetheless. It held only the names of her sister and the man she had married, but that was enough for Isaboe to make the journey across the country. Armed with information that she had received from Sister Mirium at the kirk in Edinburgh, Isaboe had learned that her sisters were living on this island, at least at one time. She hoped one of them still did.

"Sister Miriam told me that Tomas and Deidra owned a fishing business somewhere here in Orkney," Isaboe explained. "I had planned on doing some detective work and just start asking questions around the…"

But before Isaboe could explain further, a violent coughing fit interrupted her. Once the worst seemed to be over, Margaret handed her a cup of cold water as she wiped the beads of perspiration from her weak friend's forehead. Isaboe leaned back on the bed and closed her eyes.

"Will and I need to go check out the town anyway," Connor said. "We can ask around to see if any of the townsfolk have heard of this Tomas McFarland, or his business. It'll give us something to do. Will's gettin' restless."

"Why is he still here?" Margaret asked. "I know he's been a huge help to us, but I don't understand why he's still here. I would've thought he'd be long gone and back home by now."

"Why dinnae ye want him around? Dinnae ye like him?"

"I didn't say I didn't like him. It doesn't have anything to do with liking him or not. I just don't understand why he would want to stay here with us when he could go back home and be done with all of this."

"Maybe because he wants to stay. I dinnae have all the answers, so ask him yerself if ye're that curious." Connor stood and kissed Isaboe on the forehead before heading for the door. "I'll bring ye back some supper. What sounds good?"

"Some savory roasted grouse with neep and tatties sounds wonderful," Isaboe replied.

"Looks like our patient just might make it after all," Margaret said with a smile. It was the first sign that Isaboe's appetite was returning, and a good sign that she would pull through.

As Connor stood with his hand on the doorknob, though he said nothing, his smile spoke loudly. Walking back over to the bed, he leaned over Isaboe. "If I have to kill the grouse, spit and roast it myself, ye'll have it before the days over." He kissed her again, but this time full on the lips. Drawing back, he paused to stare into her eyes. "There isn't anythin' I wouldna do for ye, *Breagha*," he whispered, gently stroking the side of her face. "Please, just get better. I need ye to be well."

Breagha. Isaboe knew that Gaelic word. It meant beautiful, and she smiled up at the man who made her feel that way, even in her current condition. With a soft smile, she ran a hand across his freshly-shaven skin before locking gazes with him. "Every day is a little better, thanks to you and Margaret. And, of course, Will, too." She glanced at Margaret sitting in a chair next to her bed.

"What? Alright, enough with all this sappy emotion," Margaret exclaimed as she stood up and waved off both of their looks. "I thought you and William had some exploring to do? Get out with your sorry arse already!" She pushed Connor out the door, but not before he looked back to give Isaboe a smile and a wink.

Moving around the room, Margaret made herself busy as Isaboe slipped down beneath the covers. "Margaret, did I tell you that I felt the baby move for the first time?" she said quietly.

Margaret stopped folding clothes and sat down on the bed next to Isaboe. "When was that?"

"It was on Christmas day. I can't believe that was less than a week ago."

"Where were you at Christmas?"

"I spent Yuletide with a lovely family; the Campbells. I had intended to stay at the Scrabster Inn, but the inn keeper wouldn't hear of it and took me home with her. She had two beautiful granddaughters, and it was at their home on Christmas morning when I felt the baby move for the first time." Margaret watched her friend, silently urging her to keep speaking. "These last few months I've been so lost in my own misery that I couldn't see my way out." Isaboe cast her gaze down. "I'm ashamed to admit this, but I considered taking my own life more than once, and hadn't given any thought to the baby, not properly. But when I felt it move, I think the baby saved me, from myself and from…her."

"Oh, you dear lass!" Margaret caught Isaboe's hand and kissed it. "You're here with us now, my love."

Clasping onto Margaret's hand, Isaboe gave her a nervous smile. "But, I haven't felt the baby move since. What if something's happened? Don't you think I should have felt movement again?"

"You've been through hell, Isaboe. Don't jump to any horrible conclusions. I'm sure everything's fine. You both just need rest," Margaret said, tucking the blankets around Isaboe as she attempted to ease her friend's worry.

CHAPTER 21

FUGITIVE

Much to his relief, Connor found a restaurant that served roasted grouse, which he proudly brought back to Margaret and Isaboe's room. Though Isaboe ate only a little, it was with enthusiasm, and the heaviness in Connor's chest eased some seeing the color returning to her beautiful face.

"I feel badly that we're dining together and Will is all alone," Isaboe sighed as she leaned back against the bed. Though her appetite had improved, the simple act of sitting up and eating left her feeling drained.

"I asked him to join us, but he said it didna feel right, this bein' a ladies room and all," Connor mumbled between bites.

"Hell," Margaret scoffed. "After what we've been through, I don't think we're too worried about etiquette and protocol. Still, it's nice to know that someone out there still has manners."

Connor shot her a look, but thought best to let it go. "Actually, I think he's enjoying himself," he said. "Usually, Will's the one waitin' on everyone else's needs, but here, he's got the hotel staff waitin' on him. He's been hangin' out at the pub, sleepin' in late, and has his meals delivered to his room. He even has his beddin' changed every damn day," Connor said with a chuckle. "I think he feels a bit like he's on holiday."

"No wonder it's been so hard for me to get service here," Margaret snorted and crossed her arms. "They've all been waiting on the *vacationer!* I had to go down three times to get clean sheets brought in, and then I had to change 'em myself! No offense Isaboe, but with the way you've been sweating, I couldn't have slept on those sheets one more night."

Feeling a touch of embarrassment at Margaret's words, Isaboe noticed that Connor had focused back on his meal, avoiding Margaret's glare and offering no response to her rant. "Connor, did you and Will find out anything in town today?" she asked, breaking the uncomfortable silence. "Were you able to find anyone who knew anything about my sisters or the fishing business?"

"Aye, we did get a lead," Connor said as he downed the last swig of ale and wiped his mouth on his sleeve. "We found an 'ol fella who remembered a fishing business here in Stromness run by Tomas McFarland some years back. From what we discovered, after the business went under there was a falling-out between the sisters. Tomas and Deidra moved to Kirkwall, and the last anyone heard, Saschel was living in Duncreag. So it looks like Sister Miriam gave ye good information. For a woman of her years, her mind's still pretty sharp."

"So, when do we leave?" Isaboe asked, sitting up with renewed interest. It felt great to hear that her foolish quest had not been in vain. Perhaps she still might learn what had become of her children.

"You're not going anywhere for a while, lassie," Margaret said as she stood and began picking up the remnants of their evening meal.

"But at least it sounds like there's a good chance we can still find one of my sisters, and hopefully my children. It's good to know that all of this madness wasn't for nothing, and coming here was the right choice after all." Trying to convince herself as much as her friend, Isaboe sat nervously waiting for a response. "Don't you agree, Margaret?"

Dropping the dishes on the service table harder than necessary, Margaret turned to face Isaboe, her eyes hard. "No, I don't agree. You almost died! I'm not saying that coming here was a bad idea, but, my God girl, making this trip by yourself was *not* the right choice. If you hadn't left your damn necklace, if we didn't have the powers to track you, you would've been dead by now!"

"I, I didn't' think I had a choice, Margaret. I already told you. I left with her because I thought it was the only way to save you and Connor. I did it because—because I love you. I thought you understood." As tears welled in Isaboe's eyes, Connor opened his arms for an embrace, which she accepted gratefully.

Connor shot Margaret a glare as he held Isaboe. "It's alright, we do understand, and everythin' is gonna be just fine."

"Isaboe, I'm sorry." Margaret sat down on the bed and reached out to her friend. "I've just been so worried about you that I forgot myself. I didn't mean to speak so harshly. Forgive me?"

Isaboe drew out of Connor's arm and turned to embrace her friend. "There's nothing to forgive, Margaret. I owe you everything."

Sensing that the ladies needed a moment to themselves, Connor stood and walked over to the service table. "I'll just wheel this down to the front desk," he said, pushing it toward the door.

Margaret stood up as well and walked to the corner of the room where she picked up a pile of sheets. "It doesn't look like anyone's coming anytime soon to gather these soiled linens, so I'll go with you."

With his hand on the doorknob, Connor looked back at Isaboe. "Can I get ye anythin'? Do ye need some more tea? Do ye need a backrub? A foot rub? If anything needs rubbing, I'm yer man."

"Connor, stop," Isaboe said with a weak smile. "I'm fine. Go on. I think I'll take a wee nap, I'm a bit tired." She started to pull the covers up, then stopped, propping herself up on one elbow. "Uh, Margaret, there is one thing that you could do for me. I could use a bath this evening, if you could arrange it, please."

No sooner were they out in the hall when Connor told Margaret to leave the linens and follow him to Will's room. Though at first she protested, the look in his eyes prompted her to follow him curiously down the hall.

Will opened the door and looked carefully at both Connor and Margaret before stepping back.

"William." Margaret nodded as she passed in front of him and into the room.

"Margaret."

"Will and I found out more than just information on McFarland today. We also found this." When Connor gave Will a nod, the big man pulled a piece of paper from his vest pocket, handing it to Margaret.

Giving both men an uncomfortable glance, she hesitated before unfolding the parchment. It was a roughly drawn sketch of Isaboe with the word <u>REWARD</u> boldly printed above her likeness. "Oh my God!" Margaret's breath caught in her throat as she continued to read:

100 CROWNS FOR INFORMATION LEADING TO THE CAPTURE OF THOSE IN CONNECTION WITH THE MURDER OF A BRITISH OFFICER NEAR SCRABSTER ON THE NIGHT OF DEC. 26TH. IF YOU SEE THIS WOMAN, CONTACT THE CONSTABLE'S OFFICE OR ANY MEMBER OF THE BRITISH ARMY. CONSIDER HER AND HER COMPANIONS ARMED AND DANGEROUS.

"We found those posted all over town," Will said. "Apparently, the Brits have already been here asking questions."

"Do you think we should show this to Isaboe?"

Connor heard the fear in Margaret's words, and he saw it written across her face. "Well, she must have expected that somethin' like this would eventually show up. The question is how will she react? Do ye think she's well enough?"

"Uh, I don't know. You saw her just now. It doesn't take much to upset her." Margaret glanced from Connor to Will. "So, what do we do now?"

"We lay low and keep Isaboe in her room," Connor said calmly. "It'll be a few more days before she's strong enough to ride. So right now our best course of action is to keep our heads down and her out of sight."

"Ye ken, this looks a lot like the sketch ye showed me back at my place, remember?" Will said, looking at Margaret. "Ye have one much like this, aye?"

"Aye. What about it?"

"Because it's just a matter of time before someone remembers *us* looking for a woman that matches this same description," Connor growled.

"Aye, and then a sketch of both yer mugs will be posted all over town as well," Will finished Connor's unspoken thought.

"We have to get out of here," Margaret insisted, eyes still scanning the poster.

"Aye, and as soon as Isaboe can ride, we will," Connor said, before turning to Will. "This is the point of no return, old friend. No one would blame ye if ye turned round and headed for home and yer son. This isn't yer fight, Will, though we couldna've gotten this far without yer help. The Brits still dinnae ken about yer role in this, so either ye're in or ye're out. It might get a bit rough from here on, and I need to ken what I havta work with." Connor knew it would be good to have an old friend covering his back, but he couldn't ask Will to take such a risk.

"I already told ye that I'm in it for the long haul. Ian's been itching to prove he's a man. Now's a good time to see what's he's made of, aye? So dinnae insult me again, Mac. I ken what we're up against."

"If I thought it was just the redcoats we might have to deal with, I'd agree with ye. But before this is over, we may be encountering somethin' ye've never come up against. Ye have no idea what yer committin' to."

Will just looked at Connor stoically. That was as close to an answer Connor knew he would get, realizing that his friend had already made up his mind.

"So, I guess we'll just stay here for a few more days until Isaboe is ready to ride," Margaret said. "How far is Duncreag from here?" Though she made a good attempt to stay calm, Connor could hear the unease in her voice.

"The ol' fella said it was bout a day's ride. He said if we just follow the coastline, it'll take us right there."

"Alright, then while we stay in our room, you and William could go check that out and be back in a few days. By then Isaboe should be ready to travel."

Connor shook his head. "I won't leave Isaboe."

"It's only for a couple of days, Connor. She's already showing improvement, so don't worry. I'll take care of her," Margaret added with a reassuring nod.

"I'll not leave Isaboe, and it's not open for debate. I stay by her side until she's ready to ride, understood?" Connor said firmly.

"Understood," Margaret replied, somewhat defensively.

Connor's point was followed by a moment of uncomfortable silence before he spoke again. "Why dinnae ye two go check it out, and I'll stay here," he suggested, hoping to appease Margaret.

But she immediately shot Connor a steely glare.

"I wouldna mind getting out for a while and going for a ride," Will offered. "I'm startin' to get a bit restless just hanging around in this room. What ye say, Margaret; up for a road trip?"

Will seemed all too eager, and apparently his casual attitude struck a chord with Margaret. "Oh, sure, after getting smashed at the pub all day, you come back here and have food delivered to your door, *plus* have fresh sheets put on your bed every night. 'Tis been real tough for you, hasn't it?" she snarled, glaring at both men before she stormed out of the room.

"Does that mean we're going?" Will called out to her. Connor snickered when he heard Margaret grumbling in the hallway, something about *stupid men*.

CHAPTER 22

A LOVE WORTH WAITING FOR

Though it took some convincing on Isaboe's part, and reassurance that the fresh air would do her friend good, by the following morning Margaret had finally agreed to travel to Duncreag with Will—but not without first giving Connor a lengthy lecture on what he should do if Isaboe's condition took a turn for the worse. "Now, if her cough keeps her awake at night, give her a cup of hot tea and stir in a teaspoon of cinnamon and a shot of whiskey. Not that I suspect it will, but if her fever comes back, add this to the tea as well." Margaret held out a cloth bag filled with a mixture of herbs.

"Margaret, ye said yerself that she's gettin' better, so quit worryin'. I'll take very good care of her. She's in good hands," he said with a playful smile.

"Aye, that's what I'm afraid of." Margaret gave Connor a reprimanding glare. "You behave yourself."

"I'll be a perfect gentleman. Now get going. Buchanan left here thirty minutes ago to saddle the horses. He'll be thinkin' ye've changed yer mind."

"I still ain't sure I haven't lost my mind."

"Margaret, Will's a good man. He's had my back more than once," Connor said before giving her a polite hug. "Give him a chance, and I'm sure ye'll be friends. If ye let yer guard down a bit, ye might actually enjoy the trip." Standing back, he flashed his best, most reassuring smile.

Margaret's scoff was her only reply, but her flat, stern expression spoke volumes.

The sound of clattering china brought Isaboe out of the last remnants of sleep. With daylight shining through the lone, small window, she opened her eyes to see Connor attempting to pour a cup of tea from a hot pot, but without much success. Silently, she watched him juggling the small teacup in his hands that seemed too big and clumsy for the delicate porcelain. As she sat up and rubbed the sleep from her eyes, Connor shot her an embarrassed smile.

"Sorry, Isaboe. I tried not to wake ye, but I'm afraid I'm better suited to a basket sword than a teacup," he said, carefully placing the cup on the table next to her bed. "I promised Margaret I'd make sure ye ate, so I brought ye some sausage and tattie scones."

"What time is it?" she asked with a yawn and a stretch.

"It's almost noon. Ye've been sleepin' so sound I didna want to wake ye. Will and Margaret left a couple of hours ago for Duncreag and it looks like they'll have a good day for their ride. Is there anything I can do for ye?" Connor sat down on the bed beside Isaboe and tried to kiss her on the forehead, but she leaned back, pulling the blanket over her nose with one hand and pushing him away with the other.

"Yes, you can take a bath!" Isaboe cringed. "Connor, you smell like a wet horse!" By the blank expression on his face, she could tell he hadn't noticed the odor he carried on his person. "Are you seriously telling me you can't smell that?" she said, a slight chuckle accompanied her words.

Connor jumped to his feet and did a quick self-inspection before looking at Isaboe with a shrug. "After I walked Margaret to the stables this morning to meet up with Will, I took to groomin' the horses, and I guess I got a little on me."

"More than just a little."

"Well, sorry about that, but it wouldna be the first time we've had a wee bit of wet horse on us." With a sly smile, Connor leaned in to steal a kiss, but he was again thwarted.

"NO!" Isaboe shoved him away. "I need to use the privy and you need to go bathe. Now!" she emphasized.

"Alright, alright, I'll go take a bath," he conceded, throwing up his hands in surrender as he made his way toward the door.

Isaboe sat on the bed running her hands through her tangled hair and realized that going to bed the night before with a wet head may have been a bad idea. Her unruly hair seemed to have a mind of its own. While sweeping it back from her face, she caught a glance of Connor who was still standing at the door, watching her. "I'm so glad ye're feeling better," he said with a beaming smile. "Ye have no idea how that makes me feel."

Lost in each other's stare, they shared a silent moment until Isaboe finally broke it. "Go clean up, and don't get sidetracked. Go on." In the last few days, worry and concern had been etched across his face, but now a look of relief, and maybe a hint of happiness, shown in Connor's blue eyes, and she couldn't help but feel her own lips curl up, returning his smile, until the door closed and he disappeared.

After the trip to the privy, Isaboe ate the sausage and scones before crawling back into bed for another nap. When she woke a few hours later, feeling well-rested at last, she took some time to clean up. The bath she took the night before had cleansed her from days of sweat and exhaustion, but she also needed to wash away the wounds that still remained. She had been through hell, but in finding her way out, she'd discovered an inner strength that hadn't been there before. Isaboe hoped she could build on that small bit of courage, and in the process be able to face whatever came next.

The small, square table in the corner of her room held a bowl of water and two clean towels. Above it, a small mirror was mounted on the wall, and she noticed how thin her face looked as she brushed out her hair. Months of exposure to the elements, coupled with struggling on minimal rations, had taken its toll. Placing the brush on the table, she dropped her head and ran her hands gingerly across her swelling belly, wondering what other damage had been done that she couldn't yet see. She tried not to think about the unknown, reassuring herself that the worst was over. But a nagging seed of doubt still lingered.

Trying to focus elsewhere, Isaboe poured another cup of tea and picked up the book Margaret had left for her. It was supposed to be quite good—a quiet romance with a happy ending. That was what she needed right now, so she quickly read the first few pages before dropping it on the bed.

Thinking about her roommate brought on a warm feeling—dear, sweet

Margaret. Since they had arrived in Stromness, she had been part nurse and part nurturing friend. Margaret had even purchased new clothes for Isaboe. Suddenly recalling the pretty nightgown, also courtesy of her friend, Isaboe stepped over to the coat rack where Margaret had placed it. Removing her smock, she lifted the white gown off the hook and slipped the smooth cotton gown over her head, letting it fall easily into place. It was large enough to fit comfortably over her middle, yet flowing and feminine at the same time. Satisfied, Isaboe returned to the table and took another sip of her tea. Though no longer hot, it still warmed her. Making herself comfortable on the bed, she once again picked up the book and tried to get lost in the story. But after reading the same page multiple times without really seeing the words, she knew she wouldn't be able to concentrate and tossed it casually back onto the bed.

This time it wasn't Margaret's good heart, or Isaboe's previous uncertain thoughts that kept her from focusing on the story. It was Connor. Her mind couldn't seem to stay focused on anything other than the fact that he was somewhere nearby. It'd been a while since she'd sent him from her room. Why hadn't he come back to check on her? Feeling restless, she decided not to wait. Throwing a blanket around her shoulders, she stepped out into the hall.

Connor had just started dressing when he heard the tap at his door. He quickly pulled on his pants and threw a towel around his neck before answering. Concern shot across his face when he saw Isaboe standing in the doorway. "Darlin', are ye alright?"

"Yes, I'm fine. I just got bored. You've been gone so long I wasn't sure you were coming back. May I come in?"

"Of course, please." After Isaboe stepped in, Connor closed the door behind her. "Sorry, didna think I'd be gone so long," he said rubbing the towel across his head. "But I had to make arrangements for dinner to be brought up later, and that took longer than I expected." Placing the towel back around his neck, he ran his hands through his wet hair and away from his face. "And gettin' a bath took awhile; had to wait my turn. I was coming to check on ye as soon as I was dressed."

Dropping the blanket where she stood, Isaboe walked over to stand in front of Conner and looked up to meet his striking, blue eyes, letting her gaze dance with his. A light, clean scent wafted off his warm skin, and his damp, tangled hair hung down against his bare shoulders. Being this close, she noticed that his chest was spotted with small, faded scars, but the muscle tone underneath his skin was clearly defined, and Isaboe's gaze followed the line of thick muscle running alongside his collarbone.

Noticing the tattooed Celtic cross just below his left shoulder, she instantly had a flash of recall as she reached up and lightly traced the image with her finger. It had been the crone in the carriage who first told Isaboe; *"Seek the protector. Look for the Celtic cross."* In her own cryptic way, the old hag had predicted Connor's role in Isaboe's flight for survival long before Isaboe had ever met him. And it had been Connor who sought her out, not the other way around. In that moment, Isaboe felt a sense of overwhelming gratitude and love for this man who had saved her life, in more ways than one. "You smell better," she said with a coy smile.

"I believe that's what ye asked for. Isaboe, what're ye doing?"

"I'm in your room wearing nothing more than a nightgown, and you have to ask me that?"

Connor flipped the towel from around his neck and let it drop to the floor. Cupping her face with both hands, he took a moment to search her eyes. "Are ye sure? Ye've been so sick, and..."

"Connor, I wasn't ready before," she said, searching his eyes. "But I know what I want. After Margaret and Will return, it may be a while before we're alone again. Are you telling me you're not interested?"

"Oh, *Breagha*, there'll ner' be a day I won' be," he said, just before his mouth met hers. It was a soft kiss, full of passion and desire, and left no doubt he was interested. Wrapping her arms around his bare shoulders, Isaboe returned his kiss with the same intensity.

Without waiting for a formal invitation, Connor lifted her into his arms and carried her to his bed.

For the rest of the evening and into the next day, Connor had no problem keeping Isaboe out of sight without complaint. He'd made arrangements to have all their meals delivered to his room, and other than trips to the privy, they spent their hours under the covers, making up for lost time. Though he was concerned that she might overexert herself, Isaboe assured him that she was fine, and it didn't take much encouragement on her part to keep him focused.

A week earlier, Isaboe thought she would never feel love like this again, but now, as she lay wrapped in the protection and warmth of Connor's arms, she drifted in and out of sleep on a current of contentment. Even though she couldn't see it, there was a fixed, soft smile on her lips, and she felt it all the way to her heart. If she had to stay here forever, she'd be alright with that.

When Connor brushed her hair back and began nibbling on her ear, it brought Isaboe fully awake. "Stop it, that tickles," she giggled.

"Ye taste so good, I cannae get enough of ye," he said, easing her closer against him. As he buried his face in her hair, Isaboe shivered as she felt his breath on her neck and snuggled in tighter. With one arm over her waist to keep her close, Connor began planting soft kisses on her bare shoulder, but he suddenly pulled back when an unexpected movement rolled across her belly. "What the hell was that?"

But Isaboe knew exactly what it was, and a smile of joy lit her face. She placed Connor's hand back where it had been. "Just wait," she whispered, and it didn't take long for their patience to be rewarded when another, stronger movement rolled under her skin. "It's the baby. It's moving," she confirmed, as much to herself as to Connor.

"Uh, that's a good sign, aye?"

"Oh, aye, it's a very good sign!" she said as she rolled over and kissed him.

They lost track of time. Only their meals, brought to the door by obliging hotel staff, helped remind them that time was still passing outside the warm nest they'd made for themselves. There was no threat of British soldiers, no Fey, no agenda but each other.

Lounging on the bed with his eyes closed, Connor had one hand behind his head and the other resting on her thigh. There was a subtle, but satisfied grin on his lips, and Isaboe thought he looked more relaxed than she had ever seen him. It made her feel good knowing that she had something to do with that. Other than the sheet draped over her pulled-up knees, all the other blankets had been tossed into a reckless pile at the end of the bed.

"Will and Margaret should be back tonight," she mumbled as she nibbled on what was left of the dried fruit from their lunch. "I hope Duncreag was a good lead."

At her comment, Connor rolled over and gently tugged on her leg. "Well, then we dinnae have much time to waste." Pulling her toward him, he started kissing her face and neck, but Isaboe resisted. Giggling, she pressed her hands against his chest.

"Wait. Just...wait a minute!" she said, forcibly pushing him away. Drawing back, Connor propped up on one elbow and gave her the minute she had asked for. His hair was tossed wildly and a soft smile tugged at his lips. Isaboe couldn't help noticing the sleepy-sensual glow in his blue eyes. "I was just thinking," she said, trying to redirect his focus, "now that I'm feeling so much better, we should go out tomorrow, all four of us. Maybe we could actually go out and eat at a restaurant like real people do. It must be close to New Year's. There must be some festivities in town. Even a walk along the shore would be nice. I've been stuck in this hotel for so long I could use some fresh air. What do you think?"

As he sat up, a dark expression crossed Connor's face, and Isaboe felt the mood suddenly shift. "What is it?"

Connor rolled over and reached into a drawer of the table next to the bed. Turning back to face Isaboe, he hesitantly held out the poster.

Seeing her face on the piece of paper with the words REWARD printed above it jolted Isaboe like a punch to her stomach. Snatching the parchment from his hand, she stared at it wide-eyed as her heartbeat began to escalate. Up until this moment, she had been so immersed with being back in Connor's arms that she had almost forgotten how that came to be. "Oh my God!" she gasped. "Where did you get this? When?"

"In town yesterday. They're posted all over." Running his hand tenderly through her hair, Connor sighed. "Ye cannae go into town, love. We cannae take the chance that someone might recognize ye."

"This is awful! What are we going to do?" Isaboe dropped the paper onto the bed and stared at Connor, feeling her fear rising. "I can't stay hidden in this room forever!"

"What? Ye dinnae like these arrangements? We have food delivered to our room. We eat, fuck, and sleep, wake up and do it all over again. How's that a bad thing?" he asked, trying to break the tension.

"Seriously, Connor, we'll be on the run now. That's frightening! And speaking of all this food, who's paying for it? I don't have any money; do you?" Isaboe's earlier feeling of contentment quickly dissolved, replaced by a new dread building in her core.

"Ye dinnae need to worry yer pretty little head about any of this," Connor said as he affectionately ran a hand across her cheek. "Will and I have a plan."

Hearing him say that did help, but the price on her head complicated things. She was a fugitive now, wanted by the British army, and that was something she could never have imagined. However, the confidence she saw in his eyes gave her a bit of courage, and she attempted to push her fear aside, at least for the moment. "I'm glad we have Will around. He seems like a good man, and a good friend to do all of this for you."

"For us."

"For us. I stand corrected," she said with a half a smile, even though deep inside the anxiety still bubbled. "So what's his story? Why does he call you captain?"

Connor rolled over onto his hands and knees. "I don't...want to talk... about Will right now." Enunciating each word, he slowly approached Isaboe like a hunter stalking his prey.

This time she didn't push him away. "Again? Don't you ever wear out?" Isaboe said with a playful smile as she looked up at Connor, now hovering above her.

His tussled hair hung down, framing a face filled with the unmistakable look of desire. "Ye seem to have recovered a good deal of strength in the last twenty-four hours. Do ye not think ye can keep up with me?" Passion flashed in his blue eyes, and Isaboe watched his lips pull into a hungry grin.

"Oh, you don't need to worry about me. I can keep up with you."

"Atta girl," he said with a satisfied smile. Kissing her, she wrapped her arms around his neck and pulled him down into the bed.

chapter 23

quick trip to duncreag

Margaret and Will made good time on their way north as the prevailing winds that swept across the island helped to push the riders along the rocky coastline of Orkney. The well-traveled path frequently took them through farmland where vacant fields lay barren and brown, the soil turned under and hibernating. Signs of previous crops still lingered on the perimeter; mostly flax, bere, and hay, and due to winter's frequent rain storms that passed over daily, many of the plots had turned into mud bogs.

Keeping the pace quick, Margaret intentionally created just enough distance between her and her traveling companion to keep his friendly, idle chatter to a minimum. Eventually, Will gave up trying.

For reasons she didn't completely understand, Margaret still wasn't sure how to feel about William Buchanan. Yes, Connor trusted him, and they might not have been able to save Isaboe without his help. But his offer to pay for her hotel room as if she couldn't handle it herself, and the subsequent days he'd spent being catered to by the obliging staff had all rubbed her the wrong way, so she opted to avoid his company.

Arriving in the small community of Duncreag just before dark allowed them to find accommodations for the night. It also gave them the opportunity to dine at the only pub in this little village that was settled along the rocky shoreline above the ocean. As the unlikely couple enjoyed their meal, they found the locals willing to join in their conversation, and the mention of Saschel Cameron turned out to be a gold mine.

Saschel still lived in Duncreag, in a small bothy on a ridge overlooking the sea. The residents called her "the crazy Cameron woman". Selling herbs and oils to the desperate, she'd turned witch, if the stories were to be believed. Though no one knew the whereabouts of Deidra and Tomas, Margaret was confident that Isaboe's sister would have more information.

By early the next morning, the two riders were heading back to Stromness armed with good news for Isaboe, and for the purpose of her expedition to Orkney. The return trip was less windy, and the riders' pace more relaxed. Acquiring the information on Saschel had brightened Margaret's mood, and she found herself more inclined to tolerate her traveling companion this morning. In fact, now that she had him alone…"So, William, I've been trying to figure out Connor. What was he like before this whole bloody mess? What makes him so angry? He's like a covered kettle of hot water, and if you stoke the flame too high, the lid's gonna blow."

Will snickered at her analogy, but nodded in agreement. "I canna tell ye how many times Mac and I thought we'd seen our last days," he offered eagerly. "Fighting side-by-side, and back-ta-back, there was more than one occasion I felt the hand o' death brush by. I ken for certain that if Mac hadn't been there for me, I wouldna be alive today." Will paused as a far-away look crossed his round, bearded face. "Braden MacPherson, or as our clan called him, 'Mac-the-Fierce'…"

Margaret snorted.

"We fought some nasty battles. The idiot was our *de facto* leader, and I cannae remember a fight where he didna lead the screaming; "*Freedom for Scotland!*" Bastard would've died for Prince Charles. Actually, I thought he had until the day the two of ye walked into my establishment."

"I s'pose that's what makes for a good soldier, putting someone else's worth above your own life," Margaret said casually as she adjusted to her horse's gait. "Sometimes I think Connor feels like he's still fighting. He never left the war behind, especially since you didn't win."

"Thanks for reminding me," Will said, shooting Margaret a glare under his bushy brow. "It's hard to say with Mac. He was never an easy man to read. He's got no love for the Brits, that's for sure. And not just because *we lost the war*," he said with more emphasis than necessary. "Mac lost everything: his family, his home, his whole damn life to those bastards. When he was still a boy, the British Empire was buyin' up all the farmland in the lower Highlands for pennies, pushing out the clans and tenants who had lived there for generations. But old man MacPherson refused to sell, and the fuckers burned down the house with him inside. Mac never got over that. Cannae blame him for hatin' the Brits, aye? I believe that anger ye see is called unfulfilled revenge."

Margaret silently nodded. "So, what about you? What punishment did you endure to rejoin the *respectable* society?" she asked with genuine interest.

"I did my time as an indentured servant in America for seven years, working hard, laborious hours in the sun on a rice plantation in Carolina. It wasn't all bad. I met my wife Lora there. She worked as a maid in the owner's house. When I finally paid my debt to the King of England, and was allowed to come back home, I brought Lora with me."

"What happened to Lora?"

"She died 'bout five years ago. Doctor said it was tuberculosis."

"I'm sorry."

Will only nodded, and they rode in silence for a while before he addressed Margaret again. "The thing I cannae figure out is why Mac hasn't aged. I ken he'll tell me when he's ready, and it's got be one hell of a story, but..."

"What!" Margaret's outburst cut Will off from finishing his statement, and she pulled her horse to an abrupt halt. "Are you telling me that Connor hasn't told you? And you've committed to helping him when you have no idea what you're getting your arse into?"

Will turned on his horse and looked at her. "Well, that's what friends do, right Margaret?"

A slow smile split her face. "Yes, William, that is exactly what friends do." They shared a silent moment before she caught herself smiling at him. Noticing an internal shift, she suddenly had a different opinion of her riding companion, but she quickly brushed it aside and heeled her horse into movement. "Well, Mr. Buchanan, let me bring you up to speed. You've gotten yourself mixed up in a strange story. It's a sad one, as unbelievable to hear as it is to tell, but I swear by all that's holy, it's the truth." While the two riders continued toward Stromness, Margaret filled Will in on all the missing pieces.

The last remnants of daylight had dissipated from the horizon by the time they stabled their horses, and to Margaret's quiet surprise, the return ride had been a pleasant one. In taking Connor's advice and letting her guard down, she discovered that William Buchanan really did make for good company.

After returning to her own room, Isaboe lit all the wall sconces and the lamp beside her bed in an attempt to read. But after reading the same paragraph four times and not comprehending a single line, she gave up. Her concentration was shot and it was all Connor's fault. She could still smell his scent in her hair, and it conjured up all the images and sensations of their lovemaking, making it difficult to concentrate on much of anything else.

That changed though when Margaret briskly entered the room. Her cheeks still rosy from the cold, she was bubbling with information as she scurried about the room putting her belongings away. Still sitting on the bed under the covers, Isaboe hung on every word while Margaret related all they had discovered in Duncreag.

"And since it appears you've recovered quite remarkably, I don't see why we can't all go back just as soon as possible. I really can't get over how good you look!" she said with a bright smile as she began unlacing her riding boots. "It looks like Connor took good care of you while I was gone."

"Oh, yes. He made sure I ate well and had plenty of bed rest." Isaboe was glad Margaret wasn't looking directly at her. She was afraid that her face would give her away.

There was a knock on the door, and Isaboe heard Connor's voice before he entered. She was pleased to see that he was dressed, but the sight of him instantly made her heartbeat quicken. The thought of what they had been doing together in the other room just hours before caused her skin to tingle.

"Welcome back, Margaret. Will just stopped by and shared the news. Sounds like ye were quite successful in Duncreag." Connor shot Isaboe a wink and a quick smile, but she had difficulty just looking at him. She tried to cover the flush she felt on her face while Margaret repeated her story.

"But enough of that for now. We rode all afternoon and I'm famished! Do you think I can still get something to eat at this hour?"

"There's plenty of food in Connor's room." But the moment the words left Isaboe's mouth, she instantly regretted it. Connor shot her a questioning look as Margaret silently regarded them both. Glancing around the room, Isaboe tried to avoid Margaret's shrewd glare, but she could feel her friend's eyes on her.

"Oh, bite the dog!" Margaret finally snorted. "I expected this would happen soon enough, but you two sure didn't waste any time."

Isaboe tried to keep her face stoic, but Connor didn't bother to hide his pride. With his arms crossed, he leaned against the wall and smiled. Shaking her finger, Margaret walked over to him, her face reprimanding. "I told you she needed rest!"

"Hey, she started it," Connor said defensively.

"Connor!" Isaboe hadn't expected him to say that.

Margaret just shook her head before turning around to face Isaboe. "Well, you look better than when I left, so I guess a good roll in the hay will cure what ails ye, aye?"

"Margaret!" Shocked by her friend's quip, Isaboe felt a bit insulted that their private moment had just been exposed in a way that seemed not unlike a back-alley romp.

"I knew there was a reason I love ye, Margaret!" Connor added with a grin.

Of course, Connor doesn't mind, Isaboe thought, as she tried to recover her dignity. But the happiness she saw in his eyes melted away her annoyance, replaced with a warm feeling of love.

Walking toward the door, Margaret just shook her head. "Well the two of you may be satisfied, but I'm starvin'. I'm gonna see what's left in Connor's room."

Fumbling with the blankets, Isaboe jumped off the bed, blocking Margaret's exit. "Wait! I don't think that's a good idea."

"It's that bad?"

Connor stepped around the women. "I'll go get ye some food,

Margaret. She's right—ye really dinnae wanna go in there right now. There's a little bit of me and little bit of her all over that room." Looking like a strutting peacock, much too pleased with himself, he walked out leaving Isaboe feeling slightly embarrassed and definitely overexposed.

chapter 24

saschel

The following morning before sunrise, everyone was preparing for their travel to Duncreag. In order to keep Isaboe safely inside for as long as possible, they settled for leftover tattie scones and some dried pork strips for breakfast, along with their tea. While Margaret and Isaboe finished packing, Connor and Will took one more walk through town and along the shoreline.

Fog hovered over the dock as the sound of sailors prepping for their day at sea echoed against the stone buildings. The men had decided to set a course north that would have them riding out of Stromness during the early morning quiet, and hopefully without drawing attention. Relieved to find no new reward posters along the pier or on the streets, they briskly made their way back toward the hotel, their breath ghosting before them in the chilly winter air.

"Margaret told me yer story, Mac. I hope ye're alright with that."

Connor stopped in mid-stride. After a moment he stepped forward with a quirky smile and placed a hand on his friend's wide shoulder. "Well, since ye're still here, aye, I'm fine with that!" Margaret had accomplished what he hadn't been able to, and Connor now felt the weight of that obligation slide off his back. It had always been his intention to tell Will, but he hadn't known how to start the conversation. He also knew that he owed William Buchanan more than he could ever repay. As they made their way through the wet, empty streets, the unspoken trust they shared eased Connor's worried mind.

"It's rather a peculiar story," Will said, breaking the silence. "But it does explain why ye haven't aged."

"It's still hard for me to believe. I'm just glad I didna have tell ye myself. I was sure if I did, ye'd think I'd lost my bloody mind!"

"That's still open for debate," Will mumbled through his beard.

Chuckling, Connor nodded. "Well, I've had days that ye'd get no argument from me on that matter."

"What's this other world like?"

Connor felt the smile leave his face. Now that his friend knew his story, he wondered how much he wanted to reveal. But it seemed as if a door had been pushed open, and Connor was sharing before he realized. "Will, I saw things I cannae explain, things that weren't really there. But at the time they all seemed real, just as real as you are, just as real as this building," he said, nodding at the stone storefront they were passing. "The realm of the fey is a mysterious place, that's for sure, and the fey, well, the ones I do recall were extremely beautiful." He paused, thinking of his encounter with the dark muse, Lilabeth, "and deviously treacherous," he added darkly.

Connor suddenly wondered if he may have said too much when Will didn't respond, and the space between them felt noticeably awkward. The men continued walking in silence while scanning the side streets as they made their way back to the hotel.

But then Will finally broke the awkward quiet. "So, ye met Isaboe in this other world, and the child is yers. Do I have that right?"

"Aye, that's the short story."

"Hmm," Will murrmered, as if he were pondering this new information.

Hoping that would be the end of this topic, Connor focused on the streets, keeping a lookout for any Redcoats, but very few people, other than themselves, were out walking in the cold, early morning mist.

"Well, at least now I understand why ye traveled clear across the country," Will said casually, without glancing at Connor or breaking his stride. "And I'm glad to hear it wasn't just to get laid."

Chuckling, a smile broke across Connor's face. "Well, friend, there are some things in life worth dying for, aye? If I died today, I'd die a very happy man."

"Aye, I can see that."

After slipping quietly out of town, the four riders were in Duncreag by nightfall. Will and Margaret had made arrangements with their host from the first trip, which allowed the women to share a small cottage behind their home. No other accommodations were available, so Will and Connor had to make the most of the shelter and warmth offered by the hay bales in the barn that sat behind the cottage.

The tiny community of Duncreag sat atop the beautiful and rocky North Atlantic coastline. The scenic beauty of the land, the sea crashing against the rocks, and the thousand-mile view were spectacular, but the constant trade winds that rushed over the ridge were brutal.

Early the following morning, the small band of riders sat perched on their horses outside the rundown and unkept bothy they'd been told was Saschel's. As Isaboe looked at the stone building, trepidation bubbled in her stomach while the wind whipped at her cloak. Though this was what she had come for, she now fought the urge to turn and run. Saschel had never been kind to her; none of her sisters had. Why would it be any different after all these years? What if Saschel didn't believe her story? What if she didn't have the documents, or have any idea of what had become of Anna and Benjamin?

There was only one way to find out. When Isaboe dismounted, the others did as well. While the men hung back with the horses, the two women started walking up the path to the door of Saschel's home. The rock garden that surrounded the bothy was filled with overgrown herbs that looked neglected and leggy.

"What do you want?" The sound of an old woman's voice stopped Isaboe and Margaret in their tracks. The door of the bothy was open just wide enough to reveal a shadowed face.

"Saschel? Are you Saschel Cameron?" Isaboe asked tentatively.

"Aye, what do you want? Herbs or oils?" The door opened a bit wider to expose a woman with gray hair and an aged face. She was wrapped in a faded, torn sweater and a dark muslin skirt. Isaboe was barely able to see her sister in the old hag.

"I didn't come to buy herbs or oils. I came for information."

"I don't give out free advice. Buy something or leave!"

Saschel started to shut the door, but Isaboe stepped forward, stopping it from closing. "Please, Saschel, wait!" she blurted. "I came here looking for information on Isaboe McKinnon's children, to see if you knew what became of them."

Saschel stood in the door frame, her face still cast in shadow. Though Isaboe couldn't see them, she could feel the woman's eyes on her, sharp and searching. "Who are you, and why do you want to know?" she finally asked.

"My name is Kaitlyn. My mother was Isaboe McKinnon." Isaboe had already decided to use the same lie she had told the sisters back in Edinburgh. It hadn't felt right then, lying to Sister Miriam, and it felt just as wrong now. But she had come too far, gone through too much not to have her answers.

There was a long pause before Saschel responded. "Isaboe only had two children, and you're not one of 'em."

"She kept me a secret. I was born out of wedlock, before Isaboe married...Nathan." With a burst of guilty horror, Isaboe realized she had been so caught up in her relationship with Connor that Nathan had become a distant memory. After swallowing back her shame, she pressed on.

"Why do you want to find 'em?" The door eased open slightly.

"Because, they are my...brother and sister, we share the same mother. That makes them family. Do you have any information about what happened to them, to whom they were fostered? Can you help me at all?" Isaboe knew she sounded desperate, and she was.

A few uncomfortable moments passed before Saschel pulled the door fully open and stepped out. "If what you say is true, then that makes me your auntie." Saschel looked at Margaret, then to the men standing by the horses. "Would you and your friends like to come in?" Though her expression hadn't changed, Saschel's demeanor had lightened considerably, and Isaboe felt the tension she'd been holding in her shoulders begin to release. When she looked back at Connor and Will, they silently shook their heads. They would wait.

Inside the dreary darkness of the bothy, Isaboe and Margaret were instantly overwhelmed by the rich, poignant scent of herbs, as bundles of dried branches hung from the beams of the small home. Shelves filled with apothecary bottles lined the walls, and a large table was covered with books, tools, and bottles. Toward the back of the building were heaps of cloth bags and stacks of wooden boxes, some of which appeared to be filled with dried foliage. Intertwined among the clutter and collection of dead plants, haphazardly layered old newspapers and empty, dirty bottles finished off what looked like years of hoarding.

The sitting area Saschel offered consisted of one chair, a small table, and a wood bench covered with bundles of plant matter and various clutter, including an orange tabby-cat curled up on a dirty pillow. With one eye open, the cat scanned the newcomers, watching the women's every move and flicking its tail in warning. When Saschel gathered the clutter off the bench, the cat hissed and fled the room, startling both of her guests.

"Sorry 'bout Murphy. He don't like people much," she said, picking up the dirty cat-pillow and tossing it aside." Here, sit and I'll get us some tea."

Isaboe glanced at Margaret before hesitantly taking a seat on the now vacant bench, and they watched as Saschel scurried about what was assumed to be the kitchen, pulling three cups from a cupboard. After arranging them on a tray, she retrieved the teapot from the wood stove. Setting the tray down on the small table in front of them, she moved a bundle of dried plants off her chair and took a seat before pouring the tea.

"So, tell me, what exactly is it you're looking for, uh…Kaitlyn, right?" Saschel asked as she offered her guests a cup.

"Yes, thank you." Though initially reluctant, Isaboe smiled graciously as she took the teacup, but Margaret passed on the offer. "Well, as I said, I'm trying to find any information on how to locate Isaboe's other children, Benjamin and Anna. Sister Miriam at the Greyfriar's Kirk told me that you and Diedra had moved here to Orkney, and that you took a box of legal papers after Marta…your mother…had passed away. I was hoping there might be something in that box that could help."

"You met with Sister Miriam?" Saschel asked with a questioning stare, silently scrutinizing Isaboe. "My, you have done your research, haven't you?"

Though Isaboe didn't care for the accusatory tone in her sister's question, she let it slide. "I'm sorry to have intruded, Aunt Saschel, and my existence must be a surprise for you, but, please, do you know where this box is?"

After another moment, Saschel's face finally softened. "Aye, I do. I actually think I have it here somewhere." She turned and looked toward the towering wall of clutter that filled the back of her home.

"Do you think you can find it?" Isaboe asked apprehensively as she glanced in the same direction.

"Of course I can. It just may take me a while," Saschel said, offering the first smile Isaboe and Margaret had seen since entering the home. "Why don't you come back tomorrow and I'll see if I can find it for you by then."

"That would be wonderful!" Isaboe said with a grateful smile as she and Margaret stood. "Thank you for the tea; it had an interesting flavor."

"That would be the Yarrow mint, one of my favorites. I'll get started on searching for that box right away," Saschel said, following the two women out the door. Just before Isaboe stepped off the porch, Saschel placed a hand on her shoulder. "Kaitlyn, wait. I have something that belonged to your mother I think you would like to see. Come back in for just a moment, will you?"

"Go ahead. I'll wait with the men," Margaret said, stepping off the stoop.

No sooner had Isaboe stepped back into her sister's home than Saschel closed the door and turned on her. "Do you think you're really fooling anyone, *Isaboe?*" she said as she leaned in, her eyes wide and accusing.

"I...I don't know what you mean." Isaboe took a couple steps back. "My name is Kaitlyn. Isaboe was my mother." Though she tried to sound convincing, Saschel's statement had come totally unexpected, catching her off guard.

"You forget, Isaboe; I lived with you for twelve years. You may be a little older than I last saw you, but a sister knows her sister," Saschel hissed in a whisper as she stood uncomfortably close, staring at Isaboe with aged, hazel-colored eyes searching for the truth.

"But...but how? How could you possibly know?" Isaboe finally conceded.

"I knew it the minute you mentioned your name!" Saschel seemed so pleased at her discovery that she did a little jig before grabbing both of Isaboe's hands, looking at her with wide eyes and a big smile that was missing a few teeth. "I've got my sister back!" she sang, and gave her a hug so tight that Isaboe had difficulty breathing. Finally releasing her and stepping back, Saschel held Isaboe at arm's length and looked down at her sister's protruding middle.

"Isaboe, you're with child!" she announced.

Isaboe didn't even acknowledge her sister's statement. "But how... how do you know?" she asked, bewildered that Saschel had seen through her façade.

"Because, your belly is bulging!"

"No, no, I mean, how did you know it was me?"

"After mother came back with your children, she told us that you'd mysteriously disappeared, not a trace to be found with no clue as to what happened to you."

"You saw Benjamin and Anna? How were they?" As painful as it would be to hear, Isaboe wanted to know everything.

"Oh, Isaboe, it wasn't good. The boy was so withdrawn he wouldn't talk to anyone. And the little girl, she just cried for you all the time. It was so sad."

Fighting back her tears, Isaboe slumped down onto the wood bench.

"We didn't keep them long. Mother sent them away a few weeks later." Saschel sat next to Isaboe, taking her sister's hands. "Oh, Isaboe, I'm so sorry that Mother was so cruel to you. You didn't deserve it!" As she spoke, her face twisted into something that Isaboe thought looked like regret. "I'm sorry we were all cruel to you. You were the interloper; the pretty, glamorous, adopted sister, and it was so easy to blame you for everything that went wrong in the house. It didn't help that Mother always suspected that Father had an affair and you were the result. Can you ever forgive me?"

"It doesn't matter anymore, Saschel. I'm just glad to have found you." Isaboe wasn't completely sure about her sister's sincerity, but right now that was unimportant. "But you still haven't told me how you knew."

"When mother told me about your strange disappearance I decided to do my own investigation. Do you know what the name Faireshire means? It means *Land of the Fairies*." Saschel's voice sounded eerie, and it matched the look in her eyes. "Its whole history is full of disappearances and madness. The story was that people would disappear for years, and then suddenly reappear as if no time had passed. When I first heard you use the name Isaboe, I knew right away it was you. That's what happened to you, isn't it? You were taken by the fey folk, and now you've returned."

Isaboe only nodded. There seemed no reason to elaborate further. Saschel had apparently figured it out.

"That's what I had always believed happened to you, and now I have my sister back!" Saschel hugged her again. "I'll help you any way I can, Isaboe. I'll find that box, and then we'll find out what happened to your children."

"Oh, thank you, Saschel. You have no idea what that means to me." Isaboe hugged her sister with renewed hope.

"Your friends, do they know what happened to you?"

"Yes, they all know. They're helping me to find Benjamin and Anna. I could've never made it this far without them."

"Well, then you are very fortunate to have friends like that." The two women shared a moment before Isaboe stood up and headed for the door.

"I'll come back tomorrow then, yes?"

"Aye. I'm sure to have found it by this time tomorrow. I've been meaning to clean up this mess anyway, so, now I have a good reason." When Saschel opened the door, she was startled to see a man standing on her stoop. Catching the anxious look on her sister's face, Isaboe glanced at Connor's stern expression and quickly stepped in between them. "Connor, this is my sister, Saschel," she said lively.

He nodded, but his expression didn't change.

Full of excitement, Isaboe chatted nonstop as they rode back to the cottage. "Connor, don't you think this is good news?" Connor had been a silent observer to her enthusiasm, which wasn't unusual, but when the riders dismounted the look on his face completely squelched Isaboe's excitement.

"No, actually I think it's a little too convenient," he finally answered.

"What do you mean?" she asked as they walked their horses back to the barn.

"Think about it, Isaboe. She just happens to have the box of documents, figured out who ye are in only a few moments, and is more than willing to help ye in any way she can. Dinnae ye find that just *too easy*?" There was something haunting in his eyes, a memory of fear that left her nervous.

"Maybe you're being a bit too skeptical, Connor. You haven't even given her a chance to prove herself. After everything we've been through, perhaps it's time for something to be in our favor. I'm not saying that I don't have my doubts, and I'm not sure I completely believe her sincerity, but if she has that box of documents, I have to know."

"From the way the two of ye described the inside of her home, what makes ye think she can even find it? Something dinnae feel right."

"Well, I guess I'll find out when I go back tomorrow."

"When *we* go back," he corrected her.

"Perhaps you're taking this protector role a bit far, Connor. I don't need you to constantly stand watch over me."

He stopped and turned to face her. "Then take Margaret with ye. We really dinnae ken this woman, and I dinnae want ye in that house alone with her again." Isaboe started to protest, but he cut her off. "Isaboe, just say ye understand. I dinnae want ye to be alone with her." His gaze seemed to look right through her skin, and into her thoughts.

Isaboe sighed in resignation. "Alright, I won't." For the first time, she wasn't sure whether or not she had just lied to Connor.

Confident that he had made his point clear, Connor wrapped his arm around her waist and drew her into him, and he began to seductively trace the outline of her jaw with a smooth touch. "So, what do ye think we should do for the rest of the day?" The gleam in his eye and the grin on his face suggested none-too-subtly what Connor wanted to do.

"Well, I don't know about you, but Margaret and I are washing clothes today." Raising her chin, she turned her eyes up to his with a playful smile on her lips. "Why, did you have something else in mind?" She teased him with a matching grin.

"Aye. How long will the washin' take?"

"Most likely all afternoon."

"But ye'll be free later, aye?" he asked, sheepishly smiling down at her and running a hand through her hair.

"Sorry, Connor, not today." Isaboe gave him a quick kiss and drew out of his arms, turning back toward the cottage. "But do let me know if you need anything washed," she said over her shoulder, chuckling at the disappointment she saw in his face.

She loved Connor, but sometimes it was necessary to draw a proverbial line in the sand.

Chapter 25

Don't Poke the Bear

Isaboe's dreams of Euphoria started again that night, the same day she had been reunited with her sister.

In the dark twilight hours of early morning, and after a night of broken sleep, Isaboe laid in bed only half awake as the remnants of the dream played behind her closed eyes...

Euphoria was vivid in all of its splendor, and through a wispy fog she recognized the familiar tree-lined path. There was a tingle in the air, an energy that she only felt in her dreams. A multitude of familiar scenes flashed by quickly, but there was something different about this visit; a certain presence that had been there before was now missing. As Isaboe looked into a world she had once known, but was never really a part of, confusion and doubt swirled around in her mind.

She remembered the warm glow and heat of the bonfire—the beautiful fey dancers in their silken dresses spinning around the flames—the faint music that was no more than a whisper on the wind before it disappeared.

Suddenly she was standing in a dark room. The cavernous area smelt of rosemary, and she had the strange sensation she was not alone. Before Isaboe could investigate, the earth began to tilt and sway. Desperately grasping for something to cling to, but finding nothing, she felt the ground beneath her feet turning to sand. She watched in horror as her feet and ankles, then her calves, disappeared into the floor. Though she struggled and fought, every twisting motion only took her deeper. First her hips and waist were gone, but then the sand was lapping at her chest, pushing so hard she felt that her bones would give way. Rough sand found its way into her mouth and down her throat, choking her. She couldn't breathe! She couldn't breathe!

A bright flash of light momentarily blinded her, but in the next instant, a man's face appeared in the darkness. He was familiar, but his features were blurred. Continuing to struggle for breath, she frantically reached for the stranger. Just before slipping into the earth, Isaboe saw a hand extended toward her and made one last attempt to grab on. But she missed and was pulled under, swirling and sinking into the abyss.

Connor had just finished preparing the horses for Isaboe and Margaret when the two ladies walked into the stable, cloaked and ready to ride.

"Ye have one hour," Connor said as he helped Isaboe mount her horse. "If ye're not back, I'm coming after ye. I dinnae trust that woman, and one hour should be plenty of time to find what ye're lookin' for. One hour, Isaboe, agreed?"

Isaboe looked down at her protector whose hand was resting on her knee. An image from her dream flashed across her mind, and she took a moment to really look at him. She hadn't mentioned the dream to either Margaret or Connor, having convinced herself that it was probably nothing. "Yes alright. One hour. If she's discovered what I'm looking for, that should be plenty of time," she replied with a ring of confidence in her voice, hoping to pacify Connor's concern.

When they arrived at Saschel's home, the door was open. Margaret and Isaboe walked in to discover the strange woman standing in the middle of chaos. She had pulled nearly everything away from the back wall, and the contents lay strewn about the small interior. Piles of books, boxes, dirty bottles of oil, and bags filled with various strange objects surrounded Saschel as she pushed and kicked her way toward the door.

"Come in, come in! I've been hard at it since you left yesterday."

The bothy had been tightly packed before, but with the additional clutter, it was almost impossible to move about the room. Momentarily taken aback, Isaboe surveyed the mess. "We can see that. Any luck finding the documents?" She knew the answer, but still had to ask.

"No, but I haven't gotten though all of this side yet. It might take a while. Can I offer you ladies a cup of tea?"

Margaret and Isaboe looked at each other, realizing that this would not be a quick visit after all.

"Yes, I'll take some, but only if we can help," Isaboe replied. "What boxes haven't you gone through yet?"

Before long, Isaboe and Margaret were rummaging through old boxes and bags alongside Saschel, with an occasional squeal when a mouse scampered out. But other than some old newspaper articles from The Edinburgh Daily News, they found nothing of significance. Saschel would occasionally find something from her childhood that she had long forgotten, and she succeeded more than once in bringing Isaboe into moments of reminiscence.

Isaboe glanced over at Margaret, who had been quietly watching while the two sisters exchanged childhood stories. Knowing that Margaret probably felt like an outsider, Isaboe tried not to ignore her as Saschel chatted on. And Isaboe couldn't deny that she enjoyed soaking up the long-forgotten tales, some funny, some sad, but they were the stories of her life. It had been so long since she had been confident of her place, it was so tempting, so *comfortable*, to lose herself to nostalgia. Almost without realizing it, Isaboe let her guard down with this woman who had never been kind to her as a child, and she began to see her sister in a new light.

When a new question wormed its way into her mind, it was on her lips before she realized its emotional impact. "Saschel, what happened between you and Deidra?"

Saschel fell quiet, dropping her gaze for a moment before she looked back at Isaboe. "I was living with Tomas and Deidra, working in their bait store in Stromness. One day some money came up missing, and Deidra accused me. But I didn't do it, Isaboe, I swear! When I tried to defend myself, Deidra didn't believe me, and we got into a terrible fight. It was a few weeks later that Tomas and Deidra closed up shop and moved to Kirkwall. They left me unemployed and homeless with nothing. I had nowhere to go and no money. I sold most of the belongings they left behind, and with the little money I made, I moved here. That was years ago, and I haven't seen or heard from Deidra since."

Saschel seemed genuinely hurt, and Isaboe felt a twinge of empathy for her sister. Life had not been easy for either of them. It had just handed each of them a different basket of problems, but the end results were the same—pain, anger, and disappointment.

"Look at this," Margaret said, interrupting Isaboe's thoughts. "Henri and Marta Cameron's Personal and Business Financial Records," she said, reading the stamped gold lettering on the front of a stylish, wooden box.

"What all is in there?" Isaboe asked as she leaned forward.

Margaret lifted out a leather book and opened it. "I'm not sure, but it looks like some bank records."

"Wouldn't their financial records be with all of their other important papers? There must be something else in that box."

"I don't know, Isaboe, but we've been here almost an hour and really need to get back."

"But this box may have what I'm looking for!" Isaboe grabbed the edge of the wooden crate and pulled it toward her. "We're close to finding the rest of my parent's legal documents, I know it. The fostering papers must be in here. I just want to stay a bit longer."

"I don't think that's a good idea, Isaboe. You heard Connor."

"Well, you can go back and let Connor know everything is fine," she replied, but Isaboe could tell by the look on her friend's face that her suggestion was not well received. "Margaret, please. I'll be fine, and I won't be long, I promise."

Though she looked uncertain, Margaret finally conceded. "I can probably buy you ten minutes, but no more," she said firmly, then stood and headed toward the door, stepping over piles of clutter.

"Thank you, Margaret. I'll be right behind you."

As soon as he saw Margaret ride in without Isaboe, Connor mounted his horse, which he already had saddled. "Where's Isaboe?" he barked.

"It's alright, Connor, she's fine. They just found a box with some papers that..."

"I didna want Isaboe left alone with that woman!" he shouted, spurring his horse into a quick sprint out of the barn.

When Connor threw the door open, Isaboe and Saschel were both jolted, and the rush of the accompanying wind sent papers swirling around them. The angry Scotsman took two long, high steps over the rubble to get to them. "Isaboe, get up off the floor!" he growled, looming over them both.

"Connor, what are you…?" but before Isaboe could finish, he grabbed her by her hands and pulled her to her feet. In one fluid movement, he lifted her into his arms and plowed his way back out the door.

"Connor, put me down! What the hell are you doing?! Put me down!" Her screams fell on deaf ears as he carried her out to her horse, where he finally returned her to her feet. "Just what the hell do you think you're doing?" she spat with a lethal snarl.

"Get on your horse, Isaboe." Connor's voice was deadly calm. He looked back at the house to see Saschel standing in the shadow of the doorway, watching.

"What is wrong with you?" Isaboe shouted. "You can't just barge into someone's home like a crazed bear!"

"I said one hour or I'd come and get ye. What part of that did ye not understand? Now get on yer horse, Isaboe, or I'll put ye on it myself."

"Connor, you are being rude, ridiculous, and… *overbearing*!"

"This is yer last chance to get on that horse of yer own accord." As Connor locked gazes with her, Isaboe knew he was serious, and as much as it annoyed her, she had been swept up enough times to know that he would do it again if he chose. He had just done so.

Giving him an angry scowl, Isaboe turned and mounted her horse. Kicking it into motion harder than necessary, she bolted off down the road. Connor jumped on his horse and followed, trying to keep up with the flapping of her auburn hair.

Feeling the fury resonating off her face, she jumped down from her horse when they finally reached the barn. Storming off toward the cottage, Isaboe completely ignored Margaret and Will, only wanting to put space between herself and Connor as quickly as possible.

But Connor dismounted and stomped up behind her before she got very far. "Isaboe!" he shouted. "I told ye I didna want ye to be alone with that woman! I gave ye an order and ye disobeyed me!"

"What?" Coming to an abrupt halt and spinning around, Isaboe shot Connor a furious look. "You may be used to giving other people orders, but you don't *order* me!" she screamed.

"Oh, aye, I do! And ye'll do what I tell ye! I'll do whatever is necessary to protect ye from yer *damn, stubborn* self!" Connor shouted back.

"Protect me from *myself*? You don't get to tell me what to do!" Turning her back to him, she willed the tears from falling, though she could feel them stinging her eyes and burning her nose. *How dare he?* Connor was being completely irrational, overbearing, and overprotective, and she wouldn't be spoken to in such a manner.

Running a hand through his hair, Connor let out a deep, frustrated sigh. He walked up behind her to try again, but this time his approach was gentler. "Isaboe, when I walked into that house and saw ye sitting in the middle of all that shit, I lost it. What were ye thinking?"

She spun around to face him. "Connor, we were close to finding something before you barged in like a raging bull! You know that I'm trying to find those fostering documents."

"And ye think she has 'em?"

"Yes! She just hasn't found them yet."

Crossing his arms, Connor stared down at her. "I dinnae believe it, and I dinnae trust her. Something about her makes the hair on the back o' my neck rise, and ye're not to go over there again without me. Do I make myself clear?" Connor forcefully enunciated each word as he sternly held her gaze.

"Why don't you trust her? She's my sister—my family, and she's only trying to help me."

Connor looked like he'd been stung. "No, Isaboe, I'm yer family!" he proclaimed, tapping his chest, "Margaret's yer family! Ye haven't seen this woman in over thirty years! Ye ken nothing about her, yet ye're willin' to believe anything she tells ye!"

Unfortunately, Connor's tone was as fierce as his look, and Isaboe couldn't hold her tears back any longer. "I have to know, Connor. I have to find out," she said as the tears spilled over. "If she has those papers, I have to know. You must understand that!"

Connor's expression softened and he wrapped his arms around her, pulling her into his embrace while she cried, though her posture remained rigid. "I'm just afraid of losing ye again, *Breagha*. It'd kill me if I lost ye again."

As Connor whispered into her hair, Isaboe finally gave in, wrapping her arms around his waist. "That doesn't mean you can stop me from finding my children, or seeing Saschel again." She'd leaned her head against his chest, opting not to look at him as she made her bold statement.

Swallowing hard, Connor leaned back. Lifting her face with a gentle touch under her chin, he wiped a tear from her cheek. "Going off to search for yer children is what separated us last time, Isaboe. There must be other ways to find 'em, other than trusting that woman."

"Not that I know of, and I don't know where else to look. This is the only lead I have."

Connor hesitated, his eyes searching hers until he finally seemed to deflate. "She has one more day. After that we're on our way to Kirkwall. And yer not to be alone with her, agreed?"

Isaboe looked up at him, and did her best to maintain what control she had of the situation. "Agreed."

Seeming satisfied with her answer, Connor's stern demeanor eased, and she felt him loosen his grip as Isaboe let her head rest against his chest again. The fight was over, at least for the moment.

Sitting quietly in the barn, Will and Margaret had been silent spectators to the scene, completely invisible to the two performers who were now wrapped up in each other, oblivious to the world.

"I havta give the girl credit. She's a fiery lass to be able to stand her ground in front o' Mac. I've seen men twice her size shrink in front o' that man."

"Well, William, if you hang around long enough you'll soon discover that nothing is predictable and everything is passionate when it comes to those two. If you're not careful, you'll get caught up in their wake."

"Too late, Margaret; I already have," he said with a soft chuckle.

CHAPTER 26

DREAMS, NIGHTMARES, AND FEY ILLUSIONS

For the second night in a row Isaboe dreamed.

The forest.

The sand.

Drowning.

But tonight the figure that reached for her was more visible, and she felt a strong sense of familiarity, even after the dream faded.

Bolting upright in bed, Isaboe began taking deep breaths to calm her racing heart as she looked over at Margaret still sleeping soundly. It was hours before dawn, and she desperately wanted to fall back to sleep, though the remnants of her dream had left her feeling anxious and doubting. But before she could lie back down, the baby shifted, pressing on her bladder. Climbing quietly out of bed, Isaboe found her shoes and grabbed a wool throw to wrap around her shoulders before making her way outside to the privy.

Moonlight covered the Earth in nocturnal brightness, lighting up the barn where the men were bunked. She stared at the structure for a moment and thought about her fight with Connor as her breath ghosted before her in the cold, winter air. He had tried to make up for being such a jackass, and a slight smile crossed her lips at the thought of how affectionate and attentive he had been for the rest of the day.

All the same, Isaboe didn't feel terribly inclined to forgive him, nor did she understand why he was so suspicious of Saschel. Her sister had been kind to her, to all of them, and it bothered her that Connor should call her actions into question. He had said something about the hair rising on the back of his neck when Saschel was around, but then Connor seemed to view the entire world with suspicion.

She'd always tried to have hope for the world. Or at least she used to. With all the horrors she had experienced since falling asleep in that forest, she had become much more guarded, less naïve. Knowing that her life and her view of the world would never be the same, she wondered if she had lost something of herself. She had to learn how to live in this new world that had been thrust upon her. But at what cost?

The baby pushed again, quickly reminding Isaboe why she was out in the cold at night in the first place. She turned and briskly walked around to the other side of the cottage to where the small outhouse was lit by the moon.

When she stepped back out of the privy, Isaboe could see the silhouette of a figure in the dark only steps from where she stood. Frozen by fear, she held her breathe.

"Isaboe, I have something to show you."

"Saschel?" Isaboe said, surprised and startled at the raspy sound of her sister's voice. "What are you doing here?"

"Shhh, come with me. There's something you havta see. Come over here, by the lamp. Look what I found, Sister."

The hair on Isaboe's arms stood on end and every nerve tingled. "Did you find the fostering papers?" If Saschel had indeed found the documents, she had to know. Her curiosity drove her forward, even as her instincts screamed out in warning. *Why would Saschel come in the middle of the night?* Isaboe's disconcerting thoughts mingled and fought with her need to know.

As she followed Saschel over to the buckboard, it occurred to Isaboe that she hadn't heard her sister's approach. There had been no sound of the horse's hooves on the road, or any creaking of wooden wheels, but here she was all the same. It was also odd that Connor, whose instincts were sharper than hers, obviously hadn't heard the arrival either.

Standing in front of the buckboard, Saschel held a piece of paper under the lantern that hung from a pole mounted next to the hand-rail. Her gray hair blew wildly in the wind, and an eerie light from the swinging lantern made her look almost ghostly. "Come look at this." She waved for Isaboe to come closer.

Slowly, and with apprehension, Isaboe stepped over to the buckboard and took the piece of paper from Saschel's hand. Holding it under the light, she saw a wanted poster with her face on it, similar to the one Connor had shown her.

"Where did you get this?" Fear that the British were already this far north set her heart racing.

"What do you know about this, Isaboe? Are you involved in the murder of this officer?" Saschel eyes were wide and wild as she stared at her sister.

"He attacked me. He was going to kill me, or worse! Connor protected me."

"I knew it! I knew he did it! He killed this officer, and now you're the one wanted by the British army. Did you know about these posters?"

"Yes, but, where did you get this?" Isaboe trembled as she held the poster, realizing that they would soon be on the run again.

"A fella who buys my oils gave it to me today. Said he found it posted along the docks at Stromness. Didn't you just come from there? How did you hide from the British?"

"I...I never came out of my room. I never made it into town. I was sick. I told you that."

"Oh, I see how it is," Saschel said eerily. "That fella gets away with murder, and you're the one wanted."

"Connor? No, you have him wrong. He did it to protect me."

"No, your man's letting *you* take the fall, and he'll soon run off and leave you on your own. Just wait and see. You can't trust him!" Saschel's words were full of threat and bile.

"That's not true," Isaboe said, suddenly feeling defensive. "Connor wouldn't do that. I do trust him." Isaboe started to back away. "I need to go back inside; Margaret's waiting for me."

But Saschel reached out and grabbed Isaboe's wrist. "No! She's in on it too! Don't go back in there. Come with me, hurry!" Saschel hissed as she began dragging Isaboe back toward the buckboard.

"No!" Isaboe slapped at her sister. "Get your hands off of me! Let me go!" But before she could pull free, Saschel threw a cloth over Isaboe's face, and a pungent smell hit her senses. Though she struggled to free herself from her sister's grip, Isaboe could feel herself losing the fight as she slipped into a dark, familiar void.

Connor sat up and quickly grabbed his pistol. He sat quietly in the dark trying to catch the sound that had woken him, but heard nothing abnormal. He got up and walked over to where Will was sleeping, kicking lightly at his foot. Will sat up instantly and picked up his own weapon. He followed Connor out of the barn until the two men stood in front of the cottage, looking out into the darkness.

"What're we looking for?" Will whispered, sounding tired but alert.

"I heard somethin'."

Moments later Margaret came around the corner of the small home, still in her nightclothes. Seeing the two men standing outside in the dark, she walked briskly in their direction. "What's going on? Where's Isaboe?"

"What do ye mean?" Connor turned on Margaret. "Are ye saying she's not in the cottage?"

"No. I woke up and she wasn't in bed. I thought she was out here with you!"

Connor grimaced as panic and realization swept over all of them. Isaboe was missing.

"Will, help me saddle the horses. Margaret, get the amulet!" Connor shouted as he raced back to the barn.

chapter 27

a date with destiny

A thump to the back of her head jolted Isaboe into full awareness, but it took a few moments for her to realize that the continuous beating and grating against her back was the rocky ground she was being dragged across. Struggling to free her arms, which were bound tightly against her sides, she discovered that she was wrapped in a blanket. In a burst of panic, Isaboe thrashed and tore at the cocoon that entrapped her. When it didn't give way, she screamed.

Her head hit the ground with a jolt as the dragging came to an abrupt halt. When the blanket was ripped back, she stared up into the face of a woman she'd never seen before.

"Hello, Isaboe," the stranger said in a haunting voice. A thick, black braid hung off the woman's shoulder as she leaned over Isaboe, sneering with a red-lipped grin and dark, menacing eyes. Reaching down, she grabbed Isaboe's arms and easily lifted her up to a standing position. "We finally meet, face-to-face," the woman said in a mocking tone as she released her grip and stepped back. She had to be fey. No mortal woman had the strength to push and pull a person about as she had just done. And no other creature could be so beautiful, yet so terrifying.

As she surveyed her surroundings, it took a moment for Isaboe to find her balance. The night sky felt heavy, and gave no hint of her location. The woman was dressed in a tight, black outfit that hugged her body from her shoulders all the way down her long, shapely legs. Her black eyes sparkled in the moonlight, and they held Isaboe in an icy stare.

"Who…who are you?" Isaboe could hear the fear in her breathy words as panic bubbled up in her gut.

"I'm known by many names. Some call me Lilabeth, but you can call me your deliverer, because that's why I'm here—to deliver you."

The sultry fey woman reached out to grab her arm, but Isaboe pulled away as she shot Lilabeth a deadly glare. "What did you do with Saschel?"

"You mean that pathetic old hag? You should know that your sister was preparing to turn you in for the reward. So much for family loyalty. Don't worry about her, my dear. It's your fate now that you should be most concerned with." Lilabeth's sneer turned deadly as she clamped onto Isaboe's arm and began pulling her up a small knoll. The long stride of the fey had Isaboe stumbling to get her feet under her as Lilabeth dragged her up the hill.

"Why are you doing this? What do you want?" Isaboe screamed, though deep inside, she knew.

Lightning shot across the horizon, and for a brief moment Isaboe saw the silhouettes of large stones standing in a circle at the top of the mound. The following rumble of thunder matched the panic that exploded in her chest as she realized that the circle of stones was her captor's destination. "NO!" she screamed, twisting and digging in her heels as she struggled to break free. But the determined fey had strength beyond her stature and seemed unaffected by Isaboe's resistance. Finding a brief moment of power, Isaboe jerked her arm free and stumbled backward before standing her ground. "I denounced Lorien! You can't do this to me!"

Lilabeth chuckled. "Do you honestly think a few words will stop her Majesty from getting what she wants?" Lilabeth took a quick step toward Isaboe, once again clamping onto her arm and pulling her close. With eyes that snapped with color and energy, she glared at her captive. "The queen will have her child, with or without your cooperation," the fey said coldly, before turning and continuing to pull Isaboe up the knoll.

"*It's not her child!*" Isaboe shouted as she fought against Lilabeth's grip. "It's mine, and I'll never let her take it from me!"

"That's where you're wrong, mortal." Lilabeth stopped her progression and turned back. "You are only a vessel with the right blood-line. The child *belongs* to Lorien. If you have to die for her to get it," the fey woman leaned in, "so be it."

With a quick yank, Lilabeth resumed dragging her captive up the side of the hill where Isaboe could see small dancing lights flickering and flashing between the stones. The air was alive with energy, and she recognized the familiar tingle of faerie magic. The place was completely charged with it.

"Stop! You can't do this! NO!" Isaboe let out one more scream before Lilabeth hauled her across the threshold. In a brilliant burst of light, she was forced into the circle, and the energy began dancing around her in a frenzy, as though trying to consume her. The light pulsed with power and pulled at her from somewhere...*else*. In a last-ditch attempt to save herself, Isaboe reached out for anything to hold onto. Grabbing at the edge of a rock, she struggled for a finger hold, but her strength was no match for the magical force. As she felt her grip slipping, panic and overwhelming terror pulsed through her blood, pounding in her chest.

Just when she thought she could no longer hold on, Isaboe felt a strong hand suddenly grasping her arm, and for a moment, the forces that pulled at her lost their momentum.

Connor fought against the unnatural elements that pulled at Isaboe as he struggled to keep his hold. With all his strength, he kept his grip on her, but could not free her from the incredible energy that threatened to engulf them both.

Frantically clinging to Connor, Isaboe screamed, but her scream was drowned out by the roaring winds and the deep rumble of thunder coming from the center of the stones. The creature holding Isaboe was engulfed in a field of moving, twisting light and pulsating energy, and Connor could make out only a ghostly image of a woman melded in the raging frenzy. When the creature threw back her head and opened her mouth, her voice resonated over the knoll: "I WILL HAVE THE CHILD!"

The tiny Underlings bit and scratched at Connor like fiery bees, trying to shake loose his grasp, but he blocked the pain and held Isaboe fast. In the midst of the chaos, he caught sight of Will struggling to enter the circle of stones from the opposite side.

Fighting against the energy that desperately tried to keep him out, Will held a sword, and with massive effort, he plowed forward toward the fey creature that had not yet seen him. Will felt the bites and scratches of the Underlings, but like Connor, he ignored them and pushed on toward his target.

"Isaboe, hold on!" Connor shouted, but her grip was weakening, and he could feel her slipping from his grasp. If he could just hold on a few more moments, he could save her. He had to. There were no other options.

Will continued fighting against the violent turmoil, and was only a few feet away when Isaboe's captor caught sight of him. Holding his sword in both hands, Will lunged at the evil apparition, and his weapon found its mark. When he thrust the metal blade, it slid through the center of her abdomen, and she exploded into an all-consuming, blinding ball of light. Instantly the air was filled with an unearthly, ear-piercing sound, like the cry of a thousand banshees.

In the next moment, all sound ceased and the air fell silent. When the intense light vanished, they were thrown into darkness. As Connor quickly pulled Isaboe back across the threshold of stones, her limp body dropped to the ground. Margaret, who had been held back by the ungodly power, rushed to where her friend lay unconscious in Connor's arms.

"Isaboe! ISABOE!" Connor shouted as he shook her, but there was no response, no sign of life or breath, no indication that her heart was still beating.

Dropping to her knees, Margaret held Isaboe's hands. "No, NO, NO! Open your eyes, Isaboe! NO, this can't happen!" Margaret shook Isaboe's shoulders, but she remained unresponsive. Tears flowed from Margaret's eyes as she looked up at Connor, and her face was twisted with the same disbelief and horror as his.

Connor's worst fear had come true; he couldn't save her. After everything he had done, after all she had endured, it didn't matter. Isaboe was dead.

Sobbing as he rocked back and forth, Connor clutched Isaboe's limp body to his chest. Whispering a mindless mantra of grief, he held onto the last bit of warmth in Isaboe's body as he begged silently to have her back. In his anguish, it felt as if his heart was being ripped from his body. Will knelt down and put his hand on his friend's shoulder, but there were no words. She was gone.

Dawn's light slowly began to overtake the darkness. In the midst of his pain, Connor couldn't comprehend how Isaboe could lay lifeless, yet the world continued on. The sun will rise and the sun will set, completely oblivious to the suffering of the human spirit. He let the tears run freely down his face as the reality of his loss enveloped him.

Suddenly, cutting through the morning mist, a distant voice floated up the knoll. "Am I too late?" a woman called out. "Please, oh please, don't let me be too late!"

Through his tear-blurred vision, Connor saw a woman running toward them. Just before she reached the top of the mound, he realized who she was. "Rosalyn?"

"Am I too late?" Rosalyn demanded as she reached the top of the hill, gasping to catch her breath.

"Rosalyn, I failed her! I couldna save her! She's dead! I failed her!" Connor wailed as the pain rolled over him anew.

When Rosalyn reached down to touch his shoulder, he looked into her face and saw light and hope in her eyes. "No, Connor, she's not dead. Isaboe is still very much alive. I can feel her energy."

Connor's anguish instantly melted into a small glimmer of hope. "What do ye mean; she's still alive?"

"Isaboe is caught between the realms. Her body is here in the physical world, but her spirit is caught somewhere in there." Rosalyn pointed to the circle of stones. "I can feel her."

"What do we do? How do we bring her back?" Connor's words came out as desperate as he felt.

Rosalyn looked down at him. "We need something, something that connects you to her. Demetrick gave you a ring to mark her with. Do you still have it?" she asked.

"Aye, I carry it with me always." Connor dug into the pocket of his vest and pulled out the small pouch, dropping the ring into his hand.

"Place it in her hand and then wrap your hand around hers." As he did so, Rosalyn offered Connor a reassuring nod before sinking into her magic. Closing her eyes, she mumbled something unrecognizable before throwing her head back. Opening her arms out wide, she turned her palms upward. *"Merciful Goddess, hear my plea! I call upon all the elements of the Earth, the stars, and my ancestral spirits. Lend me your power!"*

Rosalyn lifted her voice to the sky as Connor, Margaret, and Will watched more magic erupting around them, this time with hopeful eyes. A vortex of energy began to grow in the space between Rosalyn's uplifted hands. As it grew in power and size, the energy spiral began to spin until it encompassed her entire being. But just as soon as it had begun, the vortex subsided and then vanished like vapor.

"It's not enough. She's too deeply lost in the dark. We need something else, something that can guide her back!" Searching for help, Rosalyn glanced from Connor to Margaret.

"The amulet!" they both cried out simultaneously as Margaret pulled the blue stone hanging on a green cord from around her neck. "The pixies speak to us through this. Maybe they can reach her and guide her back!"

"Yes, put that in her other hand and then wrap yours around hers, just like Connor did. Good." Rosalyn watched Margaret with approving eyes before turning to Connor. "Call to her. Let your voice guide her. There's not much time left. You have to call her back!" Rosalyn again prepared herself, repeating the same powerful words. When the vortex reappeared, this time it was larger and sparked with more energy, as if drawing strength from within itself, and from Rosalyn. The spiral of magic created a wind that whipped around the sorceress, making her appear frightening in her awesome power.

"Now, Connor. NOW!" Rosalyn cried.

"Isaboe, Isaboe come back to me! I need ye to follow my voice and come back. ISABOE!!" Connor shook Isaboe's limp form as he screamed, but still no life showed on her graying lips.

"No, no," he whispered, feeling his hope slipping away, but he wasn't done giving up. "NO, GODDAMIT!" he shouted into her face, now drained of color. "Find yer way back, Isaboe! COME BACK!" Connor cried out. "FIGHT, GODDAMIT! ISABOE, FIGHT!" he yelled at her, but she remained non-responsive. "COME BACK TO ME, ISABOE!" he screamed out one more time as he shook her shoulders.

Like a shock wave, the life suddenly burst back into Isaboe. With a violent breath, her body arched off the ground and her eyes shot wide open before she collapsed back down into Connor's arms. As the color rushed back into her face, Isaboe took a few long, deep breaths. When she opened her eyes a second time, she looked up into the faces of overwhelming relief as Connor and Margaret both shed tears of joy over the top of her.

"I heard you." Isaboe's words were weak as she reached up to touch his face. Tears still dropping from his cheek, Connor brought her hand to his lips. "It was dark, cold, and I was so afraid. But I followed the lights, and then I heard you calling me. I heard you call my name."

Isaboe and Connor stared into each other's eyes, something he had thought just moments before that he would never do again. Gently brushing his hand across her cheek, he smiled down at her. "Aye, I did call ye back, my love, and I thank the heavens that ye listened to me this time."

It took a few moments before Isaboe noticed a woman she had never seen before kneeling next to Connor, also smiling down at her. "Who are you?"

Having forgotten all about Rosalyn until just that moment, Connor turned and looked at her. He too had his own question. "How is it that ye are here, Rosalyn? I'm grateful beyond words that ye are, but, how? Why?"

Rosalyn reached out and took Connor's hand, then did the same with Isaboe. She looked at them both for a long moment before answering. "I'm here, Isaboe, because I'm your birth mother."

CHAPTER 28

TRUTHS REVEALED

Isaboe slept the rest of that day, through the night, and into the following morning. Sitting in the chair next to her bed and holding her hand, Connor never left her side. Occasionally she would awake and ask for a drink of water and give him a weak smile, but then would fall right back to sleep, resting comfortably under Connor's watchful eye.

The prior afternoon, Rosalyn had joined Connor in his vigil, quietly entering the small room where her daughter slept.

"Her birth-mother?" Connor asked quietly. "Dinnae ye think that might've been something ye should've told me before?"

"I didn't know before," she whispered, silently placing a chair next to Connor before taking a seat. "When you said her name was Isaboe, I had my suspicions, but I wasn't sure. A few days after you left I rode into Edinburgh and sought out Sister Miriam. She confirmed Isaboe's married name, and told me that you both had been there asking questions about her family. When I realized that your Isaboe and my daughter were one and the same, I followed you."

"But how?"

"When I performed the mind meld with you and took you back through the Veil of Forgetfulness, I connected to your vibration. Every being, every living thing gives off its own vibration, and each is unique. That is how I was able to track you. But I could never quite catch up. You were all over, back and forth across the country."

"Aye. Lorien kept us going in circles. But her *birth mother?* Ye ken, she's gonna have questions when she wakes."

"I know. It's a long story, so we'll take it a little bit at a time."

By late morning, Isaboe finally stirred. As she yawned deeply and started to wake, she felt fingers curled around her hand. Looking down, she saw Connor's hand wrapped around her own as he sat in a chair next to her bed. His legs were stretched out before him, his chin tucked into his chest, and his eyes closed. He was snoring. The sight of him pulled up the corners of her lips. He had been there beside her the whole time, standing guard while she slept. It reminded her why she had fallen in love with him in the first place, even with all their disagreements. She gave his hand a gentle squeeze.

Opening his eyes, Connor gave her a sleepy smile as he sat up, rubbing a hand across his face. "Good morning, sleepy head."

"Good morning, my love. How long have I been sleeping?"

"About a day, but take all the time ye need. There's no hurry. How do ye feel?"

"A little odd, but grateful that I'm here at all," she said with a smile, but then became serious when the answer to a question that had haunted her for months suddenly came crashing down upon her with clarity. "Connor, it was you, wasn't it? You were the man with me in Euphoria." As Isaboe spoke, it all became very clear, and she wondered why she hadn't seen it before. She searched his eyes for something to reassure her. "It's always been you," she realized in an explosion of light, and color, and *knowledge*. It wasn't simply in Euphoria; it was a thousand lives they had lived together. They were bonded beyond love and life. They were a pair, a couple destined to live their experiences together, life after life. Their souls were linked, and they would find each other, always. It was destiny.

"Isaboe, I wanted to tell ye, but ye were so sick with fever. Ye were so fragile. I wasn't sure about yer state of mind. I didna think ye were ready to hear everything yet. I could never find the right words, or the right time," Connor said, trying to rationalize his reason for not sharing this with her.

"That's why Will calls you captain. You served together as rebels, *twenty years ago*. That was your crime against the British. You were a Jacobite Rebel, weren't you?" The missing pieces all fell into place. "Connor, you lost twenty years, too."

"No, *Breagha*, I didna lose anything." Taking both of her hands in his, Connor leaned in and met her eyes. "I gained everything! Demetrick didna just give me back my life, he gave me you!" His unrestrained smile lit up his face, and Isaboe returned it.

"Connor, we're going to have a baby," she whispered, and her face broke into a joyful smile. Whatever doubt she had about the child's father melted away. She'd never questioned that Connor loved her. Even when she thought she carried another man's child it had made no difference to him. But now, the thought that she could look into the face of her son or daughter, knowing it would be Connor's eyes that looked back, made her heart swell.

Catching a glimpse of movement out of the corner of her eye, her gaze fell on the stranger sitting in a chair at the end of her bed, silently watching with a soft grin. Isaboe had not been fully conscious when Rosalyn had spoken to Connor the day before, but she knew enough. She knew that this virtual stranger was someone she had been quietly yearning for most of her life. They had a deep connection, though Isaboe knew nothing about this woman or what it meant to have her show up now. Locking stares with her for a long, uncomfortable moment, Isaboe finally broke the silence. "I don't even know what to ask you."

"I understand," Rosalyn said as she rose and picked up her chair, placing it on the other side of the bed next to Isaboe before taking a seat again. "And I know that I owe you an explanation, but for right now, please know that I did not give you up because I didn't want you. I was very young and on my own. I was confused, scared, and knew I wasn't capable of taking care of you. So I did the best for you that I could. On the night you were born, I left you with Sister Miriam."

"Sister Miriam was always kind to me, but she never told me about you."

"I didn't want her to. I thought it would be best if I stayed out of your life. You had a good family that gave you so much more than I ever could. As sorry as I am, I cannot bring myself to regret my choice. I had no other options at the time. With that said, I wish to ask for your forgiveness, and for not reaching out to you sooner." Rosalyn looked at her daughter with eyes that were sad and pleading.

Isaboe held the gaze of a woman she hadn't expected to meet this side of death. For a brief moment, she felt something like empathy as she read the regret in her mother's eyes. Everything was different now, and perhaps it was time to make use of this second chance, for both their sakes.

"I don't know that there is anything to forgive. You did what you had to do in order to survive. At least now I know." Isaboe and Rosalyn shared a moment of silence before Margaret interrupted, walking in with a tray.

"Well, good morning! It's nice to see you're finally awake. I brought you some tea and biscuits; you must be famished."

"Actually, I am." Suddenly realizing how hungry she was, Isaboe sat up straight in bed. "But first," she smiled at Connor, "you'll have to let go of my hand. I really need to step out to use the privy."

"The last time ye went to the privy, ye disappeared. Margaret will take ye."

"Really? I can't even pee by myself?"

"No."

"Fine," Isaboe conceded. She tried to pretend that she was annoyed, but at that moment Connor's protectiveness was deeply appreciated. She knew she would not be alive this day without him or Margaret, and along with that knowledge came an overwhelming sense of gratitude. Not only had they helped her take her life back, but she now had a family again.

Margaret assisted her from the bed, but before they even reached the door, Isaboe stopped and looked down at the puddle of water collecting at her feet. "Did...did my water just break?" she asked, shocked. "It's too soon! The baby shouldn't be coming yet! Margaret, isn't it too soon?"

"With everything you've gone through, this doesn't surprise me," Margaret said calmly as she helped Isaboe back to bed.

The truth was that no one really knew. By the look of her, Isaboe could have easily been only six months along; her pregnant belly looked quite small on her petite frame. Going months without proper nourishment, along with all the mental and physical abuse she'd endured, had taken a toll on both mother and child. The result looked to be an early birth.

Connor and Rosalyn were on their feet, anxiously standing at Isaboe's bedside.

With concern written across her face, the sorceress stepped up next to Connor. "The baby's coming. This isn't over yet," she whispered.

CHAPTER 29

THE BRILLIANCE OF BRIGHID

Other than a deep ache in the small of her back, Isaboe felt little more than anxiety for the first several hours. Margaret and Rosalyn insisted she stay in bed, and were more than willing to wait on her every need. By late afternoon, the contractions began with regularity, and by evening they were coming harder and closer together. Rosalyn confirmed that Isaboe was stretched to a healthy point, and the birth would soon begin.

Though Connor wanted nothing more than to be at her side, the women insisted that he stay out of the way. He would be underfoot, nervous, and of no help. On any other given day, he would have found an escape from his restless thoughts by grooming the horses, or taking one for a ride, but not today. He gave no thought to the animals in the barn as he paced outside the cottage, compulsively wringing his hands and then running them through his hair.

As he followed Connor a few times around the building, Will attempted to keep him occupied, but offered little in the way of conversation. Finally giving up, he made his way back to the barn and let his worried friend pace alone.

The fact that Will seemed to be at a loss for words was fine with Connor; he could focus on nothing other than Isaboe and the warning Rosalyn had spoken. Shortly after the men had been kicked out of the cottage, he intercepted Rosalyn as she was heading toward the well with a large, metal pot. "What did ye mean when ye said; this ain't over yet?" Connor asked as he followed her toward the well.

"Lorien may have failed to recapture Isaboe," Rosalyn answered when they reached their destination, and Connor began to reel in the line as she continued. "But I have little doubt that she will still try to take the child." Lifting the bucketful of water from the well, Connor placed it on the ground before looking at the sorceress. Her expression was grave, and he could see the concern in her eyes. "This baby will have a fey guardian," she added. "There is no doubt about that. The question is whether it will be a fey from the Seeling court or the Unseeling court who wins that position tonight. No, Connor, this isn't over yet."

Though he didn't completely understand what she meant, he could feel her anxiety. "What do we do?"

"Just be ready when I call you, both of you. We're going to need all of our combined strength to face what we're up against. We must be a fortress against the fey, a fortress of love if we're to protect Isaboe and the child. She needs to be completely surrounded by a circle of support—a *mortal* circle—when we bring your daughter into this world."

"My daughter? Ye ken it's a girl?" Despite his fears, hope lit Connor's face. Up until now, the baby was just an it. Now, *it* was his unborn daughter.

"Oh, it's most definitely a girl. But the process won't be easy." Rosalyn lifted one of Connor's hands, exposing the scratches and bite marks on his arms left by the Underlings when he had held Isaboe tight, preventing the fey from taking her through the circle of stones. "You think this was bad? Just wait." Rosalyn held his gaze and then dropped his hand. "But we won't be alone in our battle against this obsessed Fey Queen. We're not the only ones who want to protect this baby. We have allies."

Though he was curious, Connor didn't pursue it. He was just thankful that Rosalyn was on their side. "Have ye told Isaboe that this isn't over?"

"Oh, I'm sure she knows. The presence of fey magic is heavy in the air. I can feel its energy all over this ridge. I'm sure Isaboe feels it, too. You must recognize it as well, Connor. You've experienced it firsthand."

Connor couldn't deny that he had felt its presence. He had experienced the sensation when he scooped up Isaboe from Saschel's cluttered home only days before, and against all odds, they'd been able to stand their ground against the vicious magic. He was ready to do so again, and would do whatever it took to save Isaboe and his child.

"Braden," Rosalyn said, using his birth name. "Demetrick chose wisely when he made you Isaboe's protector. Never doubt that. If it hadn't been for you, Isaboe and your daughter would not be with us now." Rosalyn gave him a light squeeze on his arm before her face again fell serious. "So be ready when I call you. It will likely be a long night."

Less than a few hours later, the flash of lightening and crackle of energy that were all too familiar, had Connor and Will running back into the cottage before the rumble of thunder subsided. When they entered the room, the sight brought them to an abrupt halt.

Hundreds of small, twinkling, and brightly-colored lights hung suspended in the room in a brilliant display of faerie glamour, and the air was charged with energy. The lights hovered and danced about the room as if they were being carried on the wave of an unseen current.

Isaboe lay on the bed with Margaret on one side and Rosalyn on the other as they all gazed in awe at the dazzling display.

"Are ye seeing this?" Will whispered over Connor's shoulder.

"Aye, I see it."

Slowly, the lights rotated toward each other, transforming their collection of living beams into a dense spiral of energy. The brilliant vortex increased in intensity until there was no longer a distinction of any one light, but rather a mass of pulsating luminance that filled the room.

In the next moment, a beautiful woman stood where only seconds before there had been nothing but dazzling light. She was bathed in a most comforting blue aura that cast a soft glow about the room. A striking crown of tall blue and white spires swirled and danced on her head with a life of its own. Around the base of her crown, crystals and blue jewels were embedded, sparkling with white light. Her dress was a simple white gown, and in her hand was a glowing white wand. Glistening on her back was a pair of delicate, nearly-transparent wings that fluttered slightly in the ethereal power that surrounded her.

The fair-haired woman looked at each person in the room until her gaze fell upon a face she recognized. "Hello, Rosalyn." Her voice floated like music across the room, and she gave an elegant smile.

"Queen Brighid, we are honored by your presence." Rosalyn returned the queen's smile before offering a formal curtsey. "Thank you for coming."

Connor and every other astonished face in the room turned toward Rosalyn. "How long has it been?" the Fey Queen asked.

"It has been nearly fifty of my mortal years, Your Highness. I was only a child when we last met. You are just as beautiful today as you were then, my queen." Rosalyn said with dignity, somehow confident in the face of ethereal royalty.

Connor envied Rosalyn's countenance, and he suspected that this would not be the only encounter with fey royalty they would experience in their lives.

Queen Brighid appeared pleased at the compliment, fluttering her amazing wings before she glanced down at Isaboe laying on the bed. "Your daughter and your unborn grand-daughter have inspired Lorien to new levels of malicious mischief." She paused, and looking back at Rosalyn, her expression shifted slightly. "Isn't it ironic how life comes back around and pulls you into something you thought you were done with?"

A stoic expression passed over Rosalyn's face while she gathered herself enough to answer. "I'm afraid there is more than just irony and mischief at hand this time, Your Highness." Rosalyn stood tall as she addressed the queen, but spoke with reverence. "Lorien almost succeeded in taking Isaboe back into the realm of the fey. Had it not been for these brave mortals, and had I not arrived when I did, I shudder at what she would've endured. Because of Lorien, there is not a person in this room whose life has not been changed. If she succeeds and attaches one of her own as the child's fey guardian, we all know the potential outcome. I fear for this child—for all of mankind. And we have no idea what havoc could be wrought in your world if she succeeds. Can I count on your forces to join us in battle tonight?"

Queen Brighid appeared to be considering Rosalyn's request before she finally spoke. "The Council is aware of Lorien's undesirable actions. Unfortunately, they are not willing to take measures against her. Though most Underlings believe we should not interfere with the course of humanity, some fey are not of like mind."

When the queen turned to address the room, casting her regal gaze on each of them, Connor found he was unable to look away. "Such is the case with Lorien and her unscrupulous followers. Because she failed to obtain the child once before, she was determined to succeed this time. I must admit; her persistence is to be admired. Although she has attempted a number of tricks to acquire the child, Lorien underestimates all of us." When the queen spoke, her wings fluttered lightly before she turned back to address Rosalyn.

"It is not only due to your mortal influences that this young woman is still in your world today. I have not been blind to the destruction Lorien leaves in her wake." With a heavy sigh, the queen paused, looking down at Isaboe. "Against better judgment, I have intervened where others would prefer I did not. But as you have mentioned more than once, my dear, you are only mortal, and I felt you needed some assistance."

Brighid passed her wand across her face, and in a momentary twist of vision, she became an old crone with white hair. Bent over with a crooked spine, her beautiful white gown had turned into a tattered, black cloak, and the sparkling white wand was now a strangely engraved walking stick.

"*You're the old crone?*" Isaboe's words were coated with surprise, matching the look in her eyes.

"Aye. It was me that gave ye the gift of communication, and the words to set yerself free. I may not be able to stop Lorien directly, but I can make it more difficult for her." With a toothless smile, the crone turned to address the room. "Though all yer acts o' bravery did not go unnoticed, ye've not been on yer own."

Raising her cane, the old woman passed it across her face, and once again became Queen Brighid, in all of her dazzling blue splendor.

"However," she continued, "there are certain attributes mortals are born with that Lorien has not taken into consideration: your unwavering desire to be free, to make your own choices—right or wrong—and above all, your obsession with mortal love. With my power, and the combined strength of your human spirits, she will have a fight on her hands."

Brighid's smile held a hint of the crone behind the beauty, and Connor momentarily wondered about her true intentions. She was fey after all, and he caught the mysteriousness in the flash of her teeth.

As the moment passed, Isaboe moaned at the onset of another

contraction. Connor started in her direction, but Rosalyn lifted her hand, shooting him a look. He held his ground. After a few more moments with Margaret at her side, the contraction passed, and Isaboe breathed more easily.

Queen Brighid reached out her wand and gently touched it to Isaboe's belly. The tip of the wand flashed brightly for only a second before she lifted it and looked down at Isaboe. "May you both find your true purpose, and may the Goddess always watch over you both. You and your child are blessed, my dear, or cursed, depending on how this plays out," she said with a regal smile.

But Connor caught the concerned expression on Isaboe's face at the queen's words, just before she spoke again. "Lorien is coming." Brighid cast her gaze about the room. "I believe that you all have endured enough for now. I will set forces up around this cottage so you may bring the child into this world without interference. However, I cannot protect you from Lorien forever. She's been robbed twice now. Will she go for a third? Only time will tell." Then, just as suddenly as she had appeared, Brighid was gone.

Full of questions, all the eyes in the room were trained on Rosalyn, but before anyone could ask, another contraction started to build. This time Connor was at Isaboe's side, holding her hand until it peaked and waned, giving her a brief moment to relax, but not for long.

Rosalyn had moved to the foot of the bed to check the birthing progress. Looking up from the sheet draped across Isaboe's pulled-up knees, she made an announcement; "The baby's head is crowning. She's coming!" Rosalyn glanced at Will still standing at the door, appearing very uncomfortable and out of place. "William, I need you to stand guard over this room," she commanded. "If you see anything at all that seems to be from another world; *TAKE IT OUT!*"

Will immediately fell into a soldier's stance. He had been given a job he knew, even if he didn't completely understand who or what it was that he would be fighting.

With Connor on one side, Margaret on the other, and Isaboe's birth-mother acting as midwife, Isaboe delivered a tiny, but healthy, baby girl. And true to Queen Brighid's word, all stayed quiet throughout the birth. Other than the wail of a newborn babe announcing her arrival into the world, her *mortal* world, no other disturbances took place that night in the little cottage overlooking the sea.

CHAPTER 30

QUESTIONS ANSWERED, UNCERTAINTY LOOMS

The following morning Connor sat next to Isaboe on the bed as she cradled her newborn daughter who was sleeping peacefully in her arms, wrapped in a soft blanket. He could see the exhaustion on Isaboe's face, knowing she hadn't slept much since giving birth. With his arm draped over her shoulder, the former warrior tenderly stroked his lover's hair, and was captured by the awe he saw in her eyes as she stared at their perfect little girl. Framed by her hair that fell carelessly over her shoulders, Isaboe's face was softly lit by a glow from the low-burning fire. It snapped and crackled in the fire-box built into the rock wall, keeping the cottage warm. At that moment, he didn't think he could love her more.

"Isn't she beautiful?" Isaboe whispered as she stroked her daughter's tiny cheek.

"Aye, she takes after her mother," Connor whispered in return. Lifting Isaboe's hand, he kissed the back of it before bringing it to his chest. "I love ye, Isaboe. I've loved ye from the moment I met ye. *You* are my life, the reason I exist. I never want to ken a day without ye in it." Gently cupping her face with his hand, he kissed her softly, and Isaboe returned the kiss with matching affection. It was both tender and comforting. He could feel the intensity of her passion as she leaned into him, but the moment passed when they were interrupted by a whimper from the soft bundle cradled in Isaboe's arms.

"I guess we need to give this little one a name. Do you have any thoughts?" she asked looking down at her sleeping child.

"The fact that she's here at all, we should probably name her *Miracle.*"

Isaboe chuckled lightly. "Well, that's probably appropriate, but I have another name in mind—Kaitlyn. It's kind of grown on me. Kaitlyn Margaret Grant has a nice ring, don't you think?" Isaboe said with a smile, but her grin quickly melted, and he could see a question forming in her eyes. "It will be Grant, yes? Or should her surname be... MacPherson?"

"Braden MacPherson died years ago, so there's no past for either of us. But our future can be whatever we want it to be. I only want us to move forward together from here." Caressing her cheek, he paused, losing himself for a moment in her eyes. "Her name will most certainly be Grant." Connor wanted to tell Isaboe that someday her name would be Grant, too, but he had nothing to offer her, save himself and his name. That just didn't seem enough right now. Isaboe deserved more than that.

A rap on the door announced Rosalyn's arrival, and they quickly assured her that she was welcome to join them. "Margaret went to gather some breakfast for all of us, and I thought that this might be a good time to talk," the sorceress said as she pulled up a chair close to the bed.

"Good, 'cause we have some questions," Connor added.

But before he could ask, Rosalyn held up her hand. "Not yet. Your questions will have to wait. This is more important." She held both their gazes before continuing. "Your daughter is very special. I do not say this because I am her grandmother. She is special because she is a feymora."

"And what is that?" Isaboe asked defensively—a mother protecting her child.

"A feymora is a person that is both mortal and fey. Though both of her parents are mortal, your baby was conceived in the realm of the faeries, and under Lorien's manipulation. Though I don't claim to understand the extent of what Lorien had planned to do with your daughter, I'm confident that Kaitlyn will have special abilities no other child will have. And whether she finds this a gift or a curse is yet to be seen, but she will naturally be able to communicate with the fey." Rosalyn paused to let her words sink in.

"But she's quite fortunate. She will have us to help her understand what she sees and hears. She won't need to be afraid to talk to you about the strange creatures that visit her in the night and the things they say to her. She won't have to fear punishment if she is caught talking with them. Your daughter has a family that understands. For that, she is incredibly blessed."

They both regarded Rosalyn for a moment before Connor broke the silence. "Ye sound as if ye speak from firsthand experience, Rosalyn. What else dinnae we ken about ye?"

"I'd prefer to save that story for another time. I simply want you to know that she will see things in her world that you will not. From the moment she was born, this is her reality. We are not her only family."

The new parents glanced at each other before looking down at the innocent bundle in Isaboe's arms. Concern and uncertainty were etched in both of their faces.

"Rosalyn, yesterday ye said she'd have a fey guardian. Does she?" Connor asked.

"Did you not see her? She was standing in this very room!"

"You mean the woman in blue?" Isaboe asked, her eyes wide with awe.

"Yes. Queen Brighid herself is your daughter's guardian. When I called for help, I could not have imagined that she herself would appear. Do you know what this means?"

A mutual shake of their heads led to an elaboration. "Brighid's wand is a symbol of justice, leadership and purity. Though I don't claim to know what lies ahead, for Queen Brighid to choose herself as your daughter's fey guardian is unprecedented."

"What does that mean for us, and for Kaitlyn?" Connor asked hesitantly.

"Kaitlyn?" Rosalyn paused before a soft smile of acknowledgement crossed her face. "That's a beautiful name."

"Thanks," Isaboe muttered. "But, can you please elaborate. What does all of this mean? What can we expect now?"

"I honestly don't know, but the fact that Queen Brighid was here in this room means that something profound is destined for Kaitlyn's future, something of great importance to both mortal and fey." The intensity of Rosalyn's statement only created more questions, and when Connor found himself looking into Isaboe's eyes, he saw the same worry he felt.

But before any further questions could be asked, Margaret entered the room carrying breakfast. The smell of poached eggs, blood sausage, and tattie scones immediately brightened Connor's eyes, but when he reached in to steal a bite off the plate, Margaret slapped his hand. "Your breakfast is in the barn with William," she snapped.

"But it's cold out there," he whined.

"Too bad. You should be used to it by now, so get on with yourself!" Margaret pretended to swat at him before giving him a mischievous smile.

"Will and I are gonna ride out to Saschel's place to see what we can find in that rats' nest she calls a home," Connor said before kissing Isaboe and heading toward the door.

"Wait!" Isaboe called out suddenly. "I just remembered something. The events of these last few days have been coming back to me in bits and pieces. At first, it was Saschel who took me that night, but it was another woman who pulled me up the hill into the circle of stones. A fey woman, but not Lor..." Isaboe stopped herself from uttering the Fey Queen's name, "it wasn't the queen. This dark fey was wearing all black, and she was very beautiful, incredibly strong, and horribly evil." Isaboe glanced at the faces in the room before continuing. "She told me that Saschel was planning to turn me in for the reward. I don't know if she was telling the truth, but I think she might have...done something to my sister."

"Who was this fey?" Rosalyn asked. "Did she give you a name?" "She said she was known by many names, and that some call her Lilabeth, but at that moment she claimed herself as my *deliverer*." Isaboe shuddered before looking at Connor, who was still standing at the door. "Please, see if you can find Saschel, hopefully alive."

An icy-cold jolt shot down Connor's spine at the mention of Lilabeth's name, but he tried not to let his recognition show. He knew that if the dark muse was involved, it couldn't be good. Standing with his hand on the doorknob, he glanced back at the pained look on Isaboe's face. The last thing he wanted was to cause her more grief.

"We'll go look for her and those documents. If we find the papers, then we'll know if she was sincere 'bout helping ye," Connor said with a wink and a smile before closing the door. But he couldn't deny the anxiety bubbling up in his gut. Even though Isaboe had denounced Lorien, and they had all survived a horrendous ordeal, he felt a nagging doubt that they had seen the last of the Fey Queen and her nefarious sidekick.

After spending the morning and most of the afternoon in bed, Isaboe began to feel restless. Connor and Will had been gone for a long while, and they should have been back by now. Her anxiety grew as she quietly paced the one-room cottage while Kaitlyn slept on the bed. But the silence was broken when the baby awoke with a full-on cry as she realized that the space where her mother had been was now vacant.

"Oh, there, there, little wee one, mama's here. Don't cry." Isaboe laid back on the bed next to her daughter and let the babe wrap five tiny fingers around one of her own. "Did you not hear? Queen Brighid is your faerie guardian!" Isaboe paused, recalling Rosalyn's words, but she tried not to let the anxiety of the unknown diminish the joy she was currently feeling. "Though I don't know what the future will bring us, my darling child, there is one thing I do know for certain; you will never be alone, Kaitlyn. I will never leave you, and you will always know that you are loved." Whether it was the involuntary action of a newborn babe, or if Kaitlyn actually understood her mother's words, a tiny smile broke out on the baby's angelic face. Isaboe's heart swelled at the sight of it. Just six months ago she had nothing to live for. Now, she had everything. She had been given a second chance. Even though Kaitlyn's future, and whatever abilities she would have remained a mystery, Isaboe tried not to dwell on the unknown. Right now her baby was here; beautiful and perfect. And with Connor at her side she had a family again.

However, her moment of quiet reflection was short-lived when a quick rap on the door broke the solitude. A cold wind rushed in the small cottage as the door opened and Connor entered, followed by Margaret and Rosalyn.

"Will and I just came back from Saschel's place," he said. "I think ye should come outside."

Isaboe sat up and looked over the congregation that had assembled in front of her, all with solemn expressions. "Why? What have you found?" Fearing the worst for her sister, she wasn't sure she wanted to see what they had discovered.

His face stoic, Connor stepped over to the bed and extended one hand, placing the other behind Isaboe's back. Cradling Kaitlyn in one arm, she placed her free hand in his as he helped her to stand.

"Here, let me take the baby," Margaret said as she swept in and gingerly lifted the bundle from her friend's arms. Rosalyn wrapped a blanket around Isaboe's shoulders before turning to let Connor lead the way. With anxiety building in her chest, Isaboe followed him outside, but the sight of a blanketed body lying on Saschel's buckboard made her breath catch in her throat, bringing her to a halt.

"She's dead, then." Isaboe said, more as a statement than a question.

"Aye."

Isaboe's lips quivered and the tears welled up as she swallowed hard. Pulling the blanket snugly around her shoulders, she stepped up to the buckboard and looked down at the covered body.

"Ye dinnae have to do this," Connor said as he gently placed a hand on her arm.

"Yes, I do." Isaboe's words came out heavy and laced with regret before she pulled back the plain, grey blanket that covered Saschel's face. Her sister looked as if she were sleeping, but when Isaboe reached down to touch her hand, it was cold and stiff. "How did she die?" she asked, letting the tears fall that she could no longer hold back.

Connor hesitated before answering. "We found her body under the rubble in her bothy, with twine wrapped around her neck." His words come out guarded, as if he didn't want to speak them.

With tears blurring her vision, Isaboe looked up at Connor. "She was murdered in her own home?" She looked back at her sister's lifeless body. "I brought this on her."

"Dinnae do this to yerself, Isaboe. It's not yer fault."

"Isn't it?" She shot Connor a cold glare. "I was the one who demanded we come here to seek her out and made you all follow. Look at all the lives that have been affected because of my choices—lives that have been *lost!* How can you say this isn't my fault? Everything that has happened to *all of us* is my fault because I didn't listen to Margaret all those years ago!"

Connor didn't answer, only stared at her until she turned her focus back to the buckboard, trying to figure out what to do with this new lump of guilt in her gut. But it wasn't just guilt over her sister. The words she had just spewed out only made it worse. She wasn't so blind in her own pain that she didn't see the hurt in Connor's eyes. Had she not experienced the incredible event that had changed her life and everyone else's, she and Connor wouldn't be together now. It seemed clear that no matter the choices she made, or didn't make, the outcome would inevitably cause pain for the people around her.

"Forgive me, Saschel," she whispered. "I'm so sorry that I brought my curse down on you, too."

When Connor gently placed his arm around her waist, Isaboe turned to him, sobbing into his arms. "I'm sorry for everything ye've lost, Isaboe," he whispered into her hair. "I'm truly sorry yer sister was killed, and that I didna trust her."

The weight of her sister's death was a bitter realization. Even though they hadn't been close, it was confirmation that no one was safe. However, when she pulled back and looked up into Connor's compassionate blue eyes, she saw hope and strength. With him at her side, maybe this long dark chapter of her life would finally be behind her.

"Thank you," she said, offering him a weak smile. "But I'm not sure I trusted her either. I just so badly wanted to believe that she had those documents."

"It's cold out here. Let's go back inside," Connor said. Wrapping his arm around her shoulder, he began escorting her back toward the cottage when Isaboe stopped, glancing back at the buckboard.

"Can you make sure she has a proper burial, and a marker?"

"Of course. What do ye want on the marker?"

Isaboe paused, wondering what would be proper for a relative she didn't really know. "Just her name, so she's not forgotten."

CHAPTER 31

A NEW FUTURE
WITH OLD WOUNDS

Isaboe was met by the sympathetic faces of Margaret and Rosalyn as she pushed her way back into the cottage. Acknowledging them only briefly, she made her way across the room and sank down onto the bed. Her sadness felt like a heavy weight in her chest as she dropped her gaze to the floor.

"Saschel was telling ye the truth, love," Connor said as he stepped up beside the bed and pulled a folded document from inside his jacket. "After we removed her body, we found that box of legal documents ye mentioned, just before we burned most of her rat-infested belongings." He dropped the papers on the bed. "This is what ye came here looking for, *Breagha.*"

Isaboe's heart quickened as she picked up the tri-fold papers, yellowed and wrinkled with age. Hesitantly opening the documents, she scanned the legal wording until she saw the names she was looking for, Benjamin and Anna McKinnon. Though it renewed the ache in her heart to read that her children had been separated, fostered out to two different families, it was all there—names, dates, and locations—everything Isaboe needed to start the search for them.

A moment earlier she had been filled with regret and guilt. Now it was replaced with renewed hope and anticipation. When she looked up at Connor again, his eyes were soft as he smiled down at her. She could feel the tears welling up once more, but this time, they were not tears of pain. "Thank you," she said, squeezing his hand.

"We also found this," he said, tossing another bundle of documents onto the bed.

"What is it?" she asked with hesitation, but didn't pick it up.

"It's a land contract stating that Henri and Marta Cameron owned three parcels o' land in Kirkwall, though we only found one deed. I figure Tomas and Deidra took the others. From what Will and I could decipher, in order to claim that property ye just need to prove that ye're a Cameron. We found enough other legal papers to prove that, Isaboe. There's property in Kirkwall that's rightfully yers."

Staring at the yellowed papers sitting at the end of her bed, Isaboe made no attempt to reach for them. "What year were those properties purchased?" she asked coldly.

Connor opened the document and scanned it for a moment before he answered. "1732. Why's that important?"

Isaboe didn't answer right away. Her thoughts had taken her to another time. Suddenly, she was the sad little girl who shook with pain at being excluded, and it radiated from deep within her soul. "I was seven-years-old then, yet they purchased only *three* properties!" Isaboe held up her hand. "One for Deidra, one for Cecelia, and one for Saschel," she said, counting them off on her fingers. "Why not four properties? I'll tell you why. She never *wanted* me. I was never considered a real part of their family!" Seeing evidence of what she had always believed, that for Marta she had been just an obligation—not a daughter—left her mouth twisting as tears spilled freely down her cheeks. "I always knew I wasn't wanted, but how is it that after all these years she can still hurt me? All I ever wanted was a mother to love me! Why was that so much to ask for?" she shouted.

From the corner of the room, Rosalyn's voice came quietly, "Isaboe, I..."

"No! You don't get to say anything, not yet!" Isaboe cut Rosalyn off before she could finish. "I don't want their goddamn property! I don't want anything that belonged to *her!*" Isaboe wailed as she scooped her baby from Margaret's arms and returned to the bed. "Get out! All of you—get out!"

Startled by her mother's fury, Kaitlyn also began to cry. Lying back on the bed, Isaboe cradled her baby to her chest—up against her broken heart—and vowed to be a better mother than what she had been given.

Kaitlyn would see that promise fulfilled in a way that Benjamin and Anna hadn't.

After asking to be left alone with his little family, Connor laid down on the bed, easing Isaboe and baby Kaitlyn into his embrace. He held them both, softly stroking Isaboe's hair until her sobs petered out and the baby fell back to sleep.

"I'm sorry," Isaboe finally whispered. "I don't know why that bothered me so much."

"It's alright. Do ye feel better now that ye've got that off yer chest?"

Isaboe turned to look at him. "Don't you think I have the right to be angry about this?"

"I dinnae care if ye're angry. I just dinnae want ye to make yerself upset over something that ye cannae change. We can only move forward from here, love. The past is the past. We cannae change it, and we're not looking back anymore."

Careful not to wake Kaitlyn, Isaboe rolled over to face Connor. "And what are we moving forward to? What now? Since we don't have a past, and nothing to go back to, where do we go from here?" she asked, searching his eyes.

Connor didn't answer right away. He brushed her hair back and gently ran his thumb over her cheek before cupping her face in his hand, holding her gaze. "I dinnae ken yet, but we'll figure it out, I promise." Giving her a weak smile, he pulled Isaboe back into his arms, but she could sense his worry. Clinging tightly to him, with their daughter at her side, she held on to the small hope that whatever their future held, they would have the strength to face it together.

At the end of the day, shortly after the sun had set, Isaboe sat quietly alone in bed holding her baby. Kaitlyn's beautiful porcelain face glowed in the light of the fire that her father kept feeding to keep the cottage warm. Kaitlyn, who had struggled to nurse in her first day of life, had finally figured out where her nourishment came from. After a few minutes of suckling at her mother's breast, she was back to sleep.

A quick tap on the door announced Margaret's arrival. After being assured by Isaboe she was welcome to enter, Margaret breezed in and closed the door behind her. "Has the little one latched on yet?" she asked, shooting Isaboe a smile before sitting next to her on the bed.

"Yes, she just ate for the first time. Though it was hardly enough to fill a thimble, at least she took that. She's so tiny, Margaret. I'm sure she came early, but she seems alright. She looks healthy, don't you think?" The concern Isaboe felt at her daughter's early birth was valid. Problems with premature babies didn't always show right away.

"Oh, yes, she's perfect! You have nothing to worry about. You're both gonna be just fine."

Isaboe nodded, cautiously holding onto her friend's optimism. "I'm sorry that you had to sleep in the barn last night. Hopefully, you slept better than I."

"Oh, it was alright. If you remember our trip to Edinburgh, I've slept under worse conditions."

"Were you warm enough? Did you find enough blankets?"

"Stop worrying about me, I'm fine. I'm not the one who just had a baby," Margaret said firmly. "So, did Connor talk some sense into you about the property in Kirkwall? Or are you gonna stand on principle and be stubborn about it?"

"Well, since I have nothing else to my name, if I do in fact have property that's rightfully mine to claim, I can't very well turn my back on it, now can I? I may be stubborn, Margaret, but I'm not stupid. Marta may not have given me much in the way of motherly nurturing, but if I can get this from her, even after all these years, I'll take it. This property could be a new start for us and an inheritance for Kaitlyn."

"I'm glad to hear you're being reasonable. And there's a bit of fight in your voice again. That's a good sign, love." Margaret patted Isaboe's hand before turning her attention to the baby.

Isaboe quietly regarded her friend, watching Margaret run a finger over the baby's tiny hand while making soft cooing sounds. She couldn't help but wonder what her life would've been like if it hadn't been for Margaret. This woman had been there for her through the darkest period of her life—had seen Isaboe at her worst—yet Margaret fought through hell to stay by her side. Isaboe knew she didn't have the right words to tell her friend how much that meant to her, but she also knew she didn't have to. She smiled to herself at the gratitude she felt before shifting her thoughts. "What do you think of Rosalyn?"

Margaret sat up and looked at Isaboe curiously. "I'm not sure yet. She's quiet, doesn't interact with the rest of us much. She's only spoken to me a few times. But she did thank me for taking care of you, and being there for you when you came back." Margaret paused, and her face fell serious. "She told me that the fey hadn't considered that someone would be waiting for you all these years later."

"I still find it hard to believe that you did." Isaboe paused, and placed her hand on Margaret's. "I shudder to think what my life would've been like if you hadn't been there for me."

"Well, maybe it was fate that I happened to see that flyer in Aberdeen. At the time, I could hardly believe anyone would bother rebuilding Faireshire." Margaret paused again, and her warming smile returned. "But in retrospect, there just might be something to this destiny thing after all, aye?"

"I certainly don't believe it's an accident that you came into my life, dear friend. That has definitely been destiny," Isaboe squeezed Margaret's hand. "I suppose you've been spending some time alone with Will. Apparently you managed not to kill him."

"Actually, William's company isn't half bad, for a man. We've taken the time to get to know each other a bit, and he's not completely annoying."

Isaboe gave Margaret a surprised look, but with the hint of a grin on her lips, "Sounds as if you're growing fond of William."

"Now, don't go looking at me like that. I just said he wasn't annoying. I don't plan on going off and marrying the bloke!" Margaret replied with a vivid expression set somewhere between amusement and horror.

Though Margaret's statement was laced with conviction, Isaboe saw something different in her friend that she hadn't seen before, something softer, and it looked a bit like affection. But knowing Margaret like she did, she opted not to pursue it further.

"So, Rosalyn, I'm just not sure what to think about her yet. This is a woman who gave birth to me, saved my life, and helped bring my own daughter into the world, yet I know nothing about her. I don't even know what to ask her."

"Connor told me she lives in a cave."

"A cave? That's ridiculous. You don't think he was serious, do you?"

Margaret shrugged. "He said it was a nice cave, whatever that means."

"She lives in a cave, all by herself?"

"He said she has a dwarf and a giant to keep her company." Margaret shrugged again. "I don't know. She's a bit mysterious, but seems like a good woman."

"A dwarf and a giant? That's a bit odd, don't you think? But I suppose I'll find out more. Connor said she wants to come to Kirkwall with us."

Margaret nodded. "Well, that's good. It'll give you a chance to get acquainted."

"You're coming to Kirkwall with us, too, yes?"

Margaret paused, and Isaboe saw the shift on her friend's face. "Well, since William and I have been spending so much time together, we've been discussing that, and, well, we both think it's time to head south."

"What?" Margaret's words jolted Isaboe. "You're leaving me?"

The distressed look on Isaboe's face was not missed, and Margaret took her hand. "Isaboe, you're in good hands now. Connor and Rosalyn will take care of you, and…" But before Margaret could finish, tears were once more spilling down Isaboe's cheeks. "Oh, don't do that," Margaret whispered as she wiped the tears from her friend's face, giving her a sympathetic smile. "It's time, love. You don't need me anymore. You've got Connor and Kaitlyn, and it sounds like Rosalyn now, too. I need to get back to my pub. Dunivan probably thinks he owns it by now. It's time for me to go home, and for you to move on," she said with conviction. "You have a family again, love. It's what you've always wanted. It's what you've wanted since the beginning of this whole, long nightmare."

"But you *are* my family, Margaret. Both Kaitlyn and I wouldn't be here if it weren't for you. I'm not ready for you to leave me yet," she mumbled through her tears. It was pathetic and terribly clingy, but Isaboe spoke the truth she felt in her heart.

"Yes you are. You and Connor are gonna be just fine. There's not a better man anywhere to help you and Kaitlyn through whatever's to come.

Not only is he the bravest man I have ever met, he's just about as stubborn as you are. And he's more than capable of dealing with anything the two of you might throw at him—not to mention that he's completely, utterly, and ridiculously in love with you. You're gonna be fine, and this will be a good time to get acquainted with Rosalyn. Give her a chance, Isaboe. I'm sure she has quite a story, too."

Isaboe managed to pull herself together and wiped her nose before responding. "I don't know what's the matter with me today. I've been crying all day long."

"Don't be so hard on yourself, my love. With all you've been through this last year, to say nothing of the last two days, you've earned the right to a good day's cry."

Isaboe leaned forward and wrapped her free arm around Margaret's neck. "I love you with all my heart," she whispered into her friend's ear.

"I love you too, wee one."

CHAPTER 32

AND THE GREATEST
OF THESE IS LOVE

Early the following morning they were gathered back at Saschel's burned-out bothy, and though Isaboe had never been close to her sister, even when they were young, there was still the pain of loss as she looked down at Saschel's freshly covered grave. One more member of her family had been touched by the magic of the fey, but this one lost her life to it, and Isaboe felt as responsible for her sister's death as if she had done the deed herself.

Having rained hard during the night, the ground was damp and the sky still held remnants of the passing storm, but the island winds were pushing the remaining clouds out to sea. Isaboe pulled her cloak a little tighter to cut the biting chill whipping across the ridge as she stood next to the blackened stones and the burnt remains of Saschel's home. She tried to pick up her sister's essence in the winter's breeze, but only felt the bitter cold that left her heart aching.

Isaboe had intended to say a few words over her sister's gravesite, but she couldn't think of any that were appropriate. Fortunately, Margaret seemed to sense the need, and she offered up a quiet, but solemn prayer.

"Will and I are gonna saddle the horses," Connor said with his arm draped over Isaboe's shoulder, indicating that the brief service was over. "Take ye time, and we'll meet ye back at the barn." Kissing her on the forehead, Isaboe watched Connor and Will walk away, leaving her standing alone with Margaret.

Having asked Rosalyn to watch Kaitlyn, Isaboe wanted to have these few moments alone with her friend before she left. It had been the first time since Kaitlyn's birth that Isaboe had voluntarily offered the baby to Rosalyn, and the older woman appeared grateful for the opportunity to hold her granddaughter. Isaboe still wasn't sure how to feel about this strange woman, but it was a small step toward trust. Fortunately, Rosalyn seemed to respect that it would take time for Isaboe to come around. She hadn't pushed her daughter, but instead had shown gratitude for the simple moments of promise.

Margaret was dressed in her riding clothes, bundled up against the cold and ready to be on her way. As the two friends slowly strolled back toward the barn, Isaboe had one arm interlocked with Margaret's, and she struggled to keep her emotions in check. It was hard enough that Margaret was leaving her, but having just left Saschel's gravesite left Isaboe in a somber mood, and she kept her gaze to the ground, fighting the tears threatening to break free.

"I hear as soon as you're ready to ride, Connor wants to leave for Kirkwall," Margaret said cheerfully, breaking the silence.

Knowing her friend was trying to lighten the heaviness she was feeling, Isaboe nodded with half a grin. "Yes. That's the plan, anyway. I don't know what we'll do or how we'll survive when we get there. I guess we'll be living on love and prayer." She again forced a smile, but her fear for their future was real. "I'm glad Rosalyn is going to stay with us for a while, at least until we get settled in somewhere. She also offered to let us stay with her in Lochmund Hills, if we decide to head back in that direction."

Stopping to face Isaboe, Margaret took her friend's hands in her own. "And you know you'll always have a place to call home if you ever come back to Faireshire," she paused, giving Isaboe a soft smile. "There's a reason you're still here, love. You must realize that. You and your daughter have survived an incredible ordeal. If you can survive that, lass, you can survive anything. You've been given a second chance, and you need to trust that everything is gonna be fine. Have some faith in yourself, my love, and in Connor. The two of you will create a wonderful future together with a new family."

Holding back tears, Isaboe only nodded. Reaching into her cloak, she pulled out a small pouch. "Margaret, I want you to have this," she said as she dropped the blue amulet into Margaret's gloved hand.

"What? No!" Margaret exclaimed. "This was a gift to you, from the

good faerie. You don't want to give this to me. You might need it again."

"I've had enough of the fey to last me a lifetime. Besides, if what Rosalyn says is true, both she and my daughter can communicate with them, without needing this. If they can send messages to you through the amulet, then we'll always be connected, no matter how far apart we are. Margaret, I need you to take this. I can't let you go unless you do. Please, Margaret, please take it!" Now sobbing freely, she no longer tried to hold back her tears.

"Fine, alright, I'll take it. Just stop crying. I can't hold it together if you keep this up, and I'm no good with sappy good-byes," Margaret said as she wiped her nose with a hanky.

"Thank you, Margaret. I love you so much." Isaboe hugged her friend tightly before reluctantly releasing her.

"I love you too, wee one. Now, go have a good life." Tucking the amulet away, Margaret gave Isaboe one last smile before they continued toward the barn.

Hoping to arrive in Stromness before nightfall, Will had made it clear that he wanted an early start. "I'll check to see if there's any news from the mainland before we board the ferry." Will called over his shoulder while packing his saddlebags. "If there's something I think ye should ken, I'll send word back. If ye dinnae hear within three days, then there's nothing new to report. I assume ye'll want to be on yer way to Kirkwall as soon as the lass can ride, aye?" Will finished cinching the straps on his saddle and turned to see Connor pacing the barn with his fists clinched, clearly agitated. "What's wrong, Mac?"

But Connor didn't halt his pacing, or even look at Will. "I've got no plan, Will. I've been so focused on findin' Isaboe, I didna think about what to do after." When he finally stopped, Connor stared at Will, his eyes wild and filled with uncertainty. "And on top of that, now I have a baby, too. Isaboe's used to the finer things in life. What do I have to offer her—me and a horse? I've been on the road for so long that home's been wherever my bedroll hits the ground. That's not good enough for her. She deserves a real home, a place where she can lay her baby down at night—a *normal life*. But now, we're on the run. She's wanted by the British army because of me, and now I have to keep her hidden. Her face is plastered all over the British Highlands by now, and she kinda' stands out in a crowd, dinnae ye think?" He paused, trying to wrap his mind around what his next steps should be.

"What do I ken about the needs of a woman and a baby? I dinnae ken what the hell I'm doin', Will. I'm fuckin' scared shitless!"

Will crossed his arms and regarded his friend. "In all the years I've known ye, Mac, I dinnae think I've ever seen that look on yer face before. Ye've really worked yerself up into a tizzy, haven't ye?" he said with a mocking grin.

"Sorry, Will, this ain't yer problem."

"I've seen ye handle worse than this before. Ye'll figure it out." Reaching into his saddlebag, Will turned around and handed Connor a bag of coins.

Giving Will a puzzled look, Connor tossed the bag back. "I dinnae need yer charity, Buchanan!"

"It's not charity, ye jackass!" This time Will threw the bag of coins, which Connor caught before it hit him in the face. "This is for Isaboe, and the baby," he growled through his beard. "Ye're right, she deserves better than you, but ye're all she's got right now. Since ye dinnae have as much as a pot to piss in, this'll give ye a start. It's not much, but at least she won't be sleepin' on the ground. So take the money and quit whinin' like a little girl!"

An uncomfortable silence hung between the men before he spoke. "Will, I already owe ye so much, I...,"

"Dinnae make this awkward, Mac. Just take the money. I've got more at home, so shut the hell up."

Connor could only nod, but with an added grin of gratitude. "So, ye'll see that Margaret makes it back to Faireshire safely?" he said, diverting the conversation to the relief of both.

"Aye, of course. We're gonna stop off at the hostel first, make sure Ian hasn't burned the place down. We'll probably stay for a few days before headin' south."

"I ken I dinnae have to say this, but, take care of Margaret. She's kind of special to us. Both of ye have been the best friends two people could ever have. There's no way to repay what ye've have done for Isaboe and me."

"Payment's not necessary. Ye can't put a price on friendship, Mac," Will said as he held out his hand. Connor looked at the hand extended before him, then pulled his large friend into a bear-hug and slapped him on the back. William Buchanan allowed it, for a few seconds, just before the women arrived.

Meeting Connor leading her horse out of the barn, the spunky red-head took the reins. "You and I have been through hell together these last few months," Margaret said rather pointedly, just before her expression softened. "And though it's been quite the adventure, I hope to never do it again."

Connor chuckled and then pulled Margaret into his arms, giving her a warm hug. "I cannae agree with ye more. I've no words that come close to how much Isaboe and I love ye. Ye ken that, right?"

"I ken, and I know you'll take good care of your family." After giving Connor a smile and a kiss on his cheek, she turned and mounted her horse.

Isaboe watched as Will silently walked over to stand in front of her, looking slightly uncomfortable. Though she barely knew the big man, she owed her life to him as much as she did to Margaret, Connor, and Rosalyn.

"Well, I guess we'll be on our way, lass," he finally said. "It was a pleasure to have met ye, and to have been at yer service. I wish ye the best of luck." He then held out his hand.

"We don't know each other well yet, William Buchanan, and I hope someday to remedy that. But I'm currently on a mission to rebuild my family, and you have become an honorary member." Isaboe smiled warmly at him, and just as Connor had done, she opted against the handshake. Wrapping her arms around the barrel-chested man, she squeezed tightly. "Thank you."

This time Will returned the hug. "Ye're welcome, lass. Just remember, his bark is worse than his bite. Dinnae let him fool ye."

Connor walked over to Isaboe and slid his arm around her waist as

Will mounted his horse. Looking up at his friend, he said his farewell in guttural Gaelic. *"Gus an coinnich sinn a-rithist."*

"Lang may yer lum reek." Will responded with his own Gaelic farewell, and with a nod to Margaret they spurred their horses toward the road.

Will never looked back, just raised a hand as he rode off. Margaret, however, couldn't resist. She looked over her shoulder and waved one last time.

"Are ye alright?" Connor asked.

"I'm fine," Isaboe lied.

"Let's take a walk." Connor started to turn, but Isaboe hesitated and looked back at the cottage. "Kaitlyn's fine; she's with Rosalyn. Come with me, I wanna show ye somethin'."

They strolled in silence with Connor's arm draped over Isaboe's shoulders. Though the day was clear, the icy wind found its way through her cloak and it stung at her cheeks. It was the first time she had been to this part of the island, and the view of its towering cliffs plunging into the sea was breathtaking. For some reason, the sight temporarily washed away Isaboe's fears, and she let herself breathe unimpeded for the first time in weeks. As the cool, salty air enveloped her, she felt its healing energy soothing her deep, invisible wounds. Soon, they were standing at the edge of the cliff and looking into the distance at a massive rock spire that stood like a lone sentinel against the raging sea.

"That's the Ole Man of Hoy," Connor said, pointing.

"It's beautiful. It looks like a soldier protecting the land from the ocean," she said as she leaned back against him. Resting his chin on her head, Connor wrapped his arms around her as they drank in the beauty of the black, craggy cliffs. They stood like that, quietly lost in their own thoughts as the wind whipped around them and the pounding surf crashed on the rocks below.

Though Isaboe had no idea what the future held for them, the words that Queen Brighid spoke in her room on the night Kaitlyn was born continued to play over in her mind: *Two times robbed. Will she go for a third? Only time will tell.* What did that mean? Had they not seen the last of Lorien and her twisted magic? Isaboe shivered at the thought that Lorien might not be finished after all.

But right now, finding a home for Kaitlyn was their first priority. And though she knew it may be awhile, Isaboe silently held onto the hope that one day she would be able to find Benjamin and Anna as well.

"We're gonna be fine, Isaboe." As if he could read her thoughts, Connor murmured comforting words in her ear, but she was certain that he had plenty worrying him as well. She wasn't sure if he had spoken the words for her benefit, or his own.

Turning around, Isaboe slipped her arms around his waist and looked up at him. "I'm not worried. Our future is whatever we want it to be. A very wise man told me that."

Connor brushed the hair back from her face and just gazed at her for a moment before speaking. "Well, just as long as we dinnae get ourselves near-killed again, I'm good with anything that comes our way."

"I believe you were well-paid for your services," she said with a coy smile.

"Aye, that I was," Connor replied with a twinkle in his eye and grin on his face. "And I hope to keep collecting that payment for the rest of our lives," he said, snuggling her closer.

A half a year ago they were strangers, only meeting in fragmented dreams, or as ghosts of a memory long forgotten. Now they stood together as one on the edge of a ridge looking out over the crystal, blue-green sea as the wind danced around them. It wasn't the first time Isaboe had heard whispering voices in the wind, but this time they weren't speaking of fear and death, but of hope—hope for their future, and for the walk they would now take together.

She now felt ready to begin laying out plans for that new life, a life full of possibilities. But she wasn't so foolish as to believe there would be no concerns or fears, and there were certainly still many unanswered questions. Though the pain from the loss of her previous life still lingered, and Nathan's ghost occasionally still haunted Isaboe, she would work to let the anguish go. But she would never stop searching for Benjamin and Anna.

She had promised to let the past stay in the past, and owed it to Connor and Kaitlyn to do so. But more importantly, she owed it to herself. She had suffered so much loss and shed too many tears. She couldn't let the suffering and regret define her anymore. Isaboe had a future with a family again, and regardless of what may come, she was now ready for it—ready to live, and ready to love again.

Held warmly in Connor's embrace with her head resting against his chest as they looked out over the sea, she whispered. "You know what I would like?"

"Whatever ye want, my love, if it's within my power, it's yers."

Gazing up at him, Isaboe could see the intensity of the love he felt for her. She couldn't deny that when he looked at her that way with so much yearning in his baby-blue eyes, she felt a small, but undeniable, tingle fluttering deep inside. It warmed her all the way down to her toes, and in that moment, she felt whole.

"I would like you to play a tune on your whistle for our daughter. It's been too long since I've heard you play. Do you think you could do that?" she asked.

Sweeping the hair from her face, Connor looked down at her as he cupped her cheeks. His crooked grin and the sparkle in his eyes told Isaboe he felt it too. He was her other half, the piece of her life that had always been missing. It had taken her going through hell and back, and almost dying, to make her see that.

As he held her gaze, all the unspoken words they didn't need to say danced in his eyes, but to Isaboe, they spoke loud and clear. "Aye, I can do that, my love." Connor leaned his head down. "That, I can do," he whispered just before kissing her.

The End

But is it ever really over? In the words of a Fey Queen:
"Only time will tell."

ACKNOWLEDGEMENTS

Writing a story that would turn into a series of books was not what I set out to do twenty years ago, but when the characters came to life and took over the reins, I had to follow the path they blazed, and they have taken me on an incredible adventure!

However, before I could share this story with the world it required the talent of my two wonderful editors, Sara Kraft and John Thompson. Fortunately, they saw the gem in my roughly written manuscript, and with their patience and skills, helped to polish my literary work into this amazing tale. Thank you, Sara and John, for your faith in me and your creative guidance.

Another invaluable creative team member on this journey is Erik Jacobsen of Longfeather Book Design. When I first met with Erik to discuss the design concepts for this far-reaching series, I gave him just a seed of an idea. Erik's inspiring design touches surround this story, and my seed of an idea has bloomed into the work of art you are holding.

I'm also extremely grateful to Amy Fortner and Karen Ferguson, my ARC readers. What you two girls do for me is priceless!

Lastly, I want to thank my Mom for giving me that copy of *The Hobbit* all those years ago, awakening my love for fantasy literature. You've always been my greatest fan. *Love you, Momma!*

ABOUT THE AUTHOR

As far back as I can remember, I've been enchanted by the magic of the fey and fascinated by anything Scottish. My love for literary fantasy and storytelling began at an early age, and I knew I was destined to share this incredible tale with the world someday. I just hadn't expected "someday" to take so long. But as life will do, it threw some obstacles in my path as an author.

Being a career-oriented woman, I've owned and operated two successful businesses, raised two wonderful sons, and have managed to stay happily married to my best friend for over forty years. But my desire to share this story—a story that has been twenty years in the making—has always remained my golden ring.